Talking
TO THE
Moon

Talking
TO THE
Moon

JAN L. COATES

Red Deer Press

Published in Canada by Red Deer Press
195 Allstate Parkway, Markham, ON L3R 4T8

Published in the United States by Red Deer Press
311 Washington Street, Brighton, MA 02135

Library and Archives Canada Cataloguing in Publication
Coates, Jan L., 1960-, author
Talking to the Moon / Jan Coates.
ISBN 978-0-88995-562-2 (softcover)
I. Title.
PS8605.O238T35 2018 jC813'.6 C2018-900429-0

Publisher Cataloging-in-Publication Data (U.S.)
Names: Coates, Jan, 1960-, author.
Title: Talking to the Moon / Jan Coates.
Description: Markham, ON: Red Deer Press, 2018. | Summary: "Middle Grade novel about
a young girl with foster mother who discovers the multigenerational roots and meaning
of family in the historical setting of Lunenburg, Nova Scotia" – Provided by publisher.
Identifiers: ISBN 978-0-88995-562-2 (paperback)
Subjects: LCSH: Lunenburg (N.S.) -- Juvenile fiction. | Foster children – Juvenile fiction. |
Families – Juvenile fiction. | BISAC: JUVENILE FICTION / Family / Multigenerational.
Classification: LCC PZ7.C638Ta | DDC |F| – dc23

Design by Tanya Montini
Edited for the press by Peter Carver
Printed in Canada by Copywell

Red Deer Press acknowledges with thanks the Canada Council for the Arts and
the Ontario Arts Council for their support of our publishing program.

We acknowledge the financial support of the Government of Canada through
the Canada Book Fund (CBF) for our publishing activities.

ONTARIO ARTS COUNCIL
CONSEIL DES ARTS DE L'ONTARIO
an Ontario government agency
un organisme du gouvernement de l'Ontario

Canada Council   Conseil des arts
for the Arts   du Canada

www.reddeerpress.com

This novel is for my ancestors who made
the journey across the ocean,
allowing the rest of us the great privilege
of being Canadian,
and especially, this is for Gramps Mingo
who rescued the Mingo Montbéliard jug,
the inspiration for this story.

In all of us there is a hunger, marrow deep, to know our heritage—to know who we are and where we came from. Without this enriching knowledge, there is a hollow yearning. No matter what our attainments in life, there is still a vacuum, an emptiness, and the most disquieting loneliness.

— ALEX HALEY, Roots

The moon is a friend for the lonesome to talk to.

— CARL SANDBURG

Chapter 1

My real mother, Moonbeam Dupuis, disappeared on March 20th, 2008.

On my fourth birthday, 2,659 days ago.

Sir Isaac Newton died on that same date, only in 1727. He was the first scientist to notice that water could separate light into all the colors of the spectrum. Sir Isaac discovered gravity, too—the invisible force that keeps us stuck to the earth, like what roots do for trees, so we're not all the time astronaut-floating. Hugs are one of my Dislikes, but sometimes it feels like the earth's not wrapping its invisible arms around me tight enough. Like gravity and my missing mother are both avoiding me.

Part of me disappeared with Moonbeam. Since it's an inside bit, the only one who knows it's gone is me.

Me and my secret best friend, the Moon, who is likely a

man because nobody ever talks about the Woman in the Moon. The Moon is one of my Likes and a good listener, even though he never answers my very important questions:

- *Why are some kids so mean?*
- *How come Moonbeam left me behind, and where is she?*
- *Why are the rainbow colors always in the same order?*

Rainbows are like the good families in stories. All the colors are separate but together, giving each other just-right personal space. In my two foster families before Muzzy, I was always floating free in my own entire solar system of personal space. Like a falling star.

My teacher, Miss Matattall, told me I'm on the autism spectrum, which is not something pretty like a rainbow spectrum. It's more a fancy word teachers made up to describe left-out kids like me.

Muzzy says my brain's just bigger than most people's. That I'm marching to the beat of my own drum.

She says that as if it's a Like, but she's wrong. And I play the piano, not drums.

Other kids mostly make fun of me; they whisper and laugh at my grouchy old-lady face.

Whispering and laughing are two of my Dislikes.

"Ready, Freddy?"

"Almost. And my name is Katie."

I finish arranging my folded underwear in my suitcase, a row of black lined up on top of all the white, like piano keys. On top of those, I put the bookmark Moonbeam left for me. On the front it says: *Elizabeth's Books, Montague Street, Lunenburg, Nova Scotia*, and on the back, in messy writing, it says:

Every time you see the Moon, know that I'll be thinking of you, Katie.

Take good care of our Lavender Lady.

I'll tell you her story when I come back for you.

Love, Moonbeam

Our Lavender Lady, a horse-chestnut-sized rock, shaped like half a gray egg, full of hard lavender crystals, stays in my pocket to help me be brave. Bilbo Baggins kept Gollum's Ring, synonym for his Precious, in his pocket. It helped him be invisible, which would be one of my Likes.

But that could only happen in a made-up story like *The Hobbit.* I like true stories, especially the ones with happy endings. I hope what Moonbeam wrote on the bookmark is true, and that our story will have a happy ending. But sometimes being patient is hard for me.

Downstairs, Muzzy's waiting for me by the apartment door, half-in, half-out. "All set?" Her face is doing the twitchy kind of smile, the kind that says she's in a hurry to get going. Or at least I think it is. I'm better at reading books than faces.

"I hope so," I say, following her outside.

"Can you believe the magazine agreed to let me take four weeks leave?"

I nod yes, because I know that's true.

"I'm sure they felt guilty about turning down my proposal for that foreign correspondent posting. Jo-Ellen will sure appreciate our help in the café, and we'll be back before you know it."

Before you know it. Easy for her to say. She lived in Lunenburg when she was my age. It's an old, quiet little town near the ocean, not a big noisy city near the river, like Montreal.

Quiet is one of my Likes.

Moving and meeting new people are two of my Dislikes.

But maybe I'll find Moonbeam there.

In the driveway, Muzzy opens the trunk of her Honda Civic. Sea Captain Blue. It's eleven years old, like me. She grunts, lifts in our bags, then bangs the trunk closed. My eyelids flutter from the echo bouncing around inside my brain.

"What will I do while you're working in the café? Will the kids there be the whispering kind?" I fasten my seatbelt, then burrow my fingers into my jacket pocket. I wrap them snugly around my Lavender Lady, count her pointy tips with my thumb. Nine. A warm gush rushes up from my fingertips, straight up my veins. Slows my heart right down to its regular beating, instead of the pounding *pa-dum pa-dum* it does when I worry.

"Whoa!" Muzzy turns the key, then swipes the back of her hand across her forehead, like after she runs a half-marathon. Only she's sitting, not running. "Sometimes it's best to wait and see, Katie."

"Wait and see. For four whole weeks? Twenty-eight days?" I jerk ahead to make sure my seatbelt is working. "Six-hundred and seventy-two hours? And did you lock the apartment door?"

She nods. "It'll be an adventure. And we adore adventures, don't we?"

"Don't we?" I'm like Bilbo Baggins; I like my hobbit-hole and I've no use for adventures. "Like our ski trip adventure?"

"Ancient history. But we survived, didn't we?" She waves one hand at me, like she's trying to push me away without touching me, and puts the car into R for reverse. "Some things, like minor avalanches, are simply beyond our control."

I do a shoulder check. Both sides. "Nothing coming." I sigh and squint up at the sun. "Beyond our control." Synonym for one of my biggest Dislikes.

Chapter 2

I hold up my drawing to show Muzzy, then put my pencils away. My deer looks more like a cow, and my raccoon, alive not dead, looks like a fat robber cat. I get twenty-five new Felissimo colored pencils in the mail every month, all the way from Japan. I'm memorizing the color names. Lavender's Blue is my favorite. Choosing just-right colors takes too long. When I finally get to the drawing, I'm usually in a hurry.

My pencil subscription ends in sixteen months when I'll have all five hundred colors.

Unless Muzzy goes to work overseas and gives me back to the foster care people.

Worrying about that is one of my biggest Dislikes. She's my best foster mother ... so far.

"When we get to the top of that hill, you'll be able to see the backside of Lunenburg."

Backside. A synonym for bum. I lean forward and point up. "And the Moon."

• *Why do people drive so fast?*

• *Why doesn't somebody teach the raccoons, porcupines, and deer about looking right, left, and back again before they cross the road?*

• *What happened to that hour we lost when we got to New Brunswick? Will we ever get it back?*

"Yup," Muzzy says. "The very same moon that we see from our balcony in Montreal."

I check my watch. "I know Earth has only one Moon, but why is it there at 2:32 PM?"

"It's got something to do with sunlight reflecting off it. I'm fuzzy on the details." She takes both hands off the steering wheel and rubs them together. I sit on my hands to keep from grabbing the wheel. Is she excited or are her hands cold?

"What's that big white building with the Crimson Cranberry roof?"

"The Academy. I went to school there for Grades 4, 5, and 6. Just wait until you see all the pretty old houses."

I lean ahead to see the black and white Academy better, before it disappears from sight. "It's like a mansion, or a wooden castle."

"The Castle on the Hill. That's what we used to call it."

In front of a playground, a sign says: *Welcome to Lunenburg, a National Historic Site.* When I'm learning a new place, I read all the signs, in case there's important information I need to know, like where the library is, or the public washrooms.

We turn onto a skinny street. The wooden buildings are crowded together. Some of them have nametags shaped like small white houses.

Farmer Anderson House, 1877, Built by John Anderson,
Boat Builder.
Maple Bird Anderson House, Built by George Anderson, 1826.
The Tailor Shop, operated by Chas. Anderson Sr. converted to a
residence in 1898.

"How come ..."

A horn blast shuts me up. Brakes squealing jerk me ahead, then slam me back against my seat.

Muzzy shifts the car into P for park and puts down her window. "Sorry about that. Forgot about the one-way streets."

The old man in the convertible, Crocodile Green, shakes his head, then speeds away.

"Mr. Rhodenizer; I recognize his car. I used to deliver his newspaper when I was twelve." Muzzy laughs and looks at herself in the rear-view mirror. "I'm surprised he didn't recognize me."

"Why? Do you look the same now as when you were twelve? Twenty-four years ago?"

"I wish."

Muzzy's Snow White beautiful with shiny hair, Poe's Raven Black, and no freckles. People always stare at me when she says she's my mother. Because I'm freckly with frizzy hair, Apricot Brandy Brown. Kids at school call me Curly Kate. That's a coppery kind of dish scrubber, not a girl.

Built by Edward Conrad, Ship Builder, circa 1874.

Built for Eli Hopp, Carpenter, 1868.

"Do you still know a lot of people here?"

Muzzy lifts her shoulders. "I only lived here for three years, but I'm sure lots of the same people are still around. And it is a small town. Too small, sometimes, according to Jo-Ellen. Took her a while to adjust when she moved back last year after living in Montreal for so long." She pulls up to the curb just before The Brigantine Inn. Mermaid's Gown Turquoise.

Built by Stephen Morash. Shipwright, 1876.

"The houses have nametags, like the bank ladies," I say.

"So they do. Must be the original owners."

The café is the color of an old barn, Flannel Gray. Painted birds swoop across the picture window toward a black and white sign that says "The Chickadee."

The Plum Crazy Red screen door flies open and Jo-Ellen jogs down the sidewalk. She pulls open my door but she doesn't hug me. She wipes her hands on her lobster apron and high-fives me instead. Because she knows me.

"I am *so* glad you're finally here. We've been crazy busy and short a waitress for two weeks." She laughs and hugs Muzzy so tight it makes me hold my breath. "Plus, I'm always delighted to see my bestest bosom buddy."

Bosom. A synonym for breast. It's not nice to talk about breasts, but the bad boys at school do anyway. Jo-Ellen has big grapefruit breasts. Only jiggly, like water balloons. But it's not polite to stare.

Jo-Ellen winks at me, which is one of her habits. Muzzy told me it's because she is making a joke, not because she has something in her eye. "And, of course, the talented and beautiful Katie Dupuis Pearson." She opens the screen door. "Come in, come in."

"Why doesn't your place have a nametag like that?" I point to the house across the street. Celery Green.

Built by William Whitney, Boat Builder, 1885.

Jo-Ellen laughs and twists her hair, Octopus Gray, up into a bun. "Beats me, but I love that about Lunenburg, knowing who built places, and when. In these parts, that's a newish building. Let's take your things right upstairs."

Upstairs. There's barely room for both me and my suitcase between the wooden railing and the wall, Peachy Whisper Pink.

Jo-Ellen opens a white door on the left side of the hallway. "This is your room, Miss Katie. Small but cozy."

The walls are purple. Almost Lavender's Blue.

"Allie, you and I are roomies for the summer, so we can stay up late, gossiping, like the good old days. Only no pillow fights!"

Muzzy sticks out her bottom lip. Is she sad, or just pretending?

"Okay, okay. Don't stick out your *bruddle* at me, missy. Maybe one fight, but I get first hit." Jo-Ellen's blatting sheep laugh makes me want to turtle-tuck my head or cover my ears. Muzzy says that's rude, so I poke a finger in one ear and pretend I'm scratching it instead. But I don't eat the wax on my finger, like Sebastian, a left-out boy at school.

I close the door partway and lift my wheelie suitcase up onto the wheelie bed. The flowery quilt is the soft kind of material, not the scratchy static kind that makes my hair stick to my face. I unzip my suitcase and put Moonbeam's bookmark inside the bottom desk drawer, then go to the windows. The sun-dazzled ocean's right there below me, like I'm on a ferryboat. Most of the buildings are Crackling Crimson Red, and there are lots of boats in the harbor. I open one of the windows, put my nose up to the screen, and sniff; a little bit salty, a little bit horsey.

"Whoa, Bessie." A silky-looking black horse pulling an old-fashioned carriage stops out front of a hay bin that says

"Trot in Time." Bessie looks like Blackie, the horse in *The Horse Boy*, a true-story movie about Rowan, a little boy on the autism spectrum.

"We'll be down in the café. Join us when you're ready." Muzzy comes up beside me, hooks her baby finger around mine. She calls this a pinky hug. "Hope you'll love it here as much as I did when I was your age, Katie. Soon as we get a chance, we'll check out Elizabeth's Books, if it's still here."

I nod yes and squeeze her baby finger back. Her eyes are shiny, like when somebody dies in a movie. But I think she's smiling. Smiling and crying don't belong together. They're antonyms.

"Even though I didn't live here for very long, it sure feels like coming home to me."

After Muzzy leaves, I sit down at the desk, rest my chin on my hands, and stare out at all the people walking along the waterfront. Would I recognize Moonbeam if she was one of them?

Downstairs in the café, Muzzy says, "If you're interested, I found you a job already."

"Job already?" Her eyes aren't scrunched up into twinkly slits like when she's making a joke. "But I'm eleven." I sit down in the chair next to her. Sunshine Yellow with white polka dots. "Only adults have jobs. And Bessie."

"Bessie?"

"A horse who works for Trot in Time, taking people for carriage rides."

"You don't miss a trick, do you?" Jo-Ellen says.

"Bessie was not doing tricks," I tell her. "She is not a circus horse."

"Anyhow, our Grade 4 teacher, Miss Langille, has just had hip-joint replacement surgery," Muzzy says. "She's looking for a young person to help her recover."

Jo-Ellen pours more tea. "She's Aggie Mingo, now." The teapot is bird-shaped, Summer Sea Turquoise, and the tea pours out its beak like it's throwing up. "She married late in life but her husband passed a few years ago."

"Huh," Muzzy says. "I thought Miss Langille was married to her teaching job."

"Really, I think she's looking for company, too. Far as I know, she has no family other than her odd old-maid sister."

"Old Maid is a card game. You lose if you have the old maid queen at the end," I say. Miss Matattall calls that "making connections."

Muzzy nods. "But this kind of old maid is a woman who's never been married. Synonym for spinster."

"Kind of like us losers, I suppose." Jo-Ellen nudges Muzzy with her elbow. "Aggie and her sister haven't spoken to each other in years. Think there was some sort of scandal around Jessie's daughter that blew up into a family feud."

"*Family Feud* is a TV show," I say. "And what do you mean, hip-joint replacement? Replaced with what—a knee joint? An ankle? An elbow?"

They both laugh.

I shove my hands into my shorts pockets and hum inside my head, a Tom Chapin song about family trees that we did in choir. *You're probably my cousin and the whole world is our kin.* If you went back to the beginning of time, everybody in the whole world is related somehow. If I have cousins, I don't know them. But I'd like to.

"Sorry, Katie." Muzzy presses her lips together. "As people age, sometimes their joints wear out, which hurts like the devil. With technology these days, you can get an exact duplicate made of the original." I feel around inside my pockets for my own sharp hip bones. I wouldn't like them hurting like the devil, since in pictures he's always on fire, even though he's not real. My fingers slide down around my Lavender Lady. Old people are one of my Likes, the quiet gentle ones that don't look too much like skeletons.

"Maybe you should meet Aggie before you make up your mind," Jo-Ellen says. "I've already told her all about you. She's lovely."

I nod. "Lovely. Does her house have a nametag?"

Jo-Ellen taps her pointer finger on her top lip. "You know what? I can't remember, even though I've walked past umpteen times. Let's go see. I'll put up my 'Back in a Few' sign."

We stop in front of a house, Mountain Morning Blue, with Geranium Red flowers spilling out of window boxes. Rapunzel Yellow. "I always thought her place was the cutest house ever," Muzzy says. When she taps the woodpecker doorknocker, there's no answer and no nametag.

"That's strange; she must be out," Jo-Ellen says. "Or could be she has a visiting nurse with her. I've got some time before the supper crowd trickles in. Shall we do a short walking tour, then try Aggie again?"

A chipmunk scurries down a big tree, then darts into an opening between the roots. I crouch down and try to see inside, but it's a dark cave. I wonder if he gets the hiccups, like I do with strangers.

"Coming, Katie?" Muzzy closes her eyes and does deep yoga breaths as we walk. "I'd forgotten how pretty Lunenburg is. And how beachy it smells when there's a breeze."

I do yoga breaths, too. French fries. Garlic. And wet paint.

The houses look like fancy wooden cakes with paint frosting trim. I stop in front of a barn-shaped one on a corner. Tea With Milk Brown.

Altestes Haus, circa 1760, known as the oldest house in Lunenburg.

"Is this one really 255 years old?"

Jo-Ellen lifts her shoulders and both eyebrows. "A few people claim theirs is the oldest. They say a couple of houses up on York Street were built by the first settlers."

Built for John Henry Kaulbach, Sheriff, circa 1808.

Built in 1838 for John Bailly, BAKER.

"Families like the Baillys have lived here non-stop since their ancestors first came in 1753."

1753. One family living in the same town for 262 years? None of them would be looking for their real mothers or cousins. Their kin.

Chapter 3

"Come on in!" somebody calls out in a not-old-lady voice. "It's open!"

Miss Langille's on a sofa, Upsy Daisy Gold, in front of an enormous stone fireplace. She doesn't look like a skeleton, but she might if she wasn't wearing clothes. Her hair's pulled back into a ponytail, Hint of Sun White, and she wiggles the toes of her rainbow sock feet at us. "Please forgive me for not getting up to greet you, Allison, and for not having the tea kettle on. I've only just returned from an appointment. And this must be Katie. So lovely to meet you."

I squeeze my Lavender Lady and stare at the rainbow socks.

"It's so good to see you, Miss Langille!" Muzzy bends down and hugs her.

"Aggie, please. I left Miss Langille in the classroom when I retired fifteen years ago." I look up when she giggles, like the girls at school, only nicer. "And you still look like a girl, with that gorgeous thick hair. Getting old is not for the faint of heart." Aggie shakes her head, which usually means no, but I think she's smiling because her mouth's pushing up her cheeks so her eyes squint almost closed. "But, of course, it's better than the alternative."

"You haven't aged a day since you taught us all those years ago," Jo-Ellen says.

"My joints would beg to differ. I see you're admiring my socks, Katie."

I jerk my eyes away from Aggie's feet, up to the bracket-shaped wrinkles between her mouth and her cheeks, nod yes, and try to swallow my hiccups.

"My sister knit them for me, eons ago. I simply adore the spectrum, the way all the colors are separate but blending together at the same time. Don't you?"

I nod yes again and stuff my strangers-talking-to-me dancing hands into my pockets. "*Hic!* Run Oh You Great Big Irish Villain. Red, Orange, Yellow, Green, Blue, Indigo, Violet."

She nods. "I used that same mnemonic device, that nonsensical phrase, to help my students remember the colors of the spectrum."

I mumble, "Green comes after yellow and before blue. But I don't know why."

Aggie looks over the top of her round silver glasses at her socks. "My sister never was much of a one for details. More of a free thinker. But, of course, you're right—the colors are somewhat disordered."

"Disordered. A synonym for messy." I sit down beside Muzzy on the piano bench. The lid on the big wooden piano is closed so you can't see the ebony and ivory keys, which are not colors, but a type of wood and the tusks and teeth of animals like elephants. "Were you a music teacher?"

Aggie shakes her head. "In later years, I worked with children who had difficulties in school. I've always believed rainbows and music have a great deal in common. Each black note marching across the page separately until someone plays them, blending them together, like the colors in a rainbow. Don't you think?"

I nod yes.

"Katie's an excellent student," Muzzy says. "And pianist. She's also a math whiz, which, as you may recall, I was not."

"You always had a way with words; I was delighted to hear you'd become a journalist."

Muzzy gives me a pinky hug. "Katie and I are both lovers of true stories. And puzzles. We like figuring things out."

Aggie points to a table in the corner. "I could use some help with that jigsaw puzzle. A friend gave it to me as a way to pass the time while I'm on the mend."

"I can do 1000-piece jigsaw puzzles," I say, looking at the picture of the Lunenburg waterfront on the box. "But 750-piece ones like this are easier."

Aggie nods. "I see you've been kissed by plenty of angels, Katie."

I fast-look at Muzzy. She taps her nose with two fingers. "Your freckles."

"Freckles. Eighteen in the winter and twenty-nine so far this summer." I pause and wait for the next hiccup, but it doesn't come. "Even though I wear SPF 60 sunscreen. And angels aren't real."

"I do rather like the idea of angels, though," Aggie says, holding out her giraffe-freckled hands. "But of course, these are ugly age spots, not spunky freckles like yours."

"Spunky like Pippi Longstocking," Jo-Ellen says.

I keep my eyes on Aggie's age-spotted hands. "Her full name is Pippilotta Delicatessa Windowshade Mackrelmint Ephraim's Daughter Longstocking."

Jo-Ellen does one of her loud sheep laughs.

"She thought she was an orphan because her father was missing at sea, but she was lucky because he came back. I don't know about my father. My real mother is also missing, but I hope I'm not an orphan. My story is true. Pippilotta's is not. A real girl couldn't pick up a horse."

Aggie folds her hands together on her lap. "That is an excellent observation. It sounds as if you and Allison have been lucky to find each other, then."

"Are you still a storyteller, Aggie?" Muzzy asks. "I used to love hearing about your ancestor—Katrina, was it?"

Aggie puts one hand over top of where her heart probably is. "Her name is spelled like Catherine in English, but the French pronounce it 'Katrine.' I haven't thought much about her stories for a lot of years."

"Are they true stories?" I ask. "Non-fiction, like *The Diary of a Young Girl*, synonym for *The Diary of Anne Frank*?"

She nods. "These stories are even older and came from letters Catherine wrote over 260 years ago when she first came to Lunenburg as a girl. Now, Katie, speaking of horses, do you see that fearsome beast lurking in the corner behind you?"

Fearsome beast. Synonym for monster. I jerk my head around to where she's pointing. It looks like part of a shopping cart, or a grocery bundle buggy, not a monster.

"I call her Silver Streak, after a pony I once knew. The walker edition isn't nearly as peppy as the pony, but with your help, perhaps the two of you can get me back on my feet."

"If I know you, that'll be in no time at all," Jo-Ellen says.

"We shall see. In the meantime, what do you think, Katie? Or perhaps you'd like to take some time to think ab ..."

Who's humming?

I cover my ears, hum along, and look all around the room. I know the tune, but I can't think of the words. At one end of the fireplace mantel, my eyes stop on a glass case with a jug inside. Oatmeal Brown. I get up and squeeze in behind the sofa to get closer. Carved into the front, there's an old-fashioned lady wearing a bonnet and picking her nose. Is she the one humming? But she's not alive. I tilt my head and squint to get a better look, hold my ear up to the case.

Aggie looks up at me over her shoulder. "Ah. I see you've discovered one of my treasures. My little brown jug is even more ancient than me."

The humming stops. "Why is she picking her nose? Is she rude like Sebastian at my school?"

"Excellent question. Perhaps as part of your job, you could introduce me to Google; we can do some research into old pottery, unearth the jug's true story."

"I'm a Google geek." The kids at school call me Robot Girl, too, but I don't tell her that. I like robots but they're machines, not people.

"Perfect. So far, my best guess is that the woman is partaking in a pinch of snuff."

"What's snuff?"

"It's a ground tobacco product. Years ago, people inhaled it to remove the street stench from their nasal passages."

"Can you imagine?" Jo-Ellen says. "That's even more disgusting than *smoking* tobacco."

She's crowding my personal space. I step away from the fireplace.

"Agreed. Anyhow, in 1752, my ancestors carried that jug all the way from Montbéliard, France, to Nova Scotia. I inherited it from my father, who inherited it from his father, and so on, back all those decades."

Muzzy comes over to take a closer look. "Was it empty when you got it?"

"For years, everyone assumed it was just a keepsake they'd brought from the Old World. As children, we were forbidden to touch the precious family jug. Of course, when Mother and Father were out one day, my sister Jessie and I got curious."

Curious. A synonym for nosy. "Curiosity killed the cat," I say. "Curious cats sometimes get run over like the raccoons and porcupines on the highway."

"Well, we didn't die, but we may well have if our parents had discovered we'd been snooping. You'll never guess what we found inside that jug."

Guessing games are one of my Likes. "A bat? Bats can squeeze into very small dark places."

Jo-Ellen and Muzzy laugh, but Aggie shivers and shakes her head.

"Fortunately, it was not a bat. There were two things. Stuck to one side of the jug was a tightly rolled-up piece of birch bark."

"Birch bark. Is it still there?" I stand on my tiptoes and try to see through the glass case, down inside the small mouth of the jug.

Aggie lifts her shoulders and her eyebrows, then pushes both hands up in the air, like she's checking to see if it's raining. Only we're indoors. "I suppose it must be. Jessie and I were so excited, thinking we'd stumbled upon an ancient mystery."

"I remember you telling us about the Langille jug and the letters, but I don't remember this part of the story," Muzzy says.

"Upon my soul, I didn't dare tell it. My parents were still alive when I taught you. I couldn't have them discover I'd been misbehaving. I was a good little girl."

"A good little girl." Like me. "Why was the birch bark there?"

"A sensible question. It cracked when we unfurled it, but we were able to make out some words scratched into it."

"What did they say?"

"Sadly, they were written in French. We copied them out, put the birch bark back, and returned the jug to the china cabinet. Using an old French dictionary, we did our best to translate. Could you pass me that recipe card sticking out beneath the case? Please and thank you."

I slide the card out and give it to her. "I speak French. I could have read the birch bark. And why didn't the person use paper?"

"Paper wasn't nearly so common then as now. There are gaps, but you'll be able to get the general gist of the message.

"Lunenburg, September 1754

"Dear Grandmother, I have written you ... two years, but I have not found ... to send ... across the ocean. This bottle you gave us ... seed pouch ... hold my tears, but I continue to miss ... If you are living ... Our All-Seeing Heavenly Father, maybe you can hear ... reading to the Moon. The letters ... lining of the horsehide trunk ... I ... Until we meet again, I remain,

"Your Loving Granddaughter, Catherine Marguerite Langille (formerly uprooted and now transplanted)"

Uprooted. Synonym for moving. One of my Dislikes.

"So Catherine Marguerite was your ancestor?" Jo-Ellen asks.

"Great-grandmother, several times over, about eight generations back. Our family tree has very deep roots."

Deep roots. Last year in Social Studies, Miss Matattall got us to draw our family trees. Mine was the only one with no roots and just one full branch for me, plus a half-branch for

Moonbeam. Because maybe she's already dead, and that's why she didn't come back to get me.

"Catherine. Formerly uprooted and now transplanted. Why was she uprooted? And where are the letters?" I move around in front of the sofa. "I could read them. I like true stories, especially mysteries."

Aggie shakes her head, boosts herself up higher on the sofa, and closes her eyes. Is she tired or trying to make us go away, like I do when the kids at school bother me? Only Aggie's not humming.

When she opens them again, I fast-look right at her eyes, Blue Green Velvet, like my favorite fleece jacket that I still wear, even though the zipper is broken. I blink, then look back down at her disordered socks.

"After we'd retrieved the horsehide trunk from a forgotten corner of the attic, pretending that we had simply stumbled upon the letters, our parents donated the originals to the Provincial Archives, which is somewhat like a museum for papers. We did, however, have copies made of the English translations. Our discovery caused a great flurry of excitement among the history buffs in town. We were famous for a time."

"I wonder why Catherine didn't mail the letters," Muzzy says.

"That we don't know. Although I suppose postal service

then, especially transatlantic, would have been even less reliable than today. Catherine must have figured reading the letters aloud to her friend the moon was her best option. She often had questions for the moon, as well."

Questions for her friend the Moon. "Can we read the copies of Catherine's translated letters that she read to the Moon?"

Aggie shakes her head no. "Sadly, my copies have gone missing. For years, I kept them upstairs in that horsehide trunk with all my memorabilia, including Catherine Marguerite's treasures. I had such fun sharing the letters with my niece, Kitty, when she was young."

I make a connection. "Kitty was also the name of Anne Frank's diary."

Aggie nods. "You're right. Mother lived with me for several months as she had some dementia in her final years. I presume she got rid of the letters during one of her ferocious housecleaning binges."

"Did you ask for another copy from the Archives?" Jo-Ellen asks.

Aggie shakes her head no. "I've never gotten around to that."

"I would like to see your memorabilia in the horsehide trunk, please and thank you." I pick up Silver Streak from the corner and plunk it down on the floor next to Aggie. "I like old things. And history."

Muzzy puts up one hand, which means either stop or slow down. "Patience, Katie."

"Perhaps another day," Aggie says.

Jo-Ellen stands up. "You must be tired from going out to your appointment, Aggie."

Aggie frowns and pats her right hip. "I'm fine—it's my new hardware that's tired."

I put Silver Streak back in her corner. "I will take the job. I'm very good at figuring things out, washing dishes, and computers, but I am not very good at ferocious housecleaning binges, conversation, and pretending."

Muzzy laughs. "And Katie's as honest as the day is long."

Every day has twenty-four hours. Synonym for 86,400 seconds. Boring days seem longer than fun ones.

"Deal." Aggie holds out one age-spotted hand. I keep both mine in my pockets and she pulls hers back. "Of course, we don't have to shake hands since I hope we're to become friends, Katie. We can discuss your pay tomorrow." She pats her mouth and yawns. "Time for me to catch up on my beauty rest."

Beauty rest. Maybe she was beautiful before she got old. I look at my watch. "What time do you wake up in the morning?"

"That depends on whether or not it's foggy. I'll give you a jingle. Would that be all right?"

Muzzy looks at me and makes like she's holding an invisible phone.

I nod yes and rub my Lavender Lady. She feels warm. Even with my eyes on my new Royal Magenta sneakers, I can tell Aggie is staring at me.

"I have a soft spot for ginger-haired girls, Katie." She laughs but it's musical, not mean. "Several of them stand out in my memory among the hundreds of students I taught over the years."

"Ginger is a type of spice, not hair," I tell her. Ginger cookies are one of my Likes.

Back at The Chickadee, I draw a trunk with a horse head, tail, and legs. It's one of my best drawings yet. At bedtime, I push my wheelie bed closer to the windows. The Moon is bright and full. This is a poem I remember from Grade 1:

> *The Man in the Moon is a wizard,*
> *making magic and wishes come true.*
> *He comes slippery sliding down moonbeams,*
> *Some night he just might visit you!*

That couldn't really happen, but if it did, I'd like the Man in the Moon to answer some of my questions:

- *Why does the fog make you wake up at a different time?*
- *How can a trunk be made out of a horse?*

- *Did my great-grandmother several times over get left behind somewhere, too?*

- *Why was Catherine uprooted, and why was she friends with the Moon?*

- *Does Moonbeam write letters to me that she doesn't mail because she doesn't know my address?*

Chapter 4

I wake up in the dark. *What's that?* A long rumbly moaning like a giant cow mooing or the bass notes on the piano, then silence. Is it a ghost? Old houses in books sometimes have ghosts. But ghosts aren't real. I check my glow-in-the-dark watch: 7:00 AM. I count between the moans as I'm getting dressed. *One, two, three ... thirteen.* Always thirteen seconds. We're by the ocean. Do whales or seals know how to count? The spooky pattern follows me downstairs to the café.

Jo-Ellen's pouring coffee for two ladies wearing sunhats even though it's a cloudy day. "Good morning. Foghorn wake you?"

"What's it for? And where's Muzzy?"

"She's gone out for a jog before I put her to work. The Battery Point horn warns ships away from the shore when the fog rolls in. The fog eater's having its breakfast, so the horn's almost finished for the day."

I try to make a confused face. But I don't know if I'm doing it right because there's no mirror.

Jo-Ellen laughs. "That's quite a face, missy. The fog eater's what we call the sun. Its beams can gobble up even the thickest pea soup fog."

Pea soup is one of my Dislikes because it's thick and slimy, like snot.

"Speaking of eating, I made waffles—blueberry!"

I pat my stomach. Waffles are one of my Likes. Especially with berries.

The phone rings as I'm chewing my last bite, fifteen times to keep from getting gassy, since burping and passing gas—a polite synonym for farting—are rude.

Jo-Ellen puts down the phone. "Aggie says for you to walk right in, whenever you're ready."

I put my dishes in the dishwasher, then hurry upstairs to make my bed. When I'm done, I say goodbye to Jo-Ellen and go around the corner. Outside Aggie's door, I close my eyes and listen to the quiet, like just before the streetlights flicker on in our neighborhood park in Montreal. The *clip-clop, jingle-jangle* of a horse and buggy, not Bessie, makes me open my eyes and push the door open.

Aggie's sitting on the sofa, working on the jigsaw puzzle. "Good morning, Katie. How are you?"

I close the door and stand in front of it. "I am smarter than I was yesterday because I learned about the fog horn and the fog eater."

Aggie laughs. "Excellent." She pats her hip. "It's an awful thing, having to learn to walk all over again. I'm afraid I don't have the gumption I did as a toddler. The stick-to-itiveness." She lifts one skinny arm up off the sofa. Her white sweater looks rabbit-soft. Silver Streak is on the floor beside her. "The visiting nurse has told me I need more practice. Could you give me a lift, please and thank you?"

I keep my hands in my pockets and walk across the rug. Cornflower Blue. She smells like roses and she's too big for me to lift.

"There's a dear. Come in behind me, tuck one arm under my elbow, and hold my hand."

My hand feels like it's suffocating when somebody tries to hold it. Even though hands don't breathe because they don't have lungs.

But this is my job. And I want to see Catherine's treasures and the horsehide trunk. Was moving all the way across the ocean to Nova Scotia one of her Dislikes?

I take a deep breath and pull my sleeve down over my hand. I put my arm under Aggie's and help her get up. We're almost the same size. As soon as she's got both hands wrapped around

Silver Streak, I let go and follow her slippers, Red Bonnet, in slow circles through her living room, kitchen, library, and dining room. *Clunk, shuffle, shuffle. Clunk, shuffle, shuffle.* After circle number three, Aggie stops. She lowers herself slowly back down onto the sofa, then shakes off her slippers. "I'm all out of puff. But I did pretty well, don't you think?"

I nod and make my mouth push up my cheeks. You're supposed to smile at friendly people. But my face feels stiff and itchy, like when glue dries on your fingers and you need to fast-peel it off. I check my watch. "Twelve minutes and fifteen seconds. Four minutes and five seconds for each circle." But I think the last lap was slower than the first.

"I'll make it my goal to get speedier each time. Be a dear and return Silver Streak to her stable, will you?"

Stables are in barns. I try to give her my question-mark look.

"It's just a little joke. I like to pretend that corner is her stable."

After I've put the pony in the stable, I look at the snuff jug. "Will you show me Catherine Marguerite's treasures in the horsehide trunk now? Or do you have other jobs for me?"

"You've been very patient, Katie. I remember that as a trait of your mother's as well."

I stare down through the glass-topped table at her rainbow

feet on the rug. "Do you know my mother? Moonbeam Dupuis? Did you teach her at The Castle on the Hill?"

"I'm sorry, dear. I was referring to Allison. I don't believe I ever taught any students with the last name Dupuis, but Moonbeam is a most whimsical name."

"Allison is my Muzzy, my foster mother, but not my real mother." I make a fist around my Lavender Lady. "Your real mother is the person who carried you in her womb for nine months. Mine is missing. But I don't know if she is missing me."

Aggie makes a clicking sound with her tongue. She sounds like a squirrel. "I'm sorry, dear. From now on, I shall refer to Allison as your Muzzy." She points one crooked finger toward the stairs. "Now, the horsehide trunk is in a cedar chest up in the yellow bedroom. Could you bring down the splint box from the trunk, please and thank you?"

Splinters are one of my Dislikes because they can poison your blood. I rub my pointer finger and thumb together. "Do you have tweezers?"

She shakes her head and presses her lips together. "The box won't give you a splinter, although it is made of wood— smooth, thin strips of ash. The box is an integral part of Catherine Marguerite's story."

Integral. Synonym for important.

I'm already halfway up the curving skinny staircase before

she finishes talking. The room is sunny and warm, Corn Husk Yellow, with prism windows making tiny rainbows shimmer on the walls. I lift the chest lid and do a yoga breath, opening my nostrils wide. *Forest trails. Chipmunks. Pinecones.* Inside, on top of the trunk, there's a framed picture, a colored-pencil drawing of a not-smiling girl. I did a self-portrait like it when I was in Grade 4. This girl has longer hair and more freckles. The letters K.L. are printed in one corner. Maybe it's Aggie's niece, Kitty, or one of her ginger-haired students that she had a soft spot for.

The long round trunk doesn't smell like horses. The outside, Cinnamon Tea Brown, does not feel warm like a horse, and there are lots of not-shiny tacks holding the trunk together. Underneath some papers, little boxes and books, the splint box is wrapped in a flowery flannel nightie. The box is round and the size of Muzzy's cake container. It doesn't look like it's over 260 years old. I want to open it, but you aren't supposed to look at other people's things until they give you permission. This is called being nosy, even though you look with your eyes, not your nose. I take out the box, close the trunk and the chest, then go back down the fourteen stairs, holding the box with both hands.

Aggie's leaning against the back of the sofa with her eyes closed. I hold my breath and stare at her chest to make sure she's still breathing. She's very old and sometimes old people die. I start breathing again when her eyelids pop open and she pats her legs. "Right here, my dear."

After I put the box down, she says, "I hadn't noticed your beautiful eyes before. They're very unusual, bring to mind ..."

"My eyes are Prickly Pear Green," I tell her, keeping my eyes on the box. "Which is not one of my favorite colored pencils. I wish my eyes were Lavender's Blue."

"They suit your complexion perfectly," she says. "Your hair's the same color as this box."

"My hair is Apricot Brandy Brown; it's not one of my favorite colored pencils, either. The color of your hair is Hint of Sun White. I like Poe's Raven Black hair, like Muzzy's. Those are the only black and white pencils I have, so far." I sit down on the other end of the sofa and look at the puzzle pieces.

Aggie puts on her glasses and turns her knees slightly toward me. I look at the round box on her lap. The star pattern made of tiny holes on the top reminds me of Chinese checkers, a board game that uses marbles, not checkers. And you can play even if you're not Chinese.

After she traces the pattern with her pointer finger six times, Aggie closes her eyes. "I do wish I still had those letters. Like Allison, Catherine had a lovely way with words; she painted pictures with them, really. In the original French letters, we could tell from the angle of her writing that she was left-handed, like Jessie. Besides the moon, she loved rainbows and numbers and was forever counting one thing or another—acorns, waves, tears."

"I'm left-handed, too. And you have fourteen stairs."

Aggie nods and opens her eyes. "My sister and I used to play at being settlers, like Catherine. We thought of her as a friend. Do you play make believe like that?"

I shake my head no. "I'm not good at pretending, remember? A left-out boy at my school has an invisible friend. Since Catherine is dead, she would be an invisible friend, too."

"Through her letters, she seemed very real to us. We took turns being Catherine." Aggie leans back. "The other would be her cousin-sister Elisabeth, or Marie Claire, a Métis girl Catherine met here in the New World."

"Métis," I say, making a connection. "Synonym for half-French and half-Indigenous people."

Aggie nods yes. "Sometimes we persuaded our neighbor, Alex Jodrey, to play the part of Nicholas, Catherine's younger brother." She sighs. "I wish I had a better memory for details. Where do I start?"

"At the beginning: 1753," I say. "Miss Matattall told us stories have to have a beginning, middle, and end."

"That's very true. I do remember Catherine's first letter was actually dated the twenty-third of October, 1751. Before she had left France. She and Elisabeth were both the same age then as you are now. Eleven, right?"

I nod yes. "What did she look like, and why did she leave France?" I like to have lots of details when somebody is reading or telling a story, so the words turn into pictures, and it's like watching a movie in my brain. Like my brain's a DVD player. Only I don't have to plug my brain into the wall or charge its batteries.

"We can't know for certain as it was before the time of photographs, but I always pictured her with long, straight ginger hair that she wore in braids, and bright green eyes." Aggie looks at me. "A lot like yours, in fact. Like most of their farm neighbors in Montbéliard, the Langilles were of the Protestant faith, although many of the more prominent French people in the 1750s were Catholic. Protestants were sometimes treated as inferior people."

"My foster mother before Muzzy was French and Catholic. Madame LeBlanc treated me like an inferior person sometimes, and she made me go to church. Church is one of my Dislikes because it's boring."

"I suppose it depends on who is doing the preaching." Aggie closes her eyes again. "Let me see what else I can remember ... Catherine lived with her parents, David and Marie, little Nicholas, who called her Minette ..."

"French for kitty," I say.

Aggie nods yes. "... an older brother, Jean-Jacques, and dear Grandmother, to whom Catherine wrote her letters. Her friendship with the moon was a secret she shared only with her cousin-sister Elisabeth and Grandmother. They were kindred spirits."

"Kindred spirits. Like Anne Shirley and Diana Barry." My fingers find my Lavender Lady inside my hoodie pocket. If I had a cousin-sister or a grandmother, maybe I would tell them about talking to the Moon.

"Jean-Jacques was about to be recruited into the army, something David Langille, a peace-loving man, wanted to avoid."

"One of Muzzy's friends was a soldier. He got killed, though. By a landmine."

"Precisely why David Langille wanted to keep his son from serving. Just then, the British government was recruiting French Protestants to settle their new colony, Nova Scotia. Catherine absolutely did *not* want to leave her home, especially Grandmother."

"Moving and being left behind are two of my Dislikes. And why did they have to leave Grandmother in France? Did they say they'd come back for her?"

"I'm not sure, but perhaps she was not strong enough for the voyage."

"Because she was old and sometimes old people die?"

"I suppose so. In the spring of 1752, Papa was unable to resist the promise of free land. The family traveled by horse and cart to a log raft that carried them for days downriver to Rotterdam. In Holland, great ships waited to carry them across the Atlantic Ocean. The Langille family's ship was called the *Sally*."

"Muzzy gets seasick on some boats," I say. "Not canoes or pedal boats."

"Many of the settlers did, as well. Nicholas was a chatty little boy, full of annoying questions for his big sister, and excited at the prospect of seeing pirates and whales at sea. Catherine was a worrier, fearful of change." Aggie looks over the top of her glasses at me. "Wouldn't it be terrifying to leave everything you'd ever known behind, especially when you'd never seen the endless ocean before?"

I nod yes and make another connection. "Change is one of my Dislikes. I've always lived in Montreal, and my first time seeing the endless ocean was when I came to Nova Scotia."

"You seem to be adapting well." Aggie folds her hands together on top of the splint box. "Catherine kept her treasures, all part of her story, in this box. Jessie and I made a pie chart to keep track of them as they appeared in her letters. Like the letters and some of the treasures, that chart is long gone."

"Long gone." I squeeze my Lavender Lady and look at the

box. "We used pie charts, synonym for circle graphs, when we were learning fractions in Grade 3. Can we look at the treasures that aren't long gone?"

Aggie sits up straight and goes back to tracing the star on the round lid. "There were originally twelve items. I'm not sure how many are still here."

"Maybe your mother got rid of them during one of her ferocious housecleaning binges."

She laughs. "Kitty, my niece, said she had nothing to do with the disappearance, but I have my suspicions."

"Was Kitty her real name? A niece is a girl, not a cat."

Aggie leans forward and sets the treasure box in the middle of the glass table, without lifting the lid. "Kitty was my pet name for Katrina." She rubs her new hip.

"Like Nicholas's pet name for Catherine. Only in French. Can I see the treasures, please and thank you?"

"Catherine Marguerite's is a very old story." She pats the lid. "Like all history, it cannot be rushed; it must unfold and reveal itself over time."

"Over time. I will be here for twenty-four more days, 576 hours."

"Gracious me. That should be plenty of time. I'll do my best to piece the story together for you without the letters." She yawns, politely, covering her mouth with one hand. "Right now, I believe it's time for my beauty rest. Perhaps soon I'll be ready to venture out into the big wide world again. I can show you some of Catherine's favorite Lunenburg haunts."

"Haunts. Like a Halloween haunted house. Only ghosts aren't real."

"That's just a funny way of saying places where she spent time. Could you bring Silver Streak closer, please and thank you, in case I get ambitious after you've gone?"

I set the walker down next to the sofa, then go to the door.

"Oh, and we haven't discussed your salary."

"Salary." A word that sounds like celery, one of my Dislikes, but means money, one of my Likes. "I don't need any money." I stare at the closed piano lid. Does it have eighty-eight keys like Muzzy's? "Muzzy buys me what I need. Until Moonbeam comes back for me, the foster care people pay Muzzy to look after me, which is her other job besides being a journalist."

Aggie nods. "Well, I'll think of something to compensate you for your time. I'd love to hear you play the piano sometime while you're here. It hasn't been touched since Kitty left."

"Muzzy's piano is electric. I don't know how to play wooden pianos."

"Well, it's here, should you change your mind. Perhaps you could come back on Monday? Enjoy the sunshine out there!"

Like always, the Moon doesn't have any answers for me that night, but I ask the questions anyway.

- *What's inside Catherine Marguerite's splint box?*
- *Did she ever see Grandmother again?*
- *Is Aggie somebody's grandmother?*

Chapter 5

"My neighbors two doors down have a garage full of bikes their kids have outgrown," Jo-Ellen says after lunch on Saturday. "You're welcome to see if there's one your size, Katie. Other than the hills, biking is a fantastic way to explore Lunenburg."

"Are there helmets?" I ask. "In Nova Scotia, everybody wears a bike helmet, but not in Montreal."

"Good observation. I'm not sure, but you can take a look."

"Are there any bike paths or trails?" Muzzy asks. "Not that the traffic here is anything like the crazy drivers we're used to in the city."

"There's a nice woodsy trail along the Back Harbour," Jo-Ellen says. "It has some beautiful views, plus it's very safe."

"Very safe. Will I get lost?" I ask.

Jo-Ellen pushes the palms of her hands up toward the ceiling. *"Not all those who wander are lost."*

I make a connection. "*Deep roots are not reached by the frost.* Bilbo Baggins."

"Sweet!" Jo-Ellen holds up her hand.

I high-five her, silent and fast. "Really, the author J.R.R. Tolkien wrote those words since Bilbo Baggins is a made-up character. Aggie's family tree has deep roots, like in that poem."

"Like a lot of people in Lunenburg. If you do get lost, ask anyone you meet for help. The don't-talk-to-strangers rule doesn't apply here in lovely Lunenburg."

"Lovely Lunenburg." In Montreal, I never talk to people I don't know, which is almost everybody.

"Go up King Street one block, turn left, then straight to the end of Pelham, past the library. Turn left ..." While Jo-Ellen talks, I draw a map on my napkin. "... past The Knot Pub, which looks like a hobbit house, and turn right, where the old train station building is. You can get on the trail just beyond that."

Muzzy lifts her eyebrows at me. "Did you get all that?"

I hold up the map.

"Very good," Jo-Ellen says. "You haven't acquired Allison's sense of direction, which is hopeless."

"That was before," Muzzy says, pretend-punching her. "I rely on my GPS now."

I put three chocolate chip cookies and my water bottle in my backpack, Pale Periwinkle Blue, then Muzzy comes with me to the neighbor's garage. It's full of bikes and tools and smells like cat urine. And gas. Gasoline, not the gas you pass when your food is digesting. We find a black helmet that fits and a Pumpkin Spice Gold bike that's only a bit too small. "You're growing like a bad weed," Muzzy says.

"I'm sorry," I tell her, because people do not like bad weeds, especially dandelions and poison ivy.

"That's just a funny expression since weeds grow very quickly. I'm happy you're growing so tall. Let's raise the seat a little."

I stand with the bike between my legs while she adjusts the poufy black seat behind me.

"There—can you still touch the ground?"

I sit on the seat again and stretch out my legs. The toes of my new sneakers barely touch the sidewalk.

"Excellent. It's Jo-Ellen's pie-baking day, and I know she could use my help peeling and slicing the fruit. Do you mind going off on your own?"

I shake my head no.

"Does that mean you do mind going by yourself?"

I shake my head again. "I'm answering your question. No, I don't mind going off on my own. I'll stay on the sidewalk and get off and push if I meet someone walking."

She smiles and holds up her hand for a pinky finger hug. "And don't forget to come back by five o'clock."

I nod yes, then push my borrowed bike up the steep hill. The picture of the napkin map is in my brain. Miss Matattall says I have the memory of an elephant. Elephants have excellent memories because they also have very large brains. Like me. And elephants never forget people who are mean to them.

Like me. Usually.

I can't remember Moonbeam's face, or what she sounds like, but it was mean to leave me. Muzzy says she probably had a good reason. It would have to be a *very* good reason. I fast-look at each person I pass because I might recognize Moonbeam if I see her. Maybe she still lives in Lunenburg and shops at Elizabeth's Books. Would she recognize me?

Too old, too young, too many boys, men, and sniffy dogs.

After The Knot, the first part of the crunchy gravel path goes through the woods. I slow down when I see a man with a crying baby in a stroller. The man is waving his arms in the air and spinning in circles, like Joseph at my school, who is also on the autism spectrum but a different color from me. Probably red, like his face when he screams. Joseph is non-verbal, a synonym for speechless. I think he screams because he is frustrated that nobody understands him. I hope I'm at the quiet Violet end of the spectrum.

When I can't hear the baby anymore, I come to a smelly swampy part that makes me hold my breath. I count to thirty-five before I have to breathe again. I stop beside a wooden bench, rest one foot on it, and get out my water bottle. Besides birds chirping, leaves whispering, and me swallowing, it's quiet. Not-nice quiet, like when somebody sneaky at school is cheating over my shoulder.

Only I'm alone. Butterscotch might be a good name for my bike since it's the right color and butterscotch pie is one of my Likes. I wonder if Jo-Ellen knows how to make that kind. I take another drink, then start humming. The same tune I heard at Aggie's the first day. I still can't remember the words.

Oh! I spray out my mouthful of water, drop my bottle, and almost fall off my bike. Only because the slithering snake startled me, not because I'm scared. Mostly the snakes in Canada aren't dangerous, except for pets like the twelve-foot-long escaped African python that strangled two little boys in their sleep one time. A boy in my Grade 2 class told us that horrible-but-true story for his "Share and Tell." It did not have a happy ending.

Close to where the snake disappeared into the long grass, I see rainbow speckles near the bottom of a birch tree. I get off my bike and try to find the prism. When I push my bike slowly back and forth, the clear plastic reflector on the spokes spins, making the rainbows flutter. *Red, orange, yellow, green, blue, indigo, vi ...*

What's that? I jerk my head around, look up into the trees deep in the woods. A sharp tapping. Is it a woodpecker?

"Hey!"

I squint up at a big leafy tree. On a high branch, there's a stranger with long messy hair and a hammer in one hand. The don't-talk-to-strangers rule doesn't apply in lovely Lunenburg. Maybe it's a homeless person who lives in the woods. Like the ones in the park in Montreal. Some of them are friendly, but some of them are scary yellers.

The person jumps to the ground and starts crashing through the woods toward me. Hiccups heap up in my throat. I get back on my bike, hum louder, and push hard on the pedals.

Chapter 6

"Hey, you forgot your water bottle!"

I squeeze both brakes hard. It's my favorite water bottle, Dragon Fly Green. I try to get off too soon, and end up on the ground with Butterscotch on top of me. One of her pedals is digging into my leg. *Ouch.*

"Are you okay?" the person asks, reaching out one hand. I think it's a boy with long hair. His fingers have paint speckles on them. Parrot Green.

I get up by myself, brush the dirt off my shorts and legs, and check for blood, one of my Dislikes. Especially my blood.

"I'm Jack." He holds onto Butterscotch's handlebars with one hand and passes me my water bottle with the other. "Who are you?"

His sneakers were probably white when they were new. Now they're Drizzly Afternoon Gray. "Katie Dupuis Pearson." I look away and take a drink, trying to swallow my hiccups. One belches out anyway. "*Hic!* And my bike is Butterscotch. *Hic!*"

He doesn't tell me the name of his bike, if he has one. I let my eyes slide up to the middle of his wrinkly T-shirt. Sunshine Yellow. There's a picture of an old house on it, one of the frosting houses. "Is that your house? Does it have a nametag?"

He opens his mouth wide and laughs. Loudly. "That's a pretty funny first question."

I move away from him and stand with Butterscotch between my legs.

The boy tugs on the bottom of his T-shirt to smooth it out and turns around so I can read the back—Jack Jodrey & Son: We Bring History to Life.

I take one of my dancing hands off the handlebars, stuff it into my pocket, and find my Lavender Lady. "'History to life.' What does it mean? *Hic!*" I take another drink of water.

"It's my dad's business. He's Jack, too, and we fix up old houses around town, bring them back to life—for all the rich CFAs. It's my day off."

"Day off. Who are the rich CFAs?"

"CFA stands for 'Come From Away'—what we call the new people who move here."

"I'm a CFA," I say. "And I have $232.16 in the bank that I saved from my allowance, but I'm not rich. I live at The

Chickadee and I work for Aggie—*hic*—who is not a CFA. But her great-grandmother, several times over, was a CFA from France. But I don't think she was rich."

"Aggie Mingo?" Jack folds his arms across his chest. "Yeah. We did some work for her, built her a wheelchair ramp in June."

"She doesn't have a wheelchair now, but she has Silver Streak who is a walker, not a pony. And she has new hardware. *Hic!* A hip joint."

Jack laughs again and I start to pedal away.

"Hey, where ya goin'? You're funny," he says. "Too bad we don't have any peanut butter to get rid of your hiccups."

I stop pedaling and put my feet down. "Peanut butter is banned at my school because Hilary is allergic. But since she's in Montreal and I am in Lunenburg, I could eat peanut butter if we had some." Peanut butter is one of my Likes. Especially the crunchy kind.

"Being allergic would really suck. I live for peanut butter. Especially chocolate peanut butter cups. Hey, do you like fishing?"

I look at him quickly, then back down at my sneakers. "Fishing. I have never gone fishing before." I suck in some air to stop the hiccups from squeezing out. "But haddock is one of my Likes. Without bones. And salmon because it's Baby Face Pink. Why do you have a hammer?"

"I'm building a tree fort, but I was just going down to the wharf, see if the mackerel are biting. Hang on—I'll get my bike."

Hang on, a synonym for wait. He disappears into the trees. I hang on. In seventy-eight seconds, he comes back, pushing a not-new black bike and carrying a backpack with a long metal pole sticking up out of it. Charcoal Gray.

"Cyclists in Nova Scotia wear bike helmets. It's the law."

He shrugs and pats his baseball hat. "I'm good. Not much to protect by way of brains, anyway. Let's go."

Because he doesn't seem like a bad boy, I follow him back to town. He's a faster bike rider than me.

We stop only once, so fast that Butterscotch almost bumps into Jack's bike. He puts one finger up to his mouth and points into the woods. The deer is standing so still, it looks like a statue, only its big dark eyes are blinking. It's beautiful, Truffle Brown, like Jack's hair, with kangaroo ears. A crow squawks, making the deer kick up its heels. It shows us its white tail, then disappears into the trees.

"Nice, huh?"

"Nice." I nod yes. "Not like the dead ones by the highway."

"True enough."

It takes us almost six minutes to get back to town. At the corner close to the wharf, I have to hold my breath again, not because of the hiccups, which disappeared in my panting, but because of the toilet smell. Like when somebody at school forgets to flush.

I stay on Butterscotch, my sneaker toes touching the splintery-looking gray wharf boards, but Jack gets off his bike. "Public washrooms stink like the sewer, but the tourists don't seem to care. When you gotta go, you gotta go."

"Gotta go," I say.

"Gotta go already? But we just got here."

Repeating things helps me understand. Besides Robot Girl and Curly Kate, the kids at school call me Parrot Girl, too. I'm not a bird, but flying would be one of my Likes.

Jack rests his fishing rod up against part of the low rope fence all around the wharf edges. The breeze smells like the sea, fresh and cool and salty. Better than the toilet stink. A man in overalls is painting a boat named *Crystal Ann II*. Valiant Prince Turquoise is the color. If there was a *Crystal Ann I*, was she the same color? The fat gray wharf posts have pieces of rubber tire on the sides and plastic stretched across the top so they look like drums. Bongo drums.

"Why are there pieces of tire nailed to the posts?" I ask.

"Boats are all the time bumping into the piers; rubber keeps 'em from getting beat up."

Beat up. What mean kids do to other kids for no good reason.

Jack gets a little box out of his backpack. He opens it, shows me something inside that's shaped like Muzzy's silver feather earrings. "My grandpa swears by these as the best lure there is for catching mackerel. A Dexter Wedge."

"Dexter Wedge. It's iridescent," I say. Because he doesn't have much to protect by way of brains, I add, "Like a rainbow or gas that's spilled on a puddle."

"Whatever you say. Watch you don't get snagged, now." Jack hooks on the Wedge, sticks the fishing rod out to one side, snaps his wrist so the line whirs off the part that looks like a big spool of thread, and then flies out over the water. I move my bike closer to the chunky wooden edge of the wharf and watch where the line slices through the water. Sea Captain Blue.

"What are those giant crayons for?"

Jack looks at me like they do at school when I say the wrong thing. Even though I don't know why it was wrong.

I hum quietly and point to the giant orange and green crayons sticking up out of the harbor. Beach Walk Orange and Frog Pond Green.

He turns to face the water. "Oh, those. Yeah, I guess they do sorta look like crayons. They're depth markers to let boats know where the water's shallow so they can navigate around."

"Navigate around." I think Jack is eleven like me, or

maybe twelve, but he knows things like a grown-up. Maybe that's because he has an important job, bringing history to life. I eat one of my cookies while Jack fishes, a silent activity with a lot of watching and jerking the fishing rod.

"Got somethin'," he says after ten minutes. "Better back up so you don't get hit." The skinny tip of his rod bends down a bit, then the wheel part starts spinning so fast I can hardly see his fingers cranking the little handle. He pulls the rod straight up. Something's wiggling at the end of the line.

"Is it a ghost fish?"

"Even worse. Stupid squid." Jack unhooks the white fish, which looks like a baby octopus. It's still squirming as he drops it down a hole in the wharf. I can hear the splash. "No chance of catching any mackerel today. They hightail it out of the harbor when there's squid around; squid ink gets in their eyes, blinds them."

If I was a squid, I could use my ink to keep not-polite kids from staring at me. But I wouldn't want to make them blind. "Squid is the name of a boy in the book *Holes*. He has a stuffed purple octopus and wants to be a marine biologist. It's a made-up story but it seems true."

"Yeah, I think I read that one, year before last, maybe in Grade 5."

"Grade 5. I just finished Grade 5." Church bells. I count

them, then check my watch. Five o'clock. I'm late. I start fast-pushing my bike up the hill away from the wharf.

"Nice to know ya!" Jack calls after me. "Catch ya later."

I know I'm supposed to say something back, but I need to hurry. Is he trying to be my friend? Friends are supposed to share. I go back and give him my last chocolate chip cookie, then pedal away. I hear him laughing behind me. But I don't think it's mean laughing. Now, which way is Montague Street ...

- *Why do deer have such big eyes and ears?*
- *Why was the Wedge named Dexter?*
- *Does Jack want to be my friend?*

Chapter 7

"Well, I must say you're extremely punctual, Miss Katie. Just like the trains in France. If they're scheduled to arrive at 8:46, they arrive at precisely 8:46."

"Probably the people driving the trains have watches, like me." I hold up my wrist to show Aggie the watch Muzzy gave me for Christmas. It has a Lavender's Blue strap and a crescent moon under the glass face. "Time is easy because it's perfectly organized and always the same."

Aggie nods and lifts Silver Streak ahead. *Clunk, shuffle, shuffle.* "I'd never thought of time in those terms, but I suppose you're right. Twenty-four hours in a day, sixty minutes in each hour, and sixty seconds in each minute."

"And 86,400 seconds in a day." I rub the watch face with my thumb. "Time is predictable, not like people. Except for when we lost one hour, sixty minutes, on our way from Montreal."

"You'll find it again, I suppose, when you go back home.

"Go back home. In twenty-one more days."

I think Aggie's beauty rest is working because she looks more beautiful today, with her hair piled up on top of her head like a ballerina's.

After circle number six, eighteen minutes and twelve seconds, Aggie backs Silver Streak up to the sofa and sits down. She's breathing like Hilary at my school, who is allergic to peanut butter and also has asthma. "Gracious me, I'm all out of puff. How did I do?"

"Three minutes and two seconds for each circle."

"At least I improved on my time, but I'm pooped."

Poop. A synonym for feces. I look at the bathroom door over by the back porch.

"A silly way of saying I'm tired," she says. "Shall we work on the puzzle for a while?"

By the time we finish finding all the flat-edged pieces for the puzzle frame, I'm getting impatient. I want to find out what Catherine told the Moon. Was she scared to go to a strange faraway place, even though she was with her family? Was she mad about leaving Grandmother behind? Did strangers give her the hiccups?

"Can you tell me more of Catherine's story now? Please and thank you."

Aggie gets the splint box from the half-moon table beside the sofa. She taps her pointer finger up against her mouth. Either she is telling me to be quiet, which I already am being, or else she is thinking.

"Now, let me see—where were we? Wish I had that old treasure chart to jog my memory."

"Catherine's family was going by raft to Rotterdam, which is in Holland, synonym for the Netherlands, to board a ship for Nova Scotia." I sit down at the other end of the sofa. "I looked it up on Google, and it is 4,909 kilometers from Rotterdam to Nova Scotia. The Moon is more than 78.3 times that far from Earth, 384,400 kilometers, but you can't get there by boat."

"I can't even imagine such a distance," Aggie says.

"Her annoying little brother Nicholas called her Minette, which means Kitty in English, like your niece."

"Ah, yes." Aggie looks up at the jug on the mantel behind her, then back at me. I can feel her wanting me to look at her. So I do, fast. Her eyes are like Miss Matattall's, the x-ray kind that can see inside people and read faces and thoughts. My eyes are not x-ray eyes but I wish they were.

"What was the other thing inside the jug? Besides the birch bark?"

"Marvelous! I'm surprised you remembered that."

"I have a memory like an elephant."

She nods. "But we must be patient. The other jug item comes a bit later on in the story.

"Let me see if I can recall Catherine's words." She lifts one edge of the splint box lid, then puts one hand over her mouth. Why is she trying to make herself stop talking?

"Oh, my, how could I have forgotten this?" She takes a small notebook, Gothic Gold, out of the box. "Many moons ago, my sister and I wrote down some of our favorite passages from Catherine's letters." She turns the pages slowly, then shakes her head and wiggles her crooked fingers like she's playing the piano. "I had such perfect penmanship when I was young, before arthritis came to visit."

"Visitors usually go back home someday. Maybe your arthritis will, too."

"I suppose I can always hope. Let me read you this excerpt from January 2, 1752, while Catherine was still in France. Close your eyes and see if you can picture her in the attic, writing this on rough paper with her goose quill pen, a gift from Grandmother's ornery geese. I've always imagined her speaking with a charming French accent.

"*I must trust that Mama and Papa will make the best decision for all of us, yet I am a creature of habit, uncomfortable with change. And I wonder if it is true, the talk I have heard of wild beasts and wild men in the New World. Nicholas's longed-for pirates and whales may well be the very least of our troubles ..."*

Aggie does not have a charming French accent.

"I always wanted to give Catherine a hug, thinking of how frightened she must have been."

I look down at her rainbow socks. "I would like to see pirates and whales, but not wild men and wild beasts. But I don't think Nova Scotia would have wild beasts like lions and tigers."

"No, but there would have been wolves, bears, and wildcats, I suppose. And moose, which can be very dangerous. There was a farewell service at their church, which Catherine described as being more like a funeral than a celebration. Afterward, she was dreadfully heartbroken to say goodbye to Grandmother. As they were to travel separately to the New World, her cousin-sister, Elisabeth, gave Catherine her favorite moon hairclip to keep them connected. Catherine carved an owl, Chou Chou, as a gift for her cousin. Because of her big eyes, Elisabeth's pet name for Catherine was Chouette, a French word meaning ..."

"Little owl."

Aggie nods. "Good for you. Catherine and Elisabeth had a funny habit of touching noses when they said goodbye. My sister and I used to do the same ..." She stops talking and stares out the rectangle window above the piano. There's a hummingbird at the feeder.

I rub my nose. "The wings of the ruby-throated hummingbird

beat ninety times each second, and they are the only bird that can fly backwards."

"I spend a lot of time watching them; I've never seen one flying backward, but I'd like to. Anyhow, Catherine carried Grandmother's *méreau* with her on the journey, a leather disc with Jesus and his sheep carved into one side, the sun and stars on the other. The French Protestants used the *méreaux* to prove they were not Catholics, since only Protestants were welcomed by the British in the New World." Aggie pats the splint box. "Grandmother's *méreau* is among the missing items."

"Was it as big as a Frisbee, which is also a disc?" I ask.

Aggie makes a circle with her pointer finger and thumb. "The size of a large button, I suppose. Once they arrived in Rotterdam ..."

"That is an ugly name, but they have lots of tulips there."

"Indeed. It is a lovely city now, but compared to Catherine's home in Montbéliard, it was a dirty, noisy, smelly place, full of rude strangers. One of the rough sailors loading the ships pretended to be a nasty pirate and threatened to cut off Nicholas's ponytail!" She picks up the notebook. "Here's what Catherine wrote shortly after leaving Montbéliard:

"13th May, 1752: I was surprised to awaken to birdsong and sunshine this morning, as I expected I should die from a broken heart after bidding all of you farewell. It is my whimsical hope that perhaps after I read

these words to our friend the Moon, he can somehow relate them to you, Grandmother. Mama says Nicholas and I must be brave, but, despite the excitement, he continues to weep from missing you and his dear Nellie, and our long journey already threatens to be far from pleasant ..."

"Far from pleasant. Synonym for unpleasant. Was Nellie Nicholas's friend?"

Aggie shakes her head. "His pet goat. There was no room for animals on board ship, although there were plenty of uninvited rats. Don't you love the idea of the moon being able to carry Catherine's words home to her grandmother in France?"

I nod yes. "Grandmother would have seen the very same Moon as Catherine, even across the ocean. Some people think the Moon sees and hears everything, even without eyes or ears. I don't know if that is true, but lots of people believe in God, even though he's invisible, and it's almost the same thing."

Aggie nods. "You have such an interesting way of seeing things, Katie. The idea that my friends all around the world look up at the same moon as I do has always tickled my fancy." She reaches inside the splint box, then takes something out, hiding it inside her fist. Is this a guessing game, like when Muzzy gets me a treat from the corner store? I always guess black licorice because she knows that's one of my Likes.

"Is it Elisabeth's Moon hairclip?"

"No, but that's a very good guess." She opens her fist to

show me a small bag, Raccoon Dog Brown, with a drawstring pulled tight.

I sit up straight and hug my knees. "What is it?"

Aggie lets me hold the bag, then leans back into her pile of cushions.

The leather bag is soft like my old ballet shoes. "Is this really 263 years old? And why did Catherine have this little pouch?"

"Go ahead and open the drawstring."

I loosen the strings, hold it up to my nose, look inside. "It's empty. But it smells like the shoemaker's shop and the inside of your trunk."

Aggie smooths her hair back from her face, then opens the notebook. "This is one of my very favorite passages.

"30th May, 1752: Remembering your wise words of farewell gives me comfort, Grandmother, yet makes me weep. 'Roots of home for you to carry with you, my child. Memories to plant. No other place on earth shall ever smell so sweet as the place in which you were a child.' Remember? Your wise advice to hold the seed pouch close and cherish my memories whenever homesickness flooded my heart, as it does now, is most soothing. Just as you promised, I feel your love and spirit traveling with us, dear Grandmother. By the light of the Moon, I remain, as always, your loving granddaughter."

"Seed pouch? What happened to the seeds? What kind were they?"

"Acorns, horse chestnuts ... and, let me see now ... elm, lavender, and my favorite, brown-eyed Susans." Aggie rubs her new hip. "I always think of lavender as the smell of history, but I'm afraid that is a story for another day."

"Why are you afraid, and was Elisabeth's Moon hairclip the other thing inside the jug, because hairclips are long and skinny? And was the carved Chou Chou one of the treasures?"

Aggie claps her giraffe-freckled hands. "You are such a smart cookie."

"I am smart but I am not a cookie. I would only taste sweet to a cannibal or a lion, or a tiger, or maybe a wolf, since I'm made of blood and bones and muscles."

She nods. "Just an expression. But yes, the hairclip was in the jug, and later on in the splint box, but more about that later."

"And Montreal doesn't smell very sweet. More like cars and the sewer," I say.

"I'm sure you'll remember it fondly after you've grown up and moved away. Now, thinking of Catherine's voyage has made me miss visiting the waterfront. Let's take Silver Streak for another short romp. Help me get my sea legs back before you go, shall we? Then perhaps you could hang my bedding out on the line. Since I'm not getting out much these days, at least I can enjoy the fresh smells of outdoors while I'm sleeping."

After supper, I get out my old Science scribbler and use a little plate to draw a circle-shaped chart with twelve numbered spaces, like a pie. Maybe keeping track of the treasures will help jog Aggie's memory for Catherine's stories. In the first space, I write *Raccoon Dog Brown Leather Seed Pouch*. In space number two, I write *Elisabeth's Moon Hairclip*, and in space number three, I write *Grandmother's Méreau, Missing*, but I'm not sure if I spelled it right.

At bedtime, I read Moonbeam's bookmark message, then climb into bed with my Lavender Lady and find the Moon right away. Since he is as old as time, maybe he remembers Catherine Marguerite.

- *Did Grandmother's seeds and acorns grow into plants and trees?*
- *Do I have any cousin-sisters like Elisabeth?*
- *If Catherine was still alive, would she be my secret talking-to-the-Moon friend?*

Chapter 8

"How are you and Aggie making out?"

I look at Jo-Ellen. "Making out?" What the not-nice girls at school say when they talk about kissing boys.

"A synonym for getting along," Muzzy says with her mouth full, which is not polite.

"We are getting along fine," I say. "She is a very good storyteller. She says Silver Streak is trotting now instead of walking. Soon she might start galloping, or at least cantering."

Jo-Ellen laughs so hard she snorts tea out of her nose. While she's coughing, Muzzy wipes up the mess. "I'm sorry I've been so busy, Katie, but I haven't forgotten about Elizabeth's Books. We'll get there one of these evenings."

I nod yes and keep eating. After I finish my grilled cheese sandwich on homemade brown bread—fifteen bites times fifteen chews equals 225 chews—I pick up Butterscotch. I pedal slowly along the sidewalk, fast-looking at faces. I stop pedaling when I see two gray sneakers on a tall ladder. The house next door is named *Samuel Knickle, Ship's Captain, 1890s.* I think about the colors. Appassionata Purple with Kingfisher Blue trim. I push my bike up closer to the ladder, clear my throat, then cough. Jack is painting with a wide brush, but he doesn't look down at me.

I cough louder.

He keeps painting.

Maybe he found out I'm a left-out kid.

I'm about to turn my bike around, when I see the white plastic wires coming out of his ears. He notices me at the same time, pulls out the wires, and climbs down.

"Hey. I didn't hear you—listening to music. Not working today?" His white hat says Jodrey & Son, and his white overalls are covered with splotches of paint. Parrot Green.

"I helped Aggie this morning. But it's not really work."

"Painting sure is. I'm sweating like a pig."

"People sweat to cool off, but pigs usually wallow in mud to cool off," I say.

"Yeah. Guess that's a weird saying." Jack pulls a rag out of his back pocket. He dips it into a liquid that smells like the cleaner Jo-Ellen uses to scrub the café floors, then wipes his hands on the rag. "Aggie was my dad's favorite teacher ever, but I don't think he was a great student. Same as me."

"I'm a very good student," I say. "Especially in math. My foster mother, Muzzy, says my brain's bigger than most people's. I'm on the spectrum, the autism spectrum. Which is *not* like being *on* a Ferris wheel."

Jack shrugs. "No big deal. My cousin Simon is, too. Only he doesn't talk."

"Joseph at my school is also non-verbal, like your cousin Simon. He uses pictures and screaming to communicate. And sometimes hitting." One of my Dislikes.

A man who looks like Jack, but without hair, comes around the corner.

"Hey, Dad. This is Katie that I was telling you about."

"Allison Pearson's daughter?" he says. "Your mom and I were friends back in the day. I'm Jack Jodrey. Most folks call me JJ."

"Jack Jodrey, Senior," I say. "*Hic!* Allison is my Muzzy, my foster mother. My real mother, Moonbeam, is missing."

"Well, that's something you and Jack have in common."

Is Jack's mother also missing? Or is Moonbeam Jack's mother, too?

"Welcome to Lunenburg, Katie. Jack here is a good guy to show you around. He knows this town inside out."

Jack nods. "Yup."

I try to swallow my hiccups. "A sweater can be inside out, or a T-shirt. But not a town."

JJ and Jack laugh. "Too funny. I need to run over to the hardware store, anyway," JJ says, opening the door to his dusty black truck. "Have fun!"

Jack takes off his hat and starts unzipping his overalls. I turn away and look down the hill at the harbor. You are not supposed to watch other people undress, especially boys.

"No worries. I've got shorts on underneath."

I nod yes, but I don't turn around until he's finished. His long hair is in a ponytail like mine—only his is wavy and mine is frizzy.

He stuffs his clothes into a plastic bag and hangs it on his bike's handlebars. "Let's go. Want to leave your bike here with mine?"

I lock my bike to a black iron fence post. The combination is 21-03-37, which is easy to remember because 2 + 1 = 3, and 3 x 7 = 21.

"Do you know if there's a store called Elizabeth's Books on Montague Street?" I ask.

He points down the street. "Right down there, but they have really weird hours. It doesn't open until nine at night, or something crazy like that. I've never been inside, but my dad buys a lot of old books there."

Just past The Chickadee, we stop at the corner beside a Shamrock Green building with a wooden dungeon door and windows full of cooking tools. "Lunenburg is set up on a grid, you know, like graph paper for math, only massive, all kinds of huge rectangles. Montague, Pelham, Lincoln, Lawrence, Hopson, Kempt—the streets are all names of old British guys who were in Nova Scotia in 1753, I guess. The founding fathers."

"What about the old girls?" I ask. "The founding mothers, like Marie Langille, Catherine's mother?"

Jack laughs. "Men were more important back then, I guess."

"But there wouldn't have been any people without the mothers."

"So true. Guess the founding fathers never thought of that when they were naming the streets after themselves. And the wives would've had the same last names as their husbands in those days."

"Is your mother's last name Jodrey?"

Jack shrugs. "Who knows? I haven't seen her since I was about four."

About four. Like me. "I have the same last name as Moonbeam—Dupuis—but I don't know if that's her husband's last name. I use Muzzy's last name, too, so I'm Katie Dupuis Pearson, for now. Until Moonbeam comes back for me, or if Muzzy gives me back to the foster care people."

"She wouldn't do that, would she?"

"I hope not, but she is my third foster mother, so it's possible. My other foster mothers got rid of me when they fell in love with men who did not love me." I follow Jack past a brick building covered with painted sea creatures, then up a steep paved pathway cut into a grassy hill. "Also, Muzzy wants to be a foreign correspondent, a type of journalist that works overseas. It would be hard to take a kid to someplace far away, like Africa."

"I hope my mother took off to some crazy faraway place like that."

"Was your mother a journalist, too?"

Jack shrugs. "Don't know much about her. Don't care much, neither. Dad's all I need."

I can't make any connections, so I don't say anything.

"This part with the band shell has been a park forever. There's lots of music here in the summertime, mostly folk music."

"Do you like music?" I ask.

He nods. "I play guitar a little but I'm no good."

"I play piano and I'm very good," I say. "Especially when I play *Pachelbel's Canon*. Two women cried at my last piano recital. Muzzy said it was because the music made them happy, not sad."

Jack laughs. "Too bad you've got such a low opinion of yourself."

I stop walking. "But I don't. And that's not my opinion; I *am* a good pianist. I'm not as good as a boy named Kevin, who passed his Grade 9 piano exam when he was only ten. I did get a 95 on my Grade 3 piano exam, which was a lot harder than Grade 3 in school."

He puts up both hands like stop signs. "Kidding. I was just being sarcastic."

Sarcastic. I know this word, but it's like Portuguese, a language I don't understand.

"Jack!"

Near the playground at the top of the hill, a girl is windmill-waving.

Jack shouts and waves back. "Hey, Ruthie." He looks at me. "Let's go."

"Hi!" The girl is the same size as me but she has beautiful skin, Sand Patterns Brown, and long blonde hair. She looks like one of the whispering girls at my school. I cover my mouth to keep the hiccups inside. Is she Jack's girlfriend?

"Your sneakers are the bomb," she says, giggling. "I'm Ruthie."

Her Royal Magenta sneakers are twins to mine. I think she's smiling, so having sneakers that are the bomb must be different from the bombs that kill people.

"Katie's a CFA," Jack says. "Living at The Chickadee and

doing some stuff to help Aggie Mingo out for the summer."

"When I live in Montreal, I am not a CFA." I squeeze my Lavender Lady and swallow hard. "And my job is mostly keeping Aggie company and listening to her tell stories about her ancestor, Catherine Marguerite Langille, who was a CFA in 1753, and wrote letters to her grandmother back in France. The letters are lost, except for a few parts written down in a notebook."

"Awesome!" Ruthie says. "I love old stories and old stuff. I know Aggie from the market. She has a sister who makes sweet wood carvings."

"A weird witchy sister," Jack says. "She's like a hermit."

"That's mean," Ruthie says. "I've never even seen her. Have you?"

Jack shakes his head. "But I've heard stories about her chasing kids out of her woods."

"I know her name is Jessie," I say. "Aggie has lots of old stuff because she is old. *Hic!* Does your house have a nametag, Ruthie?"

She laughs. "No, I live in the boonies, out on Kissing Bridge Road, close to Jack. Want me to scare you to get rid of your hiccups?"

I shake my head no. Being scared is one of my Dislikes.

"My dad and Ruthie's mom are brother and sister." Jack says. "We're cousins."

Ruthie punches him on the shoulder. "But not kissing cousins."

I give her a quick look, but I think she's making a joke. People who want to hurt you make their eyes small and bunch up their eyebrows before they punch. Like Carter, the mean boy in my first foster family, Mrs. MacKinnon's. His fists were like hammers. Sledgehammers. He looked like a gorilla.

"See how we both have the crooked Jodrey nose?" Ruthie says.

I nod yes, then feel my own nose. It's more gumdrop-shaped than crooked. Does it look like Moonbeam's? Or my cousins', if I have any?

"Hey, I know an old Lunenburg story," Ruthie says. "Want to hear it?"

I look up quickly to see if she is talking to me, then nod yes. "Is it a true story? I read 78 books in Grade 5, 49 non-fiction, and 29 fiction. Right now I'm reading a book called *The Foreign Protestants and the Settlement of Nova Scotia,* which is longer and not as interesting as Aggie's stories, because hers are about a girl my age. I am on the autism spectrum but I'm not stupid."

Ruthie shrugs. "People always think I must be dumb because I don't go to regular school. I'm homeschooled but I don't care."

"Doesn't everybody have to go to school?" I ask. "Isn't that the law in Nova Scotia?"

"My mom's our teacher, and most of the time the kitchen table's our desk."

I would like to be homeschooled. If I wasn't a CFA, maybe Ruthie's mom could home-school me, too.

"I'm going to be a writer, or maybe an actor, or a singer. I LOVE writing stories, especially about the olden days."

"Like Catherine Marguerite's lost letters," I say. "Only they're non-fiction. Unless Catherine was making up the letters."

"Was she one of the original settlers?"

"I think so, but the story is still unfolding," I say. "History cannot be rushed."

"So true," Ruthie says. "Let's go up to the graveyard. By the Academy. I have a true story for you about a girl who died of a broken heart."

"Broken heart. Is that the same as a heart attack?" I ask, following her onto the sidewalk. "Catherine thought she would die of a broken heart when she said goodbye to her grandmother. But she was only eleven, and mostly it's old people who have heart attacks."

"I guess they're kind of the same," Ruthie says. "They can both kill you."

Some of the people we pass say hi to Jack and Ruthie. One

lady wearing a straw cowboy hat stops us to ask the time. "It's 3:30 PM," I tell her.

She takes off her sunglasses and stares at me too long. I look down at my sneakers, try to swallow my hiccups, squeeze my Lavender Lady. "Do I know you, honey, or are you just visiting?"

I want to say, "My name is Katie, not Honey," but I keep quiet so the hiccups will stay inside.

"Katie's just visiting for the summer," Jack says, looking at me. "You've never been here before, have you?"

I shake my head no. "And I live in Montreal."

"Oh. You just remind me of a girl I used to see at the Thursday market."

I squeeze my Lavender Lady harder. "Was her name Moonbeam?"

The lady laughs and puts her sunglasses back on. "I don't believe so, although her name escapes me. Her mother was a folk artist, I think. You kids have a nice day now!"

"This town's so small, everybody expects to know everybody else," Jack says. "People are nosy. Anyway, the buried girl was Sophia McLachlan. Her house was close to Aggie's."

Gravestones, Mudskipper Brown and Octopus Gray, are scattered across the lawn beside the Academy, beneath tall droopy trees.

"Gallows Hill," Jack whispers. "They used to hang

criminals up here." He points to an enormous tree as we walk across the spongy grass. "Maybe from that oak tree. They say that's the oldest tree in town, planted by the first settlers, but there's no way to know for sure."

"No way to know for sure. If the tree was cut down, they could count the growth rings," I say.

Ruthie nods. "Don't think that'll happen any time soon. Looks pretty healthy to me."

"Grandmother gave Catherine some acorns in a little leather pouch when she left France. Maybe she planted it. Is that your school?"

Jack shakes his head. "They closed the old Academy when I was in Grade 4. I go to Bluenose Academy on the other side of town, on the way to Mason's Beach."

"The *Bluenose* is the ship on the dime," I say.

"Uh-huh. The original *Bluenose*, the racing schooner, was launched here in 1921," Ruthie says. "Don't you think weeping willows are the perfect kind of tree for a graveyard?"

Weep. A synonym for cry. I nod yes. Because people weep when people die. Maybe trees do, too. Sap tears. Probably not because trees can't think or feel, because they don't have brains.

It's hard to read a lot of the dates because the headstones are too old and crumbly or covered with fuzzy moss and frilly lichen. Lemon Grass Green. Finally we come to a stone surrounded by a low black fence, with a fat broken heart being pulled apart by two chains.

Ruthie reads the headstone out loud. "Sophia McLachlan, 1865 to 1879."

"Her heart broke 136 years ago," I say.

Jack nods. "She did sewing for a rich lady who owned a seamstress shop in town."

Ruthie looks at me with wide-open eyes. Midnight Mystery Brown. "Can you imagine working all the time, especially sewing?"

I shake my head no. "I don't know how to sew; I work, but only some mornings. And I am only eleven, not fourteen like Sophia."

Ruthie puts up her hand for a high-five. "Eleven's the best age ever!"

I touch her hand quickly, then shove mine back in my pocket. Wrap my fingers around my Lavender Lady.

"Anyway," Jack says, "one day, the shop owner accused Sophia of stealing ten dollars."

"She couldn't stand living with the shame," Ruthie says, talking like an actor in a play. "So she took to her bed, spent her days weeping, becoming weaker and weaker, refusing food and drink, until finally one morning ..."

She pauses so I have to look away from the black broken heart and up at her. Her eyes are shiny "... she didn't wake up."

"Died of a broken heart from the shame she'd brought upon her family," Jack says. "And that's a true story. Uh-huh."

"True story. Uh-huh. Didn't she know it's wrong to steal?" I ask. "But ten dollars isn't very much money. One hundred dimes. Forty quarters."

"I guess it was a lot back in 1879." Ruthie laughs with her whole body. "Anyway, after Sophia's death, the seamstress lady's son confessed that he had stolen the money. Too late for poor Sophia."

"Maybe the son died of a broken heart, too. Because he told a lie. I never tell lies. I'm as honest as a boring day is long." Two brown and white striped snails are curled up together in the "S" of her name on Sophia's headstone. The Lavender's Blue violets in front of it are droopy. "After she died, do you think her parents were sorry they were ashamed of Sophia?"

"For sure," Ruthie says. "Hey, do you like swinging?"

I look to where Ruthie's pointing, at the high swings on the lawn out front of the Academy, and nod yes. Swinging is one of my Likes.

"Me, too. Let's go!"

"You should come out to my place sometime," Ruthie says while I'm unlocking my bike.

"Sometime." I try to make my face do a smile, then pedal

away. Are all the kids in Lunenburg as nice as Ruthie and Jack?

That night, only half of the Moon is visible.

- *Does it hurt to die of a broken heart?*
- *Did Moonbeam leave me behind because she was ashamed of me?*
- *Why would a road be called Kissing Bridge Road?*
- *Did Catherine grow that big oak tree from one of Grandmother's acorns?*

Chapter 9

Jo-Ellen pours Muzzy some more coffee. "Ran into Jack Jodrey at the Save Easy yesterday. Literally, with my cart, while I was searching for the cinnamon. He seemed very interested in knowing how long Allison Pearson was going to be in town."

Muzzy's face turns Tea Rose Pink, like after a run, and she tries to tuck her wavy hair behind both ears. Twice.

"I know his son," I tell Jo-Ellen. "Jodrey & Son bring history to life, and Jack Senior was Muzzy's friend back in the day."

Jo-Ellen laughs so hard she starts choking on her strawberry scone, spewing crumbs all over the table. Which is not polite. She wipes it up with a napkin. "Sorry, it's just that you sounded like a TV ad for The Discovery Channel. But the Jodreys certainly do bring history to life. JJ did most of the restoration work on The Chickadee before I opened."

"Are you hot?" I ask Muzzy. "Should I open the window?"

She covers both cheeks with her hands. "Oh, am I blushing? It's nothing—I used to be madly in love with Jack when I was a little older than you, about a hundred years ago."

She was not born a hundred years ago.

"Looks to me like that old flame could easily be rekindled." Jo-Ellen pushes herself up from the table and starts filling the salt and pepper shakers.

Why is she talking about fire?

"His marriage lasted just long enough ..."

"... to produce Jack Junior?" Muzzy gets up and starts wiping the tables, even though they already look clean. "That's ancient history. I'm not looking for romance." She wraps both arms around Jo-Ellen's not-skinny middle and rests her head on her shoulder. "Just friendship."

"You know what they say—you can catch more flies with honey than vinegar," Jo-Ellen says. "That miserable woman Jack was married to probably gave him vats of vinegar."

"She means it's better to be sweet like honey than sour like vinegar," Muzzy tells me, even though I didn't ask a question out loud.

"Jack hasn't seen that miserable woman, his mother, since he was four. Like me. But I hope Moonbeam isn't a miserable woman."

"If she's anything like you, she'd be the opposite of miserable," Jo-Ellen says.

"Happy," I say. "An antonym for miserable. I'm happy today because I'm going with Jack to Rous's Brook. After Ruthie and I help him with his fort on the Back Harbour trail."

"Why don't you bring your friends here for lunch someday?" Muzzy asks.

"I don't think they're my friends, but I would like them to be. Friends have sleepovers and share secrets. They finish each other's sentences, like you and Jo-Ellen."

Muzzy hooks her baby finger around mine. "Give it time. Doesn't Aggie need you to help her today?"

I shake my head. "I'm having two days off because she is having a sleepover with her friend from Halifax. But they won't be having any pillow fights."

"Probably a good idea. How's she doing with her hip?"

"Silver Streak is almost ready to retire. Like Aggie, who is already retired."

"Perfect! We'll have to invite Aggie over for a meal someday soon," Jo-Ellen says. "And maybe Jodrey & Son, too." She winks at Muzzy, then looks back at me and nods toward the counter. "Be sure and take some of those fresh ginger cookies to share." She opens the screen door and turns the driftwood sign around so CLOSED faces inside the café. "Another day, another dollar."

I hope she makes more than one dollar. There is nothing on The Chickadee menu that costs less than three dollars.

"Why did you pick this oak tree?" I lean Butterscotch up against a skinny birch tree across from the fort tree. Jack's saw is twanging like the rusty pulley on Aggie's clothesline.

He stops sawing and waves the saw at me. "Every board takes about an hour to cut. Stupid thing's about as sharp as a bowling ball."

"But bowling balls are smooth, not sharp."

"Exactly. Anyway, this is a good sturdy oak, no dead parts, and it's got nice, deep roots. It would suck to go to all this work then have it get wiped out in the next hurricane."

"This is not a part of the world that gets a lot of hurricanes. Tropical countries like Haiti and the Dominican Republic have an entire season of hurricanes."

"Usually that's true." Ruthie's sitting on the ground, looping a thick piece of rope around her hand and elbow. "But my parents still go on about some of the massive trees they lost during Hurricane Juan, before I was even born."

"Maybe oak trees live for a long time because they have such deep roots," I say, patting the tree's rough bark. "Like Aggie's family. Deep roots that keep them in one place. I don't have any roots. Counting Lunenburg, I've been uprooted

93

and transplanted five times in seven years. Before that, I can't remember."

Jack is back to sawing and doesn't say anything.

"Everybody has roots," Ruthie says.

"I live with Muzzy, but we don't share roots or family trees because she's my foster mother. We don't share toothbrushes, either, but she shares her last name with me."

"Oh." Ruthie's eyebrows go up in the middle. She has the kind of face that's always moving. I would like to be able to read her face. "What happened to your other parents?"

"My real mother, Moonbeam Dupuis, is missing."

"Is that her real name? It's cool."

I nod yes. "But I don't think she's missing me much. And I don't know anything about my father or his roots."

Ruthie stands up. Her eyes are shiny and she walks toward me, holding out both arms, like a TV zombie. I crouch down beside the coil of thick Poe's Raven Black rope. Hugs are one of my Dislikes.

"Oh," Ruthie says. "Sorry. Our cousin Simon isn't a hugger, either."

"Your non-verbal cousin Simon," I say. "This rope is the color of one of my colored pencils: Poe's Raven Black. Muzzy told me Poe was a poet who wrote a poem about a raven. He had a very good name for a poet, except for the missing 't' at the end. The poem is long and confusing."

Ruthie laughs and kneels down beside me.

"Have you read the book about a dog named Winn Dixie?" I ask.

"It's my favorite," Ruthie says. "It's funny and sad at the same time."

"It seems like a true story but it's not. Opal, Winn Dixie's girl, knew ten things about her missing mother. I only know two things: Moonbeam Dupuis has been to Lunenburg and she left me with the foster care people."

"Maybe she's still here," Ruthie says. "Want me to ask my parents if they've ever heard of her?"

"Okay. Since they've lived here forever, they might remember her. Have you ever made a rope ladder before?" I ask.

Ruthie picks up a piece of black plastic pipe from the pile. "Nope. But we're gonna figure it out."

Ruthie is good at knowing when to stop asking questions, but not good at tying knots. She grits her teeth together and makes bad noises, like a mad cat. "How are we supposed to get all the stupid rungs attached to the rope without cutting it?"

"Stupid is a very not-nice word," I say. "Like retarded." Two of my Dislikes.

"They're only pieces of plastic. You don't care, do you, little Mr. Pipe?" She pats the piece of pipe and laughs, so

I know the mad I hear in her voice is only pretend. Ruthie is probably very good at make-believe because she likes to act and has a lot of imagination to write stories. I am very bad at make-believe but very good at figuring things out. Like thousand-piece jigsaw puzzles. Unless one piece is missing, which is one of my Dislikes.

I take one of the pipe rungs and shove the long rope all the way through it so half the rope dangles from each end of the rung. This will be the top rung of the ladder. Then I tie the halves together in a double knot under the middle of the rung and criss-cross the two long pieces of rope through the next rung and tie another double knot. After the third rung, it's the same shape as the number 8.

"That's brilliant!" Ruthie claps her hands. "You should be an engineer or something."

"Probably I will be an engineer or maybe a concert pianist or a doctor. I haven't decided yet since I am only eleven, but they are all jobs that require right-brain thinking. The right side of my brain is bigger than the left, the same as Sir Isaac Newton, who discovered that water could separate light into all the colors of the spectrum, like a rainbow."

"Wasn't he the guy that had the apple fall on his head?"

"That is just a story, but an apple falling did help him when he was developing his theory of gravity, which is the pulling force that keeps the moon the same distance away all the time so it doesn't wander off when it's orbiting Earth, and ..."

"Look out below!"

We jump out of the way just in time as a long board comes crashing down, one corner stabbing into the dirt beside us.

"Speaking of gravity! Slippery little sucker," Jack says, jumping down after the board. "At least I got the floor almost done. How you makin' out with the ladder?"

"We are not kissing it," I say. "But we have figured out how to put it together."

Jack laughs. Ruthie holds up the first three rungs and says, "I think we'll need about twelve rungs altogether. The design was all Katie's idea."

"Sweet!" He high-fives both of us, then puts his hammer and saw in his backpack. "That'll give you something to do next time we're out here. Ready to head out to the brook now?"

We cross the road and bike along part two of the trail between walls of scratchy bushes, ducking zooming dragonflies. "Water break," Jack calls out when we get to a wooden bench looking out over the water. The Back Harbour doesn't have as many boats as the Front Harbour.

I park Butterscotch, then get my water bottle and the ginger cookies out of my backpack.

"Yum," Ruthie says. "My second favorite, after whoopie pies."

"Homemade?" Jack asks.

"Café-made," I say. "But since Jo-Ellen lives above the café, I guess they are homemade."

"You're hilarious," Jack says, taking a big bite. "Seriously."

Hilarious. A synonym for funny. "And what are whoopie pies? Like whoopie cushions that make rude noises?"

Ruthie shakes her head. "Two soft chocolate cookies with yummy white frosting in between." She closes her eyes and licks her lips. "My mom's are the best!"

We watch two people on a boat, pulling on ropes, unfolding the white triangle sails. The strong breeze makes the sails billow out like the wings of a white heron I saw once. Only bigger.

"I'd kill to have a sailboat like that," Jack says. "Instead of Dad's old dory."

"What's a dory look like?" I ask. "And killing is against the law, the same as stealing, only worse."

"It just means I'm jealous. If you think of a sailboat as being kind of like a bird, all graceful, a dory's more like an ox, a working boat, all heavy and ..."

"Clunky." Ruthie finishes his sentence for him.

"Can I see your dory sometime?"

"Sure. We keep it over at Ruthie's dock." He points to the other side of the harbor. "Just over there off First Peninsula."

"We should get going. My chore today is weeding the strawberry patch," Ruthie says, getting back on her bike. "If you're in a bad mood, yanking out weeds can be kind of fun."

"Muzzy says I'm growing like a bad weed," I say. "But that doesn't mean she wants to yank me out."

Jack closes his eyes, holds his stomach, and starts coughing. Or is he laughing?

"Are you okay?" I ask. Because he is having trouble breathing. Like Hilary when her asthma attacks her. Or maybe he's choking, and I know how to do the Heimlich Maneuver because we learned it at school.

"You're too funny," he says, gasping and starting to pedal. "And that's a good thing."

At the end of the trail, we bike up a little hill past a hospital-looking building. "Harbour View Haven" the sign says.

"The nursing home," Jack says. "Our grandpa lives there. He's got Alzheimer's."

"Did he recognize you on the weekend?" Ruthie asks.

"Nope. Kept calling me Jeffrey." Jack looks at me. "That's his little brother who died about sixty years ago."

"That's so sad," Ruthie says. "He always thinks I'm Mom. What did you do?"

"Same as I always do. Pretended I was Jeffrey."

"Aggie's mother had dementia before she died," I say. "Because she was a ferocious housekeeper, Aggie thinks she threw out Catherine's letters when she was cleaning."

"That sucks." Jack bikes past the nursing home toward a big Charcoal Gray stone. It looks like a giant gravestone. "The names of the founding families are written there—like Jodrey."

"And Langille," I say, following him and then getting off Butterscotch. "Catherine's father was David."

"They're organized by the name of the ship they came over on."

It's easy to find both names because the lists are in alphabetical order and also organized by the ships' names. I know the Langilles came on the *Sally*. Dupuis isn't anywhere.

"I asked my dad if he ever heard of somebody named Moonbeam Dupuis," Jack says.

I fast-look at him. "Did he say yes?"

He shakes his head no and gets back on his bike. "But he thought it was a pretty flakey name."

"Flakey is a synonym for falls apart easily, like Jo-Ellen's piecrust. How could a name fall apart?"

Jack laughs and pedals away. We coast down a little hill, stop by an overgrown path, and lean our bikes up against a chain-link fence.

On the gravelly beach, I look down at the trickle of water between the tall weeds. "It doesn't look like a brook."

"Well, not anymore, but it's famous for being the first place the settlers stepped on shore in 1753," Ruthie says, as we wade through the weeds down to the harbor. "Our ancestors."

"Ancestors. Your family tree roots," I say. "From 262 years ago."

She nods.

"John Rous was the captain of the *Albany*, the main ship that brought the settlers here from Halifax," Jack says. "I had to do a school project on him one time."

Down by the harbor, we sit on some boulder islands surrounded by dry, crunchy seaweed mounds that look like hay. I stare out past the Battery Point lighthouse to the open ocean, listening to the seagulls squawking and the waves splashing. Was Catherine excited when she saw her new home for the first time? Or was she scared because she was a creature of habit, uncomfortable with change, like me? I look up the hill behind me, but I can't imagine what it would look like without all the houses. I reach into my pocket and rub my Lavender Lady. She feels warm like the sun on my face.

"Morning Glories."

I look to where Ruthie's pointing to some pale flowers.

Peachy Whisper Pink. They're hard to see up against the Octopus Gray rocks.

"But it's the afternoon," I say. "And they still look glorious."

She shrugs. "I know. They're usually closed up by this time of day."

"You ever seen the ghost ship?" Jack asks.

I look up to see if he's joking but his face is straight, his eyes wide open. No winks.

Ruthie shakes her head and combs her hair with her fingers. "Uh-uh. I don't believe in ghosts. Plus I'm never down here after dark."

"Ghosts aren't real. They're something people made up to convince themselves that people don't really die," I say. "That their spirits are still alive. If everybody who ever died was floating around being a ghost, the air would be too full of them. There'd be no room for us."

"I like to imagine that my ancestors' spirits are alive in our old treasures that used to belong to them," Ruthie says.

I can't make a connection because I don't have any old treasures that used to belong to my ancestors. I squeeze my warm Lavender Lady. It's a treasure, but Moonbeam isn't exactly my ancestor.

Jack laughs. "It'd be cool, though, to talk to the ghosts of those old guys. Some people swear they've seen a ghost ship here, usually in June, around the time the first settlers arrived. I've seen the devil's fire down here, but no ghost ship."

"The devil's not ..."

"... real, either," Jack says, finishing my sentence.

"Devil's fire is what we call this algae that makes the water glow with a spooky green light," Ruthie says. "It's real, but the ghost ship's just in people's imaginations."

Jack nods. "Pretty sure they're just seeing shapes in the fog, but whatever floats their boat."

Before I can figure out what he means, Ruthie jumps up. "Come on, Katie. Last one to the bikes is a loser!"

Loser. Synonym for left-out kid. I'm the last one there but I don't feel like a loser.

Are Ruthie and Jack my friends?

Chapter 10

Aggie gives me a jingle early Friday morning and asks me to come over. She's sitting on the sofa working on the puzzle, but she's wearing a jacket and there's a suitcase on the floor beside the door.

I stand beside her and put a flag piece on top of one of the sailboats in the puzzle. "Are you going on a trip? Jo-Ellen said we should invite you for supper sometime so you won't be lonely."

"Perhaps next week. She's such a pet."

"Pets are cats and dogs, or maybe fish and hamsters. Jo-Ellen's a person."

Aggie nods and stares at the puzzle. "Just a term of endearment. She's a wonderful cook."

When she looks up at me, her mouth looks like an upside down crescent Moon, and her eyes are puffy and wet. Was she crying because her new hardware is hurting like the devil?

She pats the sofa beside her, a synonym for sit down, please and thank you.

I take off my sandals and squeeze myself back into the sofa corner. "Do you need Silver Streak? Or some medicine? I have ibuprofen in my backpack. Because sometimes I get headaches that make my brain feel like a balloon about to burst."

She shakes her head, pulls a crumpled tissue from her sleeve, then blows her nose.

"Do you have a cold? The flu?" I hold my breath, put my hands over my ears. *Pa-dum pa-dum.*

She shakes her head again. "I'm sorry, my dear. Forgive an old lady for burdening you with her troubles. I'm an old softie, always tearing up about one thing or another. It's probably nothing, but my heart's been misbehaving. Just as my hip was mending nicely. The doctor has said I need to have some tests, so I'm off to the hospital in Halifax."

I look at the splint box on the glass table. "Is your heart broken? Like Sophia McLachlan's?"

The corners of her mouth turn up and her eyes go squinty. "Not exactly. I'll possibly be gone for a week. More, if they find any serious problems that require fixing. I'm sorry I have to be away when we've just gotten started on Catherine's stories."

"I will be here for seventeen more days. Will you be gone that long?"

She lifts up her shoulders and pushes the palms of her hands toward the ceiling.

I jump up when she reaches across to pat my bare arm. "Do you need me to do anything while you're in the hospital? I could wash some dishes or hang out the laundry so your sheets will smell like outdoors."

"No, thank you. But you might give my houseplants and window boxes a drink while I'm away. The only other keeper of Catherine's stories is my estranged sister Jessie, and she ... well, she ..."

I rub my Lavender Lady hard, like she's a magic genie lantern. Except genies are only make-believe. I look at the splint box.

"S-stranged? Is that a synonym for family feud? Where does your strange sister live?"

"Just outside town."

I walk quickly to the front door. "I can take my bike, Butterscotch. Well, it's not really my bike, but I'm borrowing it from Jo-Ellen's neighbor, whose name I don't know."

"It's not that simple, Katie. Family relations rarely are. We're estranged because Jessie and I had a spat. We haven't spoken to each other in years and years."

"Years and years. There was some sort of scandal around Jessie's daughter that blew up into a family feud, but you are from the same family tree." I drop down into the velvet chair. Forest Green. "You have the same roots."

"Sometimes roots and blood ties aren't enough to keep a family together. When our parents passed, everything in our family home was divided painstakingly evenly, with the help of lawyers, of course. Furniture, dishes, antiques, photographs, papers, and letters."

"Your strange sister Jessie must be nice, even if she doesn't talk to you. She made you disordered rainbow socks and let you have all Catherine's splint box treasures. And Grandmother's snuff jug."

"She received her fair share of our family's history. I miss her dreadfully, but it is by her choice that we remain estranged. Synonym for at odds, not speaking."

I get back up and stand by the door, rubbing my Lavender Lady. I *need* to know what Catherine said to the Moon. And I *need* to fill in all the empty spaces on my pie chart. Putting the very last piece in a puzzle is the best part.

"Maybe we could send your sister an email," I say. "That's not the same as talking. It's easier because there are no faces to confuse you."

Aggie smiles. "I don't believe Jessie would be any more

adept at using technology than I, and I doubt she has the benefit of a young helper, as many Lunenburg children are frightened of her."

I fast-look at her eyes. "Frightened of her. But you're not scary. Jack said Jessie was weird and witchy. Why are Lunenburg children scared of your strange sister?"

Aggie pats the top of the splint box, like she's trying to smooth out its wrinkles—only it's already smooth, except for the holey star. "They like to pretend she's a witch." She shuts her eyes, does a little grunt. Is her new hip hurting? Her misbehaving heart? "Along the lines of the wicked witch in *Hansel and Gretel.* She was always rather odd, even as a child. Marching to the beat of her own drum."

Her own drum. Like me.

"Honest to a fault, you might say."

"I'm as honest as the day is long," I say.

She nods. "Jessie has always reveled in Mother Nature and all her bounty. In fact, she lives in the forest near the sea, across the harbor, out by Mason's Beach."

"Mason's Beach. Where's that?"

"Just down the other side of the hill that runs up alongside the golf course," Aggie says. "But she doesn't receive visitors these days. Or so I've been told."

I sit back down beside her. I can feel her staring at me,

but I keep my eyes on the floor so her X-ray eyes won't see me thinking about Google Maps.

"Jessie was always far crankier than me, which is perhaps why she pursued whittling rather than teaching as her life's vocation. She's a fairly well-known folk artist and has always preferred the company of animals and wood to that of people. Even as a child, she didn't seem to have a sense of fun. As though she was born a little old lady."

Little old lady. Like Aggie. Only crankier. "Playing at being settlers was probably a fun game. I'm making a pie chart of the treasures to help jog your memory for the stories. Does Jessie have a better memory for details than you?" I ask. "Or does she have Alzheimer's, like Jack's grandpa?"

Aggie pushes up the corners of her mouth so the crescent Moon is right-side-up, then closes her eyes and rubs the V-shaped part of her forehead in between her almost invisible eyebrows. Is she tired or thinking? I focus on her rainbow socks. *Red, orange, yellow, green, blue, indigo, violet.* Only yellow, green, and blue are disordered. Like Aggie's strange free-thinker sister.

"I don't believe she has dementia. My mind certainly isn't as razor-sharp as it once was," she says finally. "Perhaps Jessie's isn't, either, although she's five years younger than me. I suppose she still has her copy of the translated letters."

I stand up again. "Do you need me to do anything right now?"

"You could make me a nice cup of tea, if you have time."

I boil the water, pour it over a teabag in the Tea With Milk Brown teapot, and let it steep for exactly six minutes, the way Aggie likes it. Not five, not seven, exactly six minutes—360 seconds. I look away from my watch and stare out the kitchen window at the big tree in the side yard while I wait. The tree with the chipmunk cave.

Mason's Beach is just outside town, past the Bluenose Academy.

I could push Butterscotch up the steep hill.

And I don't believe in witches or fairy tales.

That night, I get out my colored pencils, open my old scribbler, and draw tiny pictures of the treasures in the chart spaces. I look up at the Moon.

- *Will Aggie's strange sister tell me the rest of the stories?*
- *Why hasn't Jessie spoken to Aggie in years and years?*
- *Is Jessie on the autism spectrum, too, because she marches to the beat of her own drum?*

Chapter 11

After supper the next day, I bike the trail along the edge of the harbor. I slow down and ring my bell when I come up behind somebody with frizzy Apricot Brandy Brown hair. When she looks back over her shoulder, I see it's an old lady who probably dyes her hair.

I stop to look at some sparkly gold seaweed in the big windows of a brick building called The Lunenburg Foundry & Engineering, Limited. After the tennis courts, I bike past a big white house with a name tag that says: *1915, Built for Captain Angus Walters, Skipper of the Bluenose*, then follow the arrow pointing to Mason's Beach. The ship parked across the harbor is *Bluenose II*, and I don't know who its captain is or where he lives.

At a smooth green part of the golf course, I have to get off and push up the steep hill. I keep my face turned away so if a ball comes, it will hit my helmet. Near the top, I stop to catch my breath and take my pulse. When it gets below 22, which is really 88 because I only counted for fifteen seconds, I look behind me, back down across the harbor at all of Lunenburg. The frosting houses, the Crackling Crimson Red buildings, the sailboats and dories, the orange and green crayons, which are really depth markers for navigation; everything looks miniature from way up here. I would like to be able to draw it all, but I would need a very big piece of paper.

By the Topmast Motel at the very top of the hill, I get back on and coast down the other side. It's not so steep, but I squeeze the brakes to keep from going too fast. Speed kills. Synonym for slow down. Besides one white mansion, there are no other houses, just a forest on both sides with some For Sale signs. When the road flattens out again by the Atlantic View Motel, I get off and push my bike across the road and along a grassy path, out toward the water. The skinny strip of gravel along the edge must be Mason's Beach. This beach isn't sandy, and there's no rushing roaring surf like at Hirtle's Beach, where Jo-Ellen took us on Sunday. The houses don't look like Hansel and Gretel witch houses. And there's no forest.

I push my bike slowly back up the hill, moving my head back and forth, side to side, staring into the dark trees. Other than a dog barking, a few cars whooshing past, and my tires crunching on the gravel shoulder, it's quiet. There's no wind, so even the trees are silent. Which is one of my Likes. But this isn't the peaceful kind of silent. More the creepy, hold-your-breath kind, like in scary movies. One of my Dislikes.

"Oh!" A shaggy dog runs out of the woods at me, tilting up his snout and barking. I act like a statue. His teeth look sharp, and he has white froth around his mouth, a sign of rabies. He's the color of a fox, Burnt Orange, but his ears are floppy, not pointy. He sniffs my bike all around, then licks the white knuckles of my left hand. It tickles.

"Woof," I say, sitting on my bike seat, squeezing both brakes, keeping one foot on the high pedal in case I need to ride away quickly. I hope I don't have to because it's uphill. "Are you a nice dog or the mean kind that rips heads off rabbits?" A boy in Grade 3 told a true story for his Share and Tell about his grandfather's dog doing that to his pet rabbit. Mean dogs are one of my Dislikes.

He or she sits beside me and looks straight up at me, with only the tip of his pink tongue showing between his teeth. Do dogs smile?

He rests one heavy paw on my knee. I shake it and look straight at his Truffle Brown eyes. He looks away. To keep me from trying to see inside his brain, maybe. "Don't worry. My eyes aren't x-ray eyes," I tell him. When he presses his head up against my bare leg, he's soft and warm, like he's been lying in the sun.

"Miranda! Git over here right now, girl!"

Girl. The raggedy voice screeches out at us from the dark woods, but I can't see who it belongs to. The dog barks once, then licks my leg and trots back across the road, disappearing into the trees. I try to wipe off the slobber blobs she left on my shorts.

Miranda. Is she Jessie's dog? I cross the road, lock Butterscotch to a signpost, Speed Limit 50, then try to jump across the narrow ditch. It's wider than I thought. About halfway up the other side, one sneaker sinks into the muck. I fall to my knees, grabbing onto a bush to keep from falling to the bottom of the deep ditch. I pull myself the rest of the way up the bank, then try to scrape the muck off my sneaker with a stick.

There's kind of a path through the tall grass but, partway along, it's blocked by a pile of broken hay bales. Are there cows or horses out here? It seems more like a place for deer and raccoons. The trees are packed close together, mostly coniferous not deciduous. I start breathing fast, like when I can't find any personal space in the middle of a crowd. I squeeze my warm Lavender Lady and tiptoe around the hay, following the flattened-out grass downhill. I look behind me when a car zooms past with its radio blaring. *Fun, Fun, Fun.* But I can't see it for the hill. I hope Butterscotch is safe. Because when you borrow something, you should always look after it.

I track Miranda's barking to where she's standing on just her back legs up against a tall tree, her front paws reaching up. Is there a raccoon? Or a squirrel? I look up, squint and blink.

Not a raccoon. Not a squirrel.

A person.

A person all dressed in black, hanging by her knees upside down from a branch. With her arms folded across her chest. Like a giant bat. Wearing a silvery cape.

Chapter 12

"Inversion therapy."

I'm hiding behind a bushy tree when the upside-down person starts talking. I know speech therapy and physiotherapy, but not inversion therapy. I put one hand over my mouth to trap the hiccups.

"Hanging upside down. Gets the blood circulating. Improves my creative potential, feeds my brain so it doesn't atrophy, landing me with the rest of the old fogies over in Harbour View Haven."

Harbour View Haven. Where Jack's grandpa lives. This is an old person, then. An old person with long Silver Sword Gray hair. But she is acting like a kid, not a cranky old lady.

She swings back and forth a few times, then grabs onto the branch with both hands, unhooks her legs, lets them dangle in the air, then drops to the rooty ground in a monkey crouch. Miranda trots over next to her and sticks her snout in underneath one of the woman's bony giraffe-freckled hands. Like Aggie's bony age-spotted hands.

The lady pushes Miranda away, stands up, and closes her eyes. She's not much bigger than me. "Give me a minute now, to get my bearings, redirect my blood flow." She shakes her head and pushes her hair back off her face, using both hands. "Dizzy as Dorothy in a twister."

"Twister. Dorothy Gale," I say, keeping my eyes on Miranda. "I know *The Wizard of Oz. Hic!* You're too small to be the Wicked Witch of the West. But you are wearing striped socks and you do look scary."

Her eyes pop open. Blue Green Velvet. Like Aggie's. "My reputation precedes me. Being known as a witch allows me to enjoy uninterrupted privacy out here ..." she makes both dark eyebrows go up "... most times. Your knees are bleeding, whoever you are." She looks away, then jerks her eyes back to my face. Like the new kids at school do when they see me for the first time. As if my face is a hard puzzle or a challenge-round mental math problem, like 23 times 24. "We met before?"

I shake my head no and look down at my knees. Blood is trickling from small cuts in both of them. "I'm Katie. I don't believe in witches. *Hic!* Or fairies, or ghosts. Blood is one of my Dislikes. Especially my blood. Do you have a Band-Aid?"

"Just Katie?"

"Katie Dupuis Pearson."

"You a CFA?"

"CFA. Come from away. *Hic!* Yes, I come from Montreal, but I'm living at The Chickadee this summer with my foster mother, Muzzy. And I know you are Jessie, Aggie's strange sister."

She lifts her eyebrows at me again. "Just let me get my clompers, now." I watch Jessie's hunched back as she turns, shoves her feet into big wooden shoes, then walks away from me, Miranda trotting after her. "Might as well come in for a cuppa. Since you're here and you don't believe in witches. Might help get rid of those hiccups."

I push the glow-in-the-dark button on my watch. I have to be home by eight o'clock, which is in one hour. "Cuppa tea? Is it the red rose kind?"

She stops and looks back over her shoulder. "Either that or eye of newt. Or maybe ear of mouse. 'Spose you're a bit young for my dandelion wine." She horse-snorts like Bessie who works for Trot in Time, then whistles for Miranda. I follow them along the path that winds deeper and deeper into the getting-dark woods.

At the edge of a clearing, she stops to wait for me. The sun is setting, finger-painting the sky. Summer Sea Blue, Daisy Mae Yellow, and Georgia Peach Pink.

And then I see her house. "*Hansel and Gretel.*" My eyes jump around, trying to see everything at once. "But no candy and cake."

She takes a bow, like an actor or a pianist. "The Gingerbread Hag, at your service. And I don't eat sugar or gluten. Called the cottage 'Hag End' when I first moved out here. You know—after Bilbo Baggins's Bag End?"

I nod yes. "Hag. A synonym for witchy old lady." Her house is all shades of green and brown, like a mossy hobbit house with round windows—only all the edges are sparkly. I get closer and see that it's crystals and beach glass. Lavender's Blue, Amber, Frog-Pond Green, and Aqua Whisper. I find my warm Lavender Lady in the corner of my pocket and run my thumb back and forth across her jagged points. *One, two, three, four, five, six, seven, eight, nine.* "Beach glass is one of my Likes. And crystals."

"You and me both. The ocean's a carver, like me," Jessie says. "Same as sandpaper on wood, its salty waves soften the sharp edges of the glass."

The gray stone path leading up to the cottage is lined with flower bushes. Clown Cheeks Pink and Toucan Yellow. The door is bursting with animals, wooden creatures carved into it. Squirrels scampering, a raccoon peeking, owls and hawks swooping, prickly porcupines, rabbits, and deer. "They look so real," I say.

"My family." Jessie pulls the door open by its snake-shaped handle. There are more animals on the inside of the door. "Easier than humans—don't give me any guff. Welcome to our humble abode."

Abode. A synonym for home. I follow her and Miranda's wagging tail inside, put my Royal Magenta sneakers next to her clompers on the braided rug.

I blink to get used to the darkness, even though two of the Oatmeal Brown log walls are mostly windows. They're full of dangling prisms, rectangles, orbs, and diamonds. Rainbows flicker everywhere.

"The spectrum," I say. "I am on the spectrum, the autism spectrum. If it's like the rainbow spectrum, I hope I am violet, like my favorite colored pencil, Lavender's Blue."

Jessie fills a black kettle with water from a bucket and puts the kettle on the woodstove. "Never heard tell of that kind of spectrum. You look white and a little freckly to me, not purple."

"A lot freckly," I say. "Thirty-six when I counted the ones on my face this morning. Thirty-seven, counting this mole by my lip."

She points her eyes up to the ceiling. "I like purple. Got a fondness for lavender, as you can tell."

I look up at the bunches of dried purple flowers hanging from the rafters. There are all kinds of wooden birds there, too: blue jays, seagulls, and an eagle. I close my eyes, then do a yoga breath, fill my lungs with Jessie's air. "Lavender is the smell of history."

"Uh-huh. Lavender's good for whatever ails you, most particularly to keep the bugs away and help you relax. I've got a nice patch of it out back, just about to blossom."

"Blossom," I say. "Synonym for flower."

She breaks off a branch of the dried lavender and holds it under my nose.

"I recognize that smell but I don't know why, and Grand-mother gave Catherine Marguerite some lavender seeds to plant."

"My mother couldn't stand the smell; thought it meant I was a hippie heathen."

I don't know what a hippie heathen is, but Jessie doesn't seem like she'd be very good at answering questions, and I don't want her to chase me away.

"Have a seat if you can find one that's empty. Let me have a gander at those knees."

I want to tell her that gander is a synonym for male goose, but I move some books and sit down on a chair that looks like it used to be hockey sticks. *Sherwood, Easton, Titan.* Miranda flops down beside me on a cushion with a low throne back that used to be part of a bed. Aubergine Purple. Aubergine is the French word for eggplant, which is one of my Dislikes. The vegetable, not the color.

Jessie trickles some cool water over my knees, then goes outside and comes back with a handful of leaves.

"Dogwood," she says, giving me one to look at. "Also known as bunchberry." I hold my breath when she presses the rest of them up against my cuts. But she doesn't touch my skin with her fingers. Her fingernails are dirty, and dirty fingernails carry germs.

The shiny little leaf has one vein in the middle, then three smaller ones on each side. It's like the teardrop leaves I drew on my family tree picture at school.

"The Mi'kmaw people taught our ancestors a thing or two about using plants for medicinal purposes. A lost art nowadays. Press on that for a few minutes, then just leave it open to the air. Tellin' people to cover up cuts is just a scam the Band-Aid people are running." She turns back to the woodstove. "Honey?"

I stretch out my legs in front of me and nod. "Honey. One spoonful, please and thank you." The mantel above the woodstove is lined with owls. "Did you make all those?"

She nods, passes me a cup of tea, then sits down on a loveseat. It matches Aggie's velvet sofa. Sunny Day Gold. "These are just my favorites. Most of my carvings I sell. I'm a whittler, but the highfalutin types call me a wood artisan. A folk artist."

"Wood artisan. A synonym for folk artist and whittler." We sit in silence, sipping our tea and staring at Miranda snoring and twitching between us. She needs her toenails cut. I keep my head down, but look up through my eyelashes when I feel Jessie staring at me again. Her eyes are the x-ray kind, like Aggie's.

"Chasing rabbits," Jessie says, poking Miranda with her striped sock toe. "Only in her dreams. More passive creature you'd never find, nowhere, no-how. More a licker than a carnivore."

"Carnivore," I say. "Meat-eater. I'm a vegetarian, except for fish. Muzzy and I are pescatarians; we eat fish but we don't catch fish, like Jack Jodrey, Junior."

"So, Katie Dupuis Pearson, what brings you to Lunenburg and, more particularly, to Mason's Beach?" She twists her silvery hair up into a bun, fastens it with a wooden clip, then picks up a knife and a small log from a basket next to the beach-stone fireplace.

"Muzzy is helping Jo-Ellen in her café, and I am working for Aggie, who has new hardware and is learning to walk again."

She looks up at me when I say Aggie's name, then starts stripping the log, pushing the knife away from her. The long curls of bark drop to the wooden floor, rustling into a pile. I'm trying to figure out if she looks happy or sad, when she squints up her eyes, presses her lips together, then says, "She send you out here to spy on me?"

I stare at one of her birds on the windowsill, a tall skinny one, maybe a heron, and think about this. Spying is something nosy people and tattletales do. Am I spying? I shake my head because spying is sneaky and Aggie didn't send me. I brought myself. "Not spying. I'm learning about Catherine Marguerite, your great-grandmother several times over. But Aggie might have a broken heart. She had to go to the hospital before she finished telling me the stories and showing me Catherine's treasures."

"Had a heart murmur when we were kids. Must be acting up." Jessie goes back to her whittling. "If the bleeding's stopped, just drop those leaves into the bucket over there by the woodstove. Real interesting girl," she says. "Not Agatha ... Catherine." She pronounces it the French way, so it sounds like Katrine. "Lots of gumption, something kids today wouldn't half know the meaning of."

"Gumption, a synonym for stick-to-itiveness," I say. "I have gumption and I am good at school, solving puzzles, and playing the piano. I am not good at conversation, imagining, or swimming."

She gives me a quick look, then goes back to her wood. "Swim like a stone myself. We used to think of Catherine as one of our friends."

"Friends share secrets and have sleepovers," I say.

"We did plenty of that. Of course, Catherine was only there in her letters and treasures. Haven't thought of that splint box since the woman formerly known as my sis ... Darn it all!" Her knife clatters onto the stone hearth, knocking over a little twig broom. She shakes her hand in the air, sending tiny drops of blood flying. Miranda jerks awake, stretches across, and licks them up. She is likely a carnivore as well as a licker.

I pick up the knife. The handle is made of stone and it's just the right shape for my hand. "Do you want me to get you some more dogwood leaves?"

She shakes her head, then digs a polka-dot hanky, Midnight Blue, out of her pants pocket and wraps it around her pointer finger. Her fingernails are short and square like mine, only dirtier. "Watch you don't cut yourself with my good knife. Made it myself. Took me a century to find the right stone to fit my hand."

"Century. A synonym for one hundred years. You must be very old."

She pokes her tongue into her cheek. It looks like she's sucking on a jawbreaker, a type of hard candy ball that's one of my Likes because they have rainbow rings inside. "That was an exaggeration. Most times I make my knives with wooden handles."

I set the stone knife down beside a wooden bowl full of sea

glass and shells. "Does Miranda chew on your carving wood, which is a habit dogs have?"

"She knows the rules—no chewing on wood that's inside the house." Jessie holds her bleeding hand above her head, like she needs to ask a question. With her other hand, she uses the twig broom to sweep the wood shavings into a pile. "Think we're about done here. I've got work to do. No time for chit-chat about ancient history."

"I want to know about Catherine and her treasures and the Moon," I say. "And Nicholas, Elisabeth, and Marie Claire. Their story, like all history, cannot be rushed." I look at my watch. "I have twenty-four hours every day, 168 hours a week, except when I'm sleeping. I am also very patient." I open the door and look back over my shoulder. "When I need to be. But I'll be going back to Montreal in sixteen days."

She squints at me. "Stubborn little piece of work, aren't you? Sound like an old schoolmarm. Try me again later in the week. Could be I'll have a change of heart, seeing as you're not a lip-flapping flutterbug like most youngsters these days."

I open my not-flapping lips to tell her thank you for the tea, then close the door behind me and stand outside, examining her family. I reach out to pat the real-looking raccoon above the little round hobbit window. He's hard, not warm and furry like Miranda, who is whining inside their abode.

I wonder what it's like living in such a quiet place with so much personal space.

I think I would like it.

In the morning, I fluff up my pillows, then find the silvery crescent Moon glowing outside my window. It looks like it's caught in the branches of a tree. I get out my scribbler and try to draw a picture of it.

- *Why doesn't Jessie speak to her sister Agatha, synonym for Aggie?*
- *Will Jessie teach me to carve?*
- *Since I'm not a lip-flapping flutterbug, will she tell me Catherine's Moon stories?*
- *Why does my Lavender Lady get warm sometimes?*

Chapter 13

"You have a wipe-out?"

"Wipe-out?" I stop counting and multiplying, trying to figure out how many squares there are in each section of the chain-link fence around the tennis courts—and look up. Jack parks his bike and sits down beside me on the bench.

"On your bike—did you have a crash?"

I follow his eyes to my scabby knees and shake my head. "I fell down in a ditch. But dogwood leaves, which don't have anything to do with dogs, are very good for stopping bleeding. Dogwood is a synonym for bunchberry." I don't tell Jack it was Jessie who told me about the dogwood leaves, because he thinks she's a weird witchy hermit.

"I know. My grandpa says the same thing. I'm just on my way to visit him. Wanna come?"

I check my watch. "I'm supposed to be back at The Chickadee

to help make oatmeal banana muffins in thirty-eight minutes. At 2:00 PM."

He shakes his head. "Do you always do what you're supposed to?"

I nod yes, then follow him, pushing Butterscotch across the crosswalk.

He looks back over his shoulder. "Let's take the Phantom Trail—it's shorter. There's a cool bunch of plants there that the Mi'kmaw people used for medicine."

There are lots of other people walking on the trail. None of them is a phantom. A synonym for ghost.

"Why is this called the Phantom Trail?"

"There's an old graveyard up ahead, the French Cemetery." Jack points to a bunch of scraggly bushes by a little-kid playground. "That's the healing garden." A small girl with Cinnamon Tea Brown skin and lots of braids is walking on some giant footprints. Sea Captain Blue. She's waving her arms like she's on the balance beam in gym class, one of my Dislikes. I'm clumsy and falling hurts.

"I know those ones are bunchberries," Jack says. "See the little white flowers?"

I lay my bike on the grass beside Jack's and walk around the garden, reading the signs.

Bunchberry—to stop bleeding; *Gold Thread*—chapped lips,

canker sores, and for sore eyes; *Teaberry*—blood thinner for heart attacks/strokes, aspirin-like; *Mullein Leaves*—steeped to treat asthma; *Sweet Fern*—poison ivy rash and rheumatism; *Juniper*—gum to heal cuts, sores, burns, treat colds/flu.

"But these are all free." I look at Jack. "Why do people buy medicine at the drugstore?"

He shrugs. "Guess it's easier than growing all these plants and learning how to use them."

"Aggie's in the hospital because her heart has been misbehaving. Maybe they'll give her some teaberries." I check my watch. "I need to hurry."

We step over a low black chain fence into the graveyard. It's not big like the one up by the Academy, and a few of the gravestones have toppled over like they're dead, too. We stop to read one with a crown carved into it. Limey Lou Green. Somebody named Elisabeth Ann who died in 1876.

"Only 139 years ago," I say. "This is not Catherine's cousin-sister Elisabeth because she would have been 136 years old in 1876."

"You're wicked at math," Jack says.

"In stories and on TV, witches are wicked. I am not."

He laughs. "Yeah, the super old grave markers are all gone, but some of the earliest settlers—the Acadians, French people that lived here even before 1753—were buried here.

Crazy superstitious people say their ghosts still roam around."

"I don't believe in ghosts," I say. "Remember?"

Jack high-fives me as we walk back to get our bikes. "My grandpa does. Swears he used to meet his own grandfather's ghost in the halls of his old house on Pelham Street. That's where he lived before he got Alzheimer's and started forgetting everything."

"Forgetting everything. One in eleven people have Alzheimer's or some kind of dementia before they die. Do you think your grandpa will remember you today? Or will he think you're his younger brother Jeffrey who died sixty years ago?"

Jack pushes his bike ahead of me, but he doesn't say anything so I use my outdoor voice. I don't shout because shouting is one of my Dislikes.

"Do you think he'll remember you?"

He turns around and waits for me. His Drizzly Afternoon Gray eyes match his sneakers. They are blinking fast. Did a bug get in his eye? Or an eyelash?

"Hope so. He was almost like a little kid at first, telling me all kinds of stories about bad stuff he did when he was younger." He stops talking and does a big swallow, even though he isn't eating anything. "But now he barely says anything. And he has to wear diapers. It sucks."

"It sucks. Like leeches that suck blood. Maybe he forgets how to talk. I would like to have a grandparent to tell me stories."

"You've got Aggie, don't you?"

I nod. "She's a good storyteller but she's not my grandmother. And they're not my family stories. We are branches on different family trees."

"You never know. Dad always says half the world's related to each other, if you went back enough generations. Maybe you're my cousin, too." Then he starts singing. "You're probably my cousin and the whole world is our kin."

"I know that Tom Chapin song," I say.

"Cool. I've been going to the Chapin Brothers concert at the Ovens Park since I was a baby," Jack says.

"I would like to see that, and I would like to have a cousin. A nice one, like Ruthie ... or you." I whisper that last part.

He pops a wheelie. "Some day when it's sunny, maybe we can take the dory out. I'll see if Ruthie can come, too."

Tuesday morning, Muzzy says, "Maybe after the café closes tonight, we can stop by Elizabeth's Books."

"I looked in the window and the sign says it's only open late," I say.

"The owner must be a real night-owl. I'm sure they've given out thousands of those bookmarks over the years, but it's worth a try."

I nod yes. But I think the owner is probably a person. In

the afternoon, I bike out to Mason's Beach again. On Saturday, Jessie told me to come back later in the week. I hope Tuesday is late enough. I'm wearing my Parrot Green raincoat because the fog eater's still asleep, and it's foggy and cloudy. Partway down the hill at the spot where Miranda found me, I stop and look into the woods, but she's not there. I lock Butterscotch to the signpost, then find a skinny, not-mucky place to get across the ditch.

It's quiet in the woods, but not creepy quiet like the first time. Now I have a movie in my brain of Jessie and Miranda and their abode. I look up every time I pass a tree with extra-big branches. Maybe Inversion Therapy is only for sunny days or evenings. Just before the clearing, I hear something that sounds like birds singing. But it's not chirpy and bouncy like staccato notes. More soft and flowing like legato notes. Separate but together at the same time, like the colors in the spectrum.

Is there a brook somewhere? I sit on the ground, leaning back against a big tree. I close my eyes and rock back and forth to the music. When I hug myself, it feels like an invisible somebody is hugging me, too. But it's not an octopus hug. It's gentle.

The fluttery music starts doing something to my throat. I feel like I'm choking, only I'm not eating anything. And I never choke because I chew every bite fifteen times.

Muzzy says her throat gets dry when she's sad and needs to cry. But I don't cry. Ever. I don't even know if I can.

When I'm sad, I like to listen to music or play the piano.

I cover my eyes and think hard, trying to get my brain to give me a memory picture. Did I used to know somebody who made music like that? And rocked me?

"Woof!"

I peer around the tree trunk into the forest. In the distance, Miranda's lying on the ground with her snout on her front paws, sweeping up pinecones and needles with her tail. Jessie's sitting on a huge mossy boulder in between some pine trees, blending in because of her Forest Green clothes. She looks like Muzzy when she meditates. Her eyes are closed and her fingers are dancing along what looks like a branch. Is it some kind of flute?

As if she heard my question, Jessie's eyes flash open. I duck back in behind the tree. The music stops. "Enjoying the free concert?"

I push myself up and slow-walk toward them. Miranda woofs, stands up, and stretches so her bum pokes up into the air. "Concerts are in big halls, like at the Place des Arts in Montreal, or in schools or churches, like St. John's Anglican in Lunenburg."

I freeze when Jessie throws open her arms, wide, like she just won a race. "*This* is my church, my sanctuary. *My* peaceful holy place. I share it with no one." She slides down off the boulder, puts on her wooden shoes, and starts fast-walking toward her cottage. "Usually." At the door, she turns around. "Well, don't just stand there. I assume you came about the stories."

I fast-walk across the clearing, slow down when I stumble over some roots, then follow her and Miranda inside. "Is that a flute?"

She takes off her clompers and holds the wooden tube out for me to examine. "A love flute. Native men used to use them for courting, trying to find a mate. I make 'em but I don't use 'em for courting. In my experience, men and misery go hand-in-hand." The corners of her mouth start to go up, but then it's like they change their mind and droop back down. "This one was an elderberry branch in its former incarnation; hollow with soft pith inside that's easy to bore out. I make 'em out of Japanese knotweed, too, similar to bamboo. Grows like wildfire, same as most weeds, and people are happy to get rid of it."

"Get rid of it. Muzzy says I'm growing like a weed. I don't think she wants to get rid of me, but she could because she's my foster mother. Mrs. MacKinnon and Madame LeBlanc both got rid of me because I'm a left-out kid, and their boyfriends didn't like me. How did you know you could make a flute out of a branch?"

"Saw a woman playing a bamboo flute up at the Boxwood Festival one year. Prettiest, most soulful music I ever did hear. She gave me a few pointers."

"Could I make a flute?" I ask. "I'm a very good pianist."

She looks at my fingers. "Doesn't look to me like you've got piano-playing fingers. Too short. How old are you, anyway?"

"I'm eleven years and 116 days old. I have very well-developed fine-motor skills but not gross-motor skills. That's what they told me when they tested me at school."

"Only ever helped one kid make a flute before." She turns and stares out the window with the dangling prisms. The sun pops out from behind a cloud, helping the crystals make tiny rainbows on the log wall beside me. I'm trying to see all seven colors when Jessie says, "Chouette."

"Catherine's cousin Elisabeth called her Chouette because she had owl eyes. But I don't think you helped Catherine make a flute because she probably died a long time before you were born."

Jessie stares at me without blinking for five breaths, like she's trying to figure something out, then shakes her head. "Never mind about that. I've got lots of knotweed kicking around. Harvested it last winter so it's had plenty of time to dry." She points with her elbow to a big slab of tree that she turned into a high table. The stools around it look like tree trunks. "Sit yourself down while I get the materials ready."

"I like to do crafts but I'm not very good at drawing, so I practice in my old scribblers with my one hundred colored pencils. I have a subscription, so pretty soon I'll be getting twenty-five new colors in the mail. But not until I go back to Montreal on July 30th."

"Bit of a chatterbox all of a sudden, aren't you? But not when we're working. You need to concentrate. Zip your lip." She makes like she's zippering up her mouth. I zip mine, too, then look around while she collects the supplies. One log wall is covered with tools. In one dark corner, there's a glass case with a mobile inside. I slide down off my stool. The dangling things are all knives, small knives with fancy carved wooden handles. *One, two three, four, five ...*

"Are you making a flute or gawking?"

"Gawking. You have sixteen knives in your collection."

Jessie pokes her tongue into her cheek, then she nods and puts a log in the woodstove. "Most of 'em even older than me. Family heirlooms." She lays the supplies out on the table; a long piece of Beach Walk Brown bamboo, which is really Japanese knotweed, a saw with a skinny blade shaped like a capital D, a long pointed metal stick, a pencil, and some pieces of sandpaper.

"Doesn't look too complicated now, does it?"

I shake my head no and keep my lips zipped.

"Now, just line up my flute with your piece of bamboo, match up this knuckle thing, which is called a node. Mark the spot where each of my finger holes are on your piece. The top one is called the blow hole, for obvious reasons."

I want to say, "Blow hole like a whale," but I don't.

"I see you're a lefty, like me," Jessie says.

"And your great-grandmother several times over, Catherine Marguerite."

After I finish the marking, Jessie puts one end of the long metal stick in the woodstove, then she uses the saw to cut off the ends of my bamboo so it's the same length as her flute. I sand the rough edges, then she gets the hot metal stick and presses the tip of it up against the bamboo where I made the pencil marks. "See how it bores right through the bamboo? Need to hold the probe perfectly straight so it makes a right angle."

A right angle. Synonym for a capital L.

"Put your hand underneath mine on the probe so you can feel how much pressure I'm using, not much. Don't want it to splinter or go through both sides."

I hold my breath, get up on my knees on my stool, and put my left hand underneath her rough, hard one. The little shreds of skin sticking out make my hand itch, but her hand is warm and holds mine firmly. Not too tight. Each time we push the probe into the bamboo, puffs of smoke fly up, then disappear when we pull out the probe, leaving a perfectly round black hole. "This is fun," I say, accidentally unzipping my lips.

She nods but keeps her eyes on the probe. When we've finished burning all seven holes, she wraps some sandpaper around the probe and shoves it inside one end of the bamboo. "This'll smooth things out." She pushes it in one end, then pulls it out the other. "Here, you try."

I poke the probe in and out for six minutes until no more white pith comes out, and Jessie says we're done.

She sits on the stool across from me, picks up her flute, and starts playing.

Since we're finished working, I say, "The scale of c."

Jessie nods. "Now, when you cover the holes, the sound is low. When they're uncovered, like this ..."

Miranda crawls into her throne bed, burrows into her blanket, and howls; I cover my ears.

"... the sound is high. Like caterwauling."

Caterwauling. A synonym for howling. Like the troop of spider monkeys at the zoo. One of my Likes when they're quiet. One of my Dislikes when they're screeching.

"Makes sense, right? It's like when you need to scream, you've gotta open your mouth wide. Although I don't expect you're the screaming type."

I shake my head no. "But Joseph is. He's a boy at my school. Can I try mine?"

"Let me test it first," she says, putting it up to her mouth. Her lips look like she's blowing out birthday candles.

"The scale of G," I say.

"No flies on you."

I run my hands up and down both arms, shooing away the flies. They must be almost-invisible no-see-ums since there are lots of those in Nova Scotia.

"Take things real literally, don't you? That's just an expression, means somebody who's quick, smart." She gives me my flute. "Press it up under your bottom lip and blow softly, like you're blowing the seeds off a dandelion puffball."

"I'm like a dandelion seed," I say.

She scrunches up her whole face. She's either confused or mad, like the kids at school when I say the wrong thing.

"Because I'm floating. I don't have any roots."

"Last time I checked, roots belonged on plants and trees, not people. Now, don't blow too hard. Think breeze, not hurricane."

Breeze, not hurricane. It takes me a long time, but when it's time to leave, I can almost play the C scale without any caterwauling. It's hard to cover the whole hole at just the right time. Whole and hole are homonyms because they sound the same but have different meanings and spellings.

Like which and witch. "Playing the piano is easier," I say, checking my watch.

She does another Bessie horse snuffle. "Well, at least with the flute, you've only got a few options for your fingers, instead of eighty-eight."

"Mostly I only use the middle three octaves on the piano. Thirty-six black and white keys." I slide down off my stool. "Because I've only been taking piano lessons for twenty-six months. Thank you for the flute-making lesson."

"Might be best if you left yours here," she says, looking out the window and patting Miranda's Burnt Orange head. "In case you want more lessons."

"Does that mean I should come back?"

"You did pretty good at keeping your lips zipped. Could be we'll get around to one of Catherine's stories, too. Used to have a little notebook we wrote the best parts down in."

"Was it yellow?"

She nods.

"Aggie keeps it in the splint box." I open the door and look at her carved animal family for a minute. Sixty seconds. Then I turn around and look right at her. "Are you somebody's grandmother, Jessie? A person, not an animal?"

She gets up and starts cleaning up. "I seem like the grandmotherly type to you? Apple pies and lullabies?"

"Grandmothers are old and they know lots of things," I say. "Like you."

"You're honest, I'll give you that, Chouette," she says, stuffing her hands into her green overall pockets.

"My name is Katie," I remind her. "Why do you call me Chouette? I'm not an owl."

She waves her hand, like she's trying to push me out the door. "As you pointed out, I'm old. I get confused. Maybe sometime you're here, you can meet Chou Chou, my little saw-whet owl friend. A real one, not that one carved into the door. You remind me of Chou Chou, with those big eyes of yours, and your feline face."

Feline. A synonym for cat. "A group of cats is called a clowder. But I don't know why. And Chou Chou was the name of the owl Catherine carved for her cousin-sister Elisabeth. I would like to know what happened to Catherine next, after she got uprooted. And I would like to see what else is in the splint box, so I can fill in all the spaces on my treasure chart, but Aggie's still away."

"You're a *trotsy* little thing, don't give up easy when you're hankering after somethin'."

"A group of owls is called a parliament. I think because they're wise like the people in the government are supposed to be. Only Muzzy says they're mostly not."

Jessie pokes her tongue into her cheek again and nods. "Real interesting. I'll see you when I see you."

I close the door and walk down the path into the woods, looking around for Jessie's little saw-whet owl friend, Chou Chou. I keep saying my new Moon question out loud so I'll remember it at bedtime. "Why does Jessie call me Chouette?"

Chapter 14

Muzzy gives me a pinky hug and I wrap my dancing fingers around my Lavender Lady while I wait for the man to look up from the book he's reading. The person who owns Elizabeth's Books is not a lady named Elizabeth. It is a man named Chris. He looks like a hobbit, and he has 5,000 movies to rent and more than 30,000 books, mostly used, to sell. And I don't know how many newspapers, but a lot.

Finally, he looks up, pulls his glasses down to the end of his nose, and says, "May I help you?"

I squeeze my lips together to keep the hiccups inside, then take the bookmark out of my backpack and show it to him. "I'm trying to find my missing mother. She probably looked like me, only older." I swallow a hiccup. "I know she was here one time because she left me this." I can't find the picture of Moonbeam that is probably stored somewhere in my brain, so

I can't describe her to him, but I wish I could.

Chris pushes his glasses back up. "I used to have bookmarks like that. Can't say for sure when it was, but quite a while ago, I'd say. More than a decade." He stares at me for a long time, rubbing his beard, then shakes his head. "Can't think of any customers resembling you right off hand. I get a lot of people passing through. I can call you if anyone comes to mind."

I tell him thank-you and Muzzy gives him her cell phone number. We look at the books and Muzzy rents a movie for Jo-Ellen—*Turner & Hooch*. The dog on the front is the same color as Miranda. "Jo's been in love with this actor, Tom Hanks, forever. How about an ice cream for a bedtime snack?"

We walk across the street to Sweet Treasures, which is right beside another bookstore called Lexicon Books. We don't go in because it has regular hours, so it's closed. I get homemade Toasted Coconut on a waffle cone, and Muzzy buys a little box of candy that says it's lobster poop to take back to her boss in Montreal. I think that is a joke. I don't know what real lobster poop looks like, but the candy looks like chocolate-covered peanuts.

"I wonder if Chris has read all those books," I say as we walk back to the café.

"Jo-Ellen told me he worked on boats at sea for a lot of years. I'm not sure how long he's had the shop."

I squeeze my Lavender Lady. "Maybe Moonbeam found the bookmark in a book she got somewhere else. Maybe she was never even here in Lunenburg."

"Do you think she was here?" Muzzy asks.

I nod yes. "But I don't know why I think that."

"Sometimes gut instincts are all we have to work with. I've been asking people I meet, but nobody seems to remember a person named Moonbeam Dupuis."

"Maybe she changed her name or maybe it's a nickname. Synonym for pet name. Aggie's niece was named Katrina but Aggie called her Kitty."

"Names can get a little confusing. When I'm researching an article, I sometimes have trouble tracking people down because they've changed their name for various reasons. And sometimes people just don't want to be found."

I read some of the house nametags out loud as we walk. I'm still looking for Dupuis. *"Built in 1790, Hammett Hotel."* Only now it's a gift store called Mosaic, with a window full of the fish-shaped cream pitchers Jo-Ellen uses in the café. That doesn't make sense because fish aren't even mammals.

• *Did Moonbeam used to have a different name?*

"Thank you, Jo-Ellen. Such a delicious supper after almost a week of hospital food. That was quite possibly the most scrumptious chowder I have ever enjoyed." Aggie wipes the corners of her mouth with her napkin. "And, Allison, those biscuits were light as air." She pats where her belly would be if she had one. But, except for her bosom, she's skinny like me.

"I'm teaching Allie everything I know about baking," Jo-Ellen says, winking at Muzzy. "You know what they say about the way to a man's heart being through his belly."

Muzzy laughs and gets up to clear the table. "There are plenty more strawberries and whipped cream if ..."

Aggie laughs. "Oh, no, thank you. Dr. Wellwood has suggested I cut back on fat and salt. If I eat one more bite, I'm certain I shall blow up." She puffs out both cheeks so her wrinkles disappear, then blows out some air.

"Blow up. That only happens in cartoons," I say. "People blowing up like balloons from eating too much."

"Just an expression, Katie. A silly one at that." Aggie's mouth opens like she's about to yawn, but she uses her hand to hide it. Because yawning in public isn't polite. Like burping and farting. "It's past my bedtime, I fear. Will you walk me across the street, Katie? Please and thank you. The doctor has finally given me permission to retire Silver Streak very soon; this could be his last outing for a while. And you and I have some business to discuss."

Muzzy walks to the door with us. "I'm so glad you're okay, Aggie. I'll be out when you get back, Katie."

"Out where?"

"Just for a walk with a friend."

Jo-Ellen pokes her with an elbow, then winks at me.

Why is that a joke? I didn't know Muzzy had any other friends in Lunenburg besides Jo-Ellen. As soon as the screen door of The Chickadee snaps shut behind us, I ask Aggie, "What business?"

"I finally contacted the Archives while I was in Halifax. They're apparently short-staffed this summer; it could be weeks before they can respond to my request for a copy of the letters."

"But they're your letters. You gave them to the Archives, didn't you?"

She pushes her Rapunzel Yellow door open and nods back at me. "Sadly, that doesn't give me any higher priority on their wait-list. As well, my doctor has suggested I rest as much as possible this week, so you won't need to help me with my walking."

"But what about the stories? And the treasures?"

"I'll let you know if I'm feeling up to it. For now, we shall just have to be patient."

Patient. Sometimes that's a hard thing for me to be. Because she doesn't ask, I don't tell her about meeting Jessie.

Chapter 15

"Don't grab onto the oars like you're trying to strangle them. Pretend they're little birds. Sparrows or something."

I try to do like Jack tells me, but my hands are small. The oars are long and don't feel anything like the baby robin I tried to rescue once after it fell out of its nest. We're rowing backward across the Back Harbour, and Jack's sitting behind me with his own oars. On the dock, Ruthie's jabbing both thumbs up in the air. A synonym for "Good work!"

"Think of your arms as loose ropes for the first part of the stroke. We call it the catch. Let your legs do the work."

"I am trying," I say. "But my arms are like threads, not ropes."

"You'll get the hang of it. Each stroke has a pattern or a rhythm. Catch, middle, finish. Catch, middle, finish."

I twist my head around to see how he's doing it, but it's hard to row and watch at the same time.

"Not so deep. You're rowing like you're catching crabs."

I stop rowing and stare at the dripping end of one oar. "Is it possible to catch crabs with an oar?" Crabs are one of my Dislikes. Mr. Munroe, the gym teacher, makes us do the crab walk, and I'm always the slowest crab.

Jack laughs. "Just a way to make fun of beginners. But it's a lot less work if you don't dig so deep."

"You're doing great!" Ruthie shouts. "Not choppy at all."

Catch, middle, finish. Catch, middle, finish. I pull on the oars and lean back, stretching out my scratched-up legs. I'm wearing my black sandals with the covered toes to hide my strange toes. Like E.T.'s fingers, a boy at school said. I'm not an alien, because I was born on the planet Earth. I close my eyes. *Catch, middle, finish. Catch, middle, finish.* It's almost like swinging; there is a rhythm to it.

"That's it. You're getting the hang of it now," Jack says. "We're actually gliding instead of hopping."

Back at the floating dock, my arms and legs feel wobbly when I stand up. I unzip my Burnt Orange life jacket and drop it into the dory, then grab onto one of the silver dock handles. Jack's already on the dock, tying up the dory. I step up onto the edge of the boat, the gunnel, just as a noisy motorboat zooms past.

"No!"

I try to catch my balance, bang one knee on the gunnel, then splash into the water, a belly-flopper. I come up sputtering, kicking my legs, trying to grab onto the side of the boat, but it's too high up. Overtop of my own splashing and gasping for air, I hear a bigger splash.

Then Jack's beside me, sticking his arms in under mine, dragging me back to the beach. "It gets shallow real quick. Chill."

"Chill. You don't need to tell m-m-me to ch-ch-chill." I try to keep my teeth from chattering. "This water is iceberg c-c-cold."

"Are you okay?" Ruthie reaches out her hand, helps me stand up on the gravel shore. "Oh, your watch!"

"It's waterproof, and I *can* swim." I cough and feel around in my pocket for my Lavender Lady. "Dog-paddle. But surprises are one of my Dislikes. And water up my nose."

"Let's go up to my place and get you some dry clothes." Ruthie puts her hoodie around my shoulders.

I nod and squeeze some of the water out of my T-shirt. Wish I'd worn my bathing suit.

"If you're good to go, I've gotta get back to work." Jack finishes tying up the dory, then puts on his painter's hat and sneakers. "Saving up for a new bike. Won't be able to earn any money when I'm away at camp next week."

Next week. I will be leaving Lunenburg in less than two weeks, eleven days. I wring some of the water out of my hair. "Thank you for saving me and for being my friend."

"Get outta town." Jack turns away and speed-walks over to our bikes.

"But we already are out of town," I say, my soggy sandals making fart sounds.

Ruthie and I push our bikes up the hill. "Why is your street called Kissing Bridge Road?"

"Back in the olden days, when the men went off to hunt or cut trees outside the log fence, the palisade, their families would come here to this bridge to see them off. Kiss them goodbye, I guess."

"I wonder if Catherine ever kissed Papa goodbye out here."

"Probably. It was more dangerous outside the palisade, because the Mi'kmaw people, called savages by the settlers, didn't like the British taking their land."

"Taking their land. The Mi'kmaw people were here first?"

"Uh-huh. For a very long time."

"But that's stealing. Stealing is against the law."

"I know, right?"

"Maybe the law was different then."

Ruthie lives on a farm, and the yard is full of clucking

chickens running around, pooping, and pecking at seeds scattered everywhere.

"Are they your pets?" I squint up at the Flannel Gray silo, because the swirling chickens make me dizzy.

Ruthie shoos them away so she can pull open the back door. "Except for the egg layers; they're only around for a little while before ..." She stops talking and makes a slicing motion across her throat. She is good at explaining things with her hands.

I follow her inside. "I don't eat meat, and I've never met a real chicken before," I say. "Do you use their feathers for pillows? In France, Catherine had a quill pen made from a feather from one of Grandmother's ornery geese."

Ruthie shakes her head, digs around in a laundry basket on the kitchen table, then passes me some clothes. "These should fit. I just took them in off the line before I went to meet you guys." She opens a cupboard door, then covers her nose and sneezes. "If you can believe it, I'm allergic to feathers."

"Me, too. They make me sneeze."

Ruthie laughs. "We *must* be related. Here's an old pair of flip-flops and a towel; you can get changed in the pantry."

The clothes are stiff from being on the clothesline, but they're dry and they smell like outdoors, but not chicken poop. The flip-flops are too small, but better than bare feet. Whoever's chore it was to sweep the dirty pantry floor must've forgotten.

Ruthie gives me a plastic bag for my wet clothes, then says, "Want to see something neat?"

"Okay. I like neat things. I always keep my room neat."

"I share with my two little sisters, so my room's a disaster."

Hurricanes, tornadoes, and tsunamis are disasters. Her room is messy but it's not a disaster.

She picks her way between the piles of clothes on the floor, opens the closet door, and gets out a cereal box. Special K.

"I only like Cheerios, plain, not honey nut," I say.

She laughs. "It's not really cereal inside."

"Oh. Where are your sisters?"

"I think Mom took them to the library."

"The library. On Pelham Street." Three dolls are having a tea party on the windowsill. Except dolls can't drink tea because they're not alive. "Is it nice having sisters because then you always have friends?"

Ruthie shrugs. "Sometimes, but I could use a little more personal space."

I nod. "Personal space is one of my Likes. Especially at school."

She opens the cereal box. "My dad was taking apart the old Langille family homestead up in Blockhouse, and he found these inside one of the walls."

"Maybe it was Catherine's house. Her last name was Langille."

"Maybe. We have Langilles on our family tree, too."

Ruthie takes a crumpled tissue ball out of the cereal box and sets it on the bed between us. "I like to imagine that these belonged to one of my ancestors, more than two hundred years ago. A girl my age."

One of the combs is small and square and made of wood. Some of the thick teeth are missing or broken off. The other comb is shaped like a capital I with tiny teeth along both sides. It looks like it's made of Miss Muffet Ivory-colored plastic, but plastic wasn't invented two hundred years ago.

"What's this one made of?" I ask, touching it with my pointer finger.

"Bone. They had to use whatever they could find to make stuff. I counted all the tiny teeth once. I forget exactly, but there's more than a hundred—only lots of them are broken. Mom said it was probably used as a nitpicker."

I try to give her my question-mark look.

She lifts her eyebrows. "That's a funny face. Sometimes my grandpa calls fussy people nitpickers. But nit is another name for lice eggs. Do kids at your school get lice?"

I nod and scratch my head. "But not me."

"Cool. Supposedly lice like clean hair, anyway. Everything's supposed to have a purpose, but I've never been able to think of one for lice."

"Maybe their purpose is to give somebody a business selling nitpicker combs."

She laughs and wraps the combs back up in the tissue. "Maybe."

"Maybe." I check my watch and stand up. "It's time for me to go now."

"Oh. Already? I thought we could just hang out for a while. Since I'll be away at camp next week."

Hang out for a while. What friends do.

I check my watch again. "I told Muzzy I would be home by 4:00 PM. Thank you for letting me borrow your clothes and for showing me your messy room and your neat combs. Aggie keeps Catherine's treasures in a splint box, not a cereal box."

"Nice. I love old stuff. I can spend hours imagining their stories."

I follow her downstairs.

Ruthie stops in front of a big framed picture on the living room wall. "Here's our family tree—pretty big, huh?"

"Pretty big." I lean in closer and find Ruthie's name, stitched in Plum Crazy Red above a twig attached to her family's branch. Jack's is stitched in Summer Sea Blue on a different branch.

"I have so many cousins, I can't keep track of them all. Just my favorites, like Jack. The names by the roots are our ancestors. The first settlers."

"My roots are invisible," I say.

"Like real tree roots. You can't usually see most of them but you know they're there, holding the tree in place and feeding it."

"Missing people roots are harder to find." I give her back the flip-flops and put on my wet sandals. I get on Butterscotch, hook my bag of wet clothes over the handlebars, and fasten on my helmet.

"I'll email you when we get back from camp," Ruthie says, shooing away the pecking chickens.

I nod yes, then squeeze my brakes all the way down her driveway.

I can't see the Moon at all that night, but I know he's not missing, just hiding.

• *Am I a twig on a big branchy family tree, like Ruthie and Jack?*

Chapter 16

Aggie gives me a jingle in the morning. "Would you like to come over for a cup of tea? I've already made a pot."

I tell Muzzy I'll be back before lunchtime and walk to Aggie's.

"Where's Silver Streak?" I look at the empty corner that was her stable.

Aggie hooks her cane over her arm and claps her hands. "She has been put out to pasture for a well-earned rest."

"Won't she rust? Like the handlebars on Jack's bike?"

"Just a little joke. The point is, I'm a free woman again; I'm not exactly in racing form, but I'm doing as well as could be expected for a reconstructed old girl."

"Old girl. Muzzy is in racing form because she runs half-marathons."

"I don't think I'll ever quite get up to Allison's speed."

The handle of her wooden cane is a bird's head. "It's a loon," she says, sitting down on the sofa and pouring the tea. "Jessie carved it for Father a long time ago. It was one of her first projects."

I think of Jessie but I don't tell Aggie about my visits. If she asks me, I will tell her. But I won't tell her that it's more fun at Jessie's because that would be mean. I sit down at the other end of the sofa and start working on the puzzle. There are too many Sea Captain Blue and Crackling Crimson Red pieces. "Ruthie told me your sister makes awesome carvings."

"Ruthie Ernst? Lovely girl. I know her family from the market. They sell beautiful vegetables and baked goods. Her father is in the record books as being the world's strongest man at one time."

"Really? I would like to meet him. I've never seen a real giant before."

"Surprisingly, he's not as big as you might expect. A gentle giant."

"Ruthie and Jack Jodrey are my friends. They're telling me Lunenburg stories, too."

"That must be JJ's son. Is Jack as mischievous as his father was? And as powerful? JJ was a champion dory racer as a young man. As was his father before him, Alex Jodrey."

I nod yes. "Jack is teaching me how to row his dory. But

I don't think I will be a champion. Muzzy used to be in love with JJ back in the day."

Aggie nods and spills some of her tea onto her saucer. "I do remember that."

I pour some extra milk into my *Bluenose* teacup.

"I hear you've met Jessie."

"Jessie." I fast-look at her. "But I didn't tell anybody about Jessie. Not even Muzzy. Not yet. Because nobody asked."

"Lunenburg is a very small town. A neighbor mentioned she'd seen your orange bike parked alongside the Mason's Beach road. I don't mind, you know."

"Pumpkin Spice Gold, not orange," I say. Should I tell her about Jessie and Miranda and the flute? Would she let me borrow the splint box and the notebook?

"Did Jessie agree to have a turn sharing Catherine's stories with you?"

I nod yes. "She said she might since I'm not a lip-flapping flutterbug like most youngsters these days."

Aggie presses her lips together. "Sounds like she hasn't changed much."

"And she calls me Chouette, even though I am a girl, not a baby owl."

Nobody says anything for a long time, but I can feel Aggie staring at me.

Finally, she stands up and tells me to sit tight, a synonym for wait. She goes upstairs slowly, holding on to the railing. She comes back down, carrying a round box that looks like a fancy birthday cake, Baby Soft Pink and Frog Pond Green.

"This was my mother's." She sits down and takes off the lid. Inside, there's a green hat covered with silky pink flowers. "She wore this straw beauty when she was Queen Annapolisa back in 1940. The flowers are apple blossoms." Aggie puts it on over her Hint of Sun White hair. It doesn't look like a crown, but it's pretty.

"Was your father King Annapolisa?" I ask. "And were you a princess?"

She laughs. "That's an excellent question but, to the best of my knowledge, the Apple Blossom Festival only ever had queens. And 1940 was before my time." She puts Catherine's splint box inside the hatbox. It fits perfectly. "I think you should take this with you to Jessie's."

"To Jessie's. But what if I drop it? Or what if I trip and fall on it? I'm a klutz."

She aims her x-ray eyes at me.

I close my eyes and shove my hands into my pockets. "Some of the kids at school say that."

"Mean kids are as perennial as daisies, although not so nice. I have no doubt you'll take very good care of these living bits of my family history, Katie. I expect Jessie will enjoy seeing Catherine's treasures again, as well. She's been living all alone in the woods since Kitty left, more than a decade ago. I'm sure she's enjoying having a young girl around again."

"But Jessie is an old maid and, in her experience, men and misery go hand in hand, so how could she have a daughter, synonym for your niece?"

Aggie laughs. "Sometimes these things happen. I don't think Jessie intended to be a mother and, to be perfectly honest, I'm not sure if I still do have a niece."

"Is she missing, like my real mother, Moonbeam?"

"Yes, I suppose she is. Kitty was part of the reason Jessie and I had a falling-out." Aggie's eyebrows are squeezed together so they look like one. Her eyes are shiny. "But that was all a long time ago." She puts the hatbox into a heavy plastic bag with handles. "I know I can trust you not to peek."

"Thank you, Aggie." I stand up, keep my chin down, and look up through my eyelashes.

She's looking at me the way Muzzy looks at puppies in the pet store window. When she reaches out like she's going to touch my hair, a synonym for patting, I step back, holding the bag in front of me.

"It's my pleasure, my dear. Please tell my sister hello from me. I miss her."

At bedtime, Muzzy notices the hatbox on my white dresser. "What's this lovely thing?"

I yawn but I don't cover my mouth because it's Muzzy. "It's a very long story," I say, yawning again. "And I'm very sleepy right now."

She gives me a pinky hug and a nose tap. "Me, too. It can wait until morning. Sleep tight, Katie."

I nod yes. After she leaves, I stare up at the banana-shaped Moon. A synonym for crescent Moon. It looks like a right bracket in math. If I had a grandmother, I would like to write letters to her.

> *Dear Grandmother (or Nana, or Grandma, or Grammy),*
>
> *Do you know where your daughter Moonbeam is?*

That's all I can think of because I'm too tired. And I can't see my grandmother's face. It's hard to write a letter to somebody you've never met.

Chapter 17

In the morning, I carry the hatbox down to the kitchen. Jo-Ellen's taking a pan of cinnamon buns out of the oven. "They smell like Christmas," I say.

Muzzy laughs. "That's the only time I ever bake cinnamon buns. Or anything, in fact."

"What kind of treasure have you got there?" Jo-Ellen puts the buns on a wire rack, then wipes her sweaty face, Apple Pudding Pink, on her lobster apron.

"Catherine Marguerite Langille's treasures. But peeking is not allowed." I set the hatbox down on the table and lift off the cover. "The hatbox belonged to Aggie's mother. And Aggie is letting me borrow this very old splint box while her strange sister Jessie is telling me the rest of Catherine's stories."

Muzzy puts up one hand, synonym for please stop talking. "Hang on a sec. Who's Jessie?"

I take a bite of hot cinnamon bun, chew it fifteen times, wash it down with some cold milk, and then explain.

When I get to the part about Jessie and the flute-making lesson, Jo-Ellen lifts both eyebrows at Muzzy.

"Jessie Langille's a bit of an odd duck," Jo-Ellen says when I'm finished talking. She winks at me. "And I don't mean that she has webbed feet and quacks. It's just a way of describing a person who marches to the beat of her own drum."

"Like me. Except I play piano. And flute."

She nods, then looks at Muzzy. "Jessie's an individual. She took to the woods out by Mason's Beach years ago and rarely comes out. I haven't laid eyes on her since I moved back from Montreal. But her whimsical carvings are delightful. She gets somebody to sell them for her at the Thursday market."

"Are you sure it's safe for you to be going out there on your own?" Muzzy has the up-and-down W between her eyebrows that she told me means she's worried. That is easy to remember because worried starts with W. "A customer mentioned he'd seen a coyote along the bike trail to Mahone Bay. I wish you'd told me what you were up to."

"I didn't tell you because you didn't ask. Jessie has Miranda, who is a dog, not a coyote. Some kids are scared of Jessie," I say. "But she likes me because I can keep my lips zipped and I'm not a flutterbug like other youngsters."

They both laugh. "I love that expression," Jo-Ellen says.

"And I'm very responsible, and I want to hear the rest of Catherine's stories. Her treasures bring history to life, like Jodrey & Son."

Muzzy looks at Jo-Ellen, who is nodding. "Well, I guess it's okay. But make sure you let me know when you're going out to Jessie's."

"All right." I put the hatbox back in the bag, then put the bag into my backpack. Carefully. "I'm going there now. Jack and Ruthie are away at camp and Silver Streak is retired, so I have lots of free time."

"Be home in time for lunch at noon hour," Muzzy says, smiling. "Please."

"Noon hour." I check my watch. "That only gives me 202 minutes. I need to hurry."

Miranda's waiting for me on the other side of the ditch, woofing and wagging. Maybe she could smell me coming from far away. Some breeds of dogs have a sense of smell that's ten million times stronger than people. Humans having tails would be one of my Likes, because tails make dogs easier to read than people. I lock up Butterscotch and get across the ditch without falling, and follow Miranda down the path. The cottage door is open. Jessie is sitting on a stool at the high table with her back to me.

"Don't just stand there with your mouth open, catching flies," she says, without looking at me. "Come in."

"Come in." I don't see any flies, just an orange and black Monarch butterfly. I close my mouth anyway and walk over beside her.

She's wearing a gray glove on the hand holding a piece of wood. The hand holding her stone knife has only a glove thumb. "Working on a saw-whet. Folks at the market can't seem to get enough of the little critters. Chou Chou was real good at posing for me when I was first learning to carve 'em. Have to admit they are cute as a bug's ear."

"Cute as a bug's ear. Do bugs have ears?"

"Just an expression." She nods toward the windowsill, which is full of carved birds and animals. "She still shows up from time to time, checking to make sure I'm getting it right, I expect."

I thought it was a carving, but the little owl is staring straight at me with her not-blinking eyes. Toucan Yellow. Her face is heart-shaped, and her head looks too big for her body. Maybe Chou Chou has a big brain, like me and elephants.

Jessie stands up, takes off her glove and glove thumb, sweeps the wood chips into a basket, then sets the carving on the floor near the woodstove. She slips her little knife into a leather pouch, then stands in the middle of the room, holds

out one arm, and whistles. Chou Chou lifts her wings, flies
over, and lands right on Jessie's shoulder. Her feathers are
Hint of Sun White and Cinnamon Tea Brown. Jessie reaches
across with her other hand and pats the owl's round head like
a kitten. Chou Chou looks very soft; I would like to touch her
but I'm a scary stranger. I don't want her to get the hiccups.

"I'm an owl whisperer," Jessie whispers. "She trusts me
since I rescued her when she was just a day or so old. Must've
been the runt and Mama owl kicked her out of the nest."

"Kicked her out of the nest," I whisper back. "Moonbeam
kicked me out. She left me with the foster care people."

Jessie shakes her head and makes the same tongue-clicking
squirrel sound as Aggie. "Young people today. No sense of
responsibility."

"Muzzy says Moonbeam probably had a good reason to
leave me," I say.

"What kind of name is Moonbeam, anyway?"

"A cool name," I say, borrowing Ruthie's words. "More
interesting than Katie."

"Humph. I've had a few loved ones leave me over time. It's
never easy."

"Never easy. Synonym for always hard."

"Anyhow, Miranda sniffed out this little girl down by the
brook. Spring before last, it was." She squats down so Miranda

and Chou Chou can touch, nose to beak. Like Catherine and Elisabeth. "She helps keep the place clear of mice."

"I didn't know owls and dogs could be friends," I whisper. "They're so different."

"You never can tell which critters are gonna hit it off." She stands in the doorway and Chou Chou flies away. "Same as people. I'll teach you to listen for Chou Chou's voice some evening. It's not like a regular owl, and a far cry from those screech owls that just about scare the gizzard out of a person. The male sounds like a saw being sharpened, which is how the saw-whet got its name, W-H-E-T being another word for sharpen."

"Sharpen. A synonym for whet. W-h-e-t, a homonym for w-e-t."

She leans her head up against the doorframe. "We spend many a starry night out here, me and Chou Chou, just listening to the night music and talkin' to the Moon."

I unzip my backpack slowly and take out the hatbox. "I talk to the Moon, like Catherine Marguerite. He is a very good listener but he never answers me."

"I always say you take your friends where you can find 'em." Jessie laughs then turns around. "Well, looky here. Mother's Apple Blossom Queen hat."

I shake my head no and take off the lid.

She drops back down onto her work stool. "Surprised Agatha trusted me enough to allow you to bring the treasures out here."

"Catherine's treasures help bring history to life," I say, setting the hat box on the table. "And I told Aggie you're having a turn telling me Catherine's stories. She said to tell you hello. She misses you."

"Must be gettin' soft in her old age."

I nod yes. "Aggie is an old softie. She's forever tearing up about one thing or another."

"Bit of a bawl baby when we were kids. Now, let me get my specs." Jessie pulls a pair of round wire glasses out of her shirt pocket and puts them on. Specs. A synonym for glasses. Her plaid shirt has too many colors to figure them all out.

Jessie sits down on the loveseat. "Let's make ourselves at home, shall we?"

"This is your home but not mine."

"Sure enough. But take off your shoes and sit down anyway."

I sit down beside her on the loveseat, with the splint box in between us.

"Do you still have your copies of the letters?"

She shakes her head.

"Then why do you need your glasses to *tell* a story?"

"Help me think, for some strange reason. Habit, I guess. Now, how far did you and Agatha get?"

I pull my knees up under my chin and hug my legs. "They were almost on the ship. The *Sally*."

"Good enough. Did you get to the sad part?"

"About leaving Grandmother and Nellie in France?"

She shakes her head. "Somethin' else." She takes a tall book, Truffle Brown, off a shelf beside her. When she opens it, I see that it's really a box. The only things inside are a raggedy cloth bag and a tall carving that looks like a girl holding the Moon. Jessie covers the carving with the bag and closes the box quickly. "Made this box myself when I first took up the knife." *Catherine Marguerite Langille's Letters to Grandmother, 1752-1754* is carved on the front in fancy letters. "As a tribute to my great-grandmother so many times over, her being a fellow whittler and all. Used to keep my copy of the letters in it, until they disappeared. Seems they up and grew legs and walked right out the door."

"Did your mother, who was a ferocious housekeeper, get rid of the letters?"

She laughs so loud it wakes up Miranda. I blink fast as the echo bounces around in my brain. "That what happened to Agatha's? Serves her right, always trying to be everybody's favorite, taking Mother in and all, instead of putting her in a home."

"Jack Jodrey's grandfather is in a home because he has Alzheimer's."

"Alex Jodrey. Used to be a real good friend of mine, once upon a time."

"What's the cloth bag inside the box?" I ask. "And the carving?"

She opens the book box a crack and passes me the bag. "Catherine's flax sack that she used to carry her writing materials. It's in fair shape for being around 260-plus years. And the carving is in the category of 'mind your own beeswax.'"

"I don't have any beeswax to mind."

"Nicer way of saying mind your own business. Expression came from the olden days when women used to sit by the fire, gossiping and making beeswax candles." She puts the flax sack back inside the book box.

"Oh. Will you tell me one of Catherine's stories now?" I ask.

"Which of the treasures do you already know about?"

"Only three. The leather seed pouch, Elisabeth's Moon hairclip, and Grandmother's *méreau*. The pie chart you and Aggie made to keep track of the treasures is also missing, but I started making my own to help jog Aggie's memory. It has nine empty spaces."

Jessie lifts the splint box lid just enough to peek inside, then does a horse snort and pulls something out. "Why on earth would Agatha send me this?"

It's the framed colored-pencil drawing of the girl, K.L.

"I saw that inside the horsehide trunk. Who is it?"

Jessie rubs her forehead and looks back and forth between me and the picture for ten breaths before she puts the picture inside the book box. "Also in the MYOB category."

MYOB. Synonym for don't be nosy.

"Now, where were we?" She takes the little notebook out of the splint box and turns the pages, shaking her head. "Agatha had such perfect printing. No wonder she turned into a teacher. Here's a bit from May 30th, 1752, just before they set sail.

"To distract myself from seeing my homeland disappear in the distance as the Sally set sail, I began to count the waves splashing up against the side. I wondered if there were enough numbers in the world to count all the waves between the Old World and the New. And the tears."

Jessie looks at me. "Can't you just feel her sorrow?"

"It would be impossible to count that many waves," I say. "Or tears. I never cry."

"Not ever?"

"Not ever. A synonym for never. I didn't cry when we left Montreal to come to Nova Scotia. And I don't remember if I cried when Moonbeam left me with the foster care people."

Jessie makes the squirrel noise with her tongue and looks through the notebook. "Here's a longer bit, from August 4th, 1752. The voyage took much longer than six weeks. They ended up being on board for seventeen weeks, all told."

"One hundred and nineteen days." I lean back and close my eyes. "Two thousand, eight hundred and fifty-six hours."

"I have not written for some time as most days we are tossed about on the sea swells like leafy twigs in a gale. Being thrown violently from our berths below deck leaves us with bruises and, for some, broken bones. I believe it has rained for almost forty days and forty nights. I can only pray the Sally proves to be as seaworthy as Noah's Ark.

"Pressing your lavender sachet to my nose, Grandmother, provides some solace from the stench of retching, vinegar, and mold. Scurvy, which the sailors call mouth-rot, has begun to spread due to our constant consumption of salted meat and porridge, and the absence of vegetables. Ship's fever, or typhus, has already taken several lives.

"Supplies are scant and the rock-hard ship's bread, on which Papa cracked a tooth, is rife with worms and spiders. We collect rainwater when we can as the cask water is black and foul. Some drink Geneva instead, but Father says we must not touch spirits. We add vinegar to the water, but most often we use it to scour our mossy berths.

"How I long for the taste of your fresh oat bread and a mouthful of water from the sparkling stream. This supposed six-week voyage has become a never-ending test of both our endurance and our faith."

I sit up straight and open my eyes. Interrupted movies and stories are two of my Dislikes. "Our endurance and our faith.

Muzzy needs a lot of endurance to run races. I would not like to eat hard bread with bugs."

"You and me both."

"It only took us fifteen hours to drive here from Montreal. And we ate in gas station restaurants. And how could they drink Geneva since that's a city in Switzerland?"

Jessie makes her face even more wrinkly than usual. Does she smell something bad? I look at Miranda who is sleeping by the door, because sometimes dogs make bad smells. "It was their name for gin, a type of alcohol. Catherine also wrote a funny bit about Nicholas having a hard time using the 'head,' basically a hole acting as a toilet. With the water splashing up on his behind, he was scared to death of falling smack-dab into the ocean."

"Sometimes at parks, I have to use a stinky outhouse, which would be like the head, but without the ocean underneath."

Jessie nods, then she takes off her specs and rubs her eyes. "Thinking of the head reminds me of a not-so-funny part. A horrible disease called typhus killed off a lot of the passengers making their way across the ocean."

"Anne Frank also died of typhus, but in a concentration camp. Her diary is a famous non-fiction book."

Jessie nods. "Sad story, that one. Anyhow, Catherine's description of little tykes dying at sea from the great fever was one of the saddest letters. Heartbreaking."

I think of the broken heart at Sophia's grave. "But how did they bury them if they died at sea?"

"She described that in detail. Space was scarce on board, so after a proper church service, they just wrapped them up in a blanket, laid them out on a plank, and tipped them into the ocean. The smallest ones made barely a splash."

"At least they were already dead so they wouldn't feel the cold."

Jessie pokes her tongue into her cheek. "Guess that's a good, sensible way to look at it."

"Is there a treasure that goes with that chapter of Catherine's story?"

"There used to be. Let me see, here ..." Jessie lifts one side of the lid. She squeezes her dark eyebrows together so her eyes are almost shut, then closes the lid. "Used to be that lavender sachet was in here, but it must've sprouted legs like my copy of the letters."

I rub my fingers across my Lavender Lady. "I know lavender is a color, and sashay is a step I learned in ballet, but what is a lavender sashay?"

"This sachet has a different spelling: s-a-c-h-e-t. It's a little sack or sometimes a pillow. Remember how Grandmother included some lavender seeds in the little leather pouch? Its scent is real calming, healing, even. A lavender sachet under my pillow helps me sleep."

"Since the sachet is missing, could I see another one of the treasures? Please and thank you."

"What time of day is it?"

I check my watch. "It's 10:32 AM. I have to be home in eighty-eight minutes."

"All righty, then." She turns her back to me so I can't see her looking through the splint box. "This was always my favorite." When she turns back around, she's unwrapping something inside a piece of plaid pajama material. It's a tiny knife. "Grandmother was teaching Catherine to whittle before they left. She carved this knife handle specially to fit Catherine's hand." Jessie stops talking and stares at her knife collection. "Catherine had a hard time trying to carve a wooden Nellie goat for Nicholas while they were at sea forever. That goat carving used to be in the box, too. How did Catherine put it now?"

Miranda woofs, like she's answering the question.

"Right. Thank you, Miranda. She longed for Grandmother's help in learning to coax a creature's soul from a simple piece of wood. Think that's what made me set my sights on becoming a carver."

Miranda rests her snout on my leg and I pat her warm head.

"S'pose you'd like to hold it, would you? Careful with the rusty blade."

The wooden handle is a perfect tiny owl, Tobacco Brown, standing on the broken blade. I turn it over and stroke the owl's round head with my pointer finger. The little owl fits perfectly into the palm of my hand, like Grandmother had carved it just for me. I close my eyes.

I hold the owl knife up to my ear. Is it humming? I look at Jessie. Is it her humming?

"It's like holding a piece of living history in your hand, isn't it? These old things help bring Catherine's spirit to life."

Spirit. A synonym for ghost. Is it Catherine's ghost humming? I don't answer Jessie because I'm busy noticing a warm spot on my leg. My Lavender Lady.

"Can you teach me to carve an owl like this?" I ask. "I'm not a very good artist, but I might be a good carver."

Jessie wraps the knife back in its flannel and puts it away. "Possible. But right now, I've gotta get back to work." She puts the splint box and the book box on the shelf and sits down at her worktable. "And didn't you say you had to be home by mid-day?"

I get up and put on my sneakers. "Should I come back tomorrow?"

"Suit yourself, Chouette. You know where to find me."

That night, in the fourth space of my splint box chart, I write *Grandmother's Lavender Sachet, Missing*. In number five, I write,

Catherine's Owl Carving Knife, and *Nellie Goat, Missing* in space number six.

The Moon is very bright. A long-ago scientist named Galileo decided the dark spots that make the wise face of the Moon were seas. I don't know why, but scientists call the dark spots *maria,* almost the same name as Catherine's mother. After telescopes were invented, they found out the Moon is actually dry and dusty. But I don't mind.

- *Did anybody in Catherine's family get tipped into the sea?*
- *Does missing your grandmother feel the same as missing your real mother, even if you can't remember what she looks like?*
- *Is the girl in the picture Kitty, Aggie's niece, synonym for Jessie's daughter Katrina?*

In case the Moon decides to answer me, I'm listening hard and don't hear Muzzy come in behind me.

"Are you talking to yourself?"

I keep my eyes on the Moon and think about this. "Yes and no," I say finally.

"You know you can always talk to me." My bed creaks as she sits down behind me. "About anything."

So I tell her about Catherine's missing letters that she read to the Moon, and her treasures. Which takes a very long time. But I don't tell her that I talk to the Moon, too.

She's yawning by the time I'm finished. "That's so lovely

of Aggie and Jessie to share their family history with you."

"The stories and treasures bring history to life. Like Jack and his father, Jack Jodrey, Senior. JJ, who was your friend back in the day."

She nods. "Exactly. Don't stay up too late."

I sit up and touch my nose to hers. A synonym for pinky hug. After Muzzy leaves, I get out Moonbeam's bookmark. I read her words out loud to the Moon.

"Every time you see the Moon, know that I'll be thinking of you, Katie.

Take good care of our Lavender Lady.

I'll tell you her story when I come back for you.

Love, Moonbeam"

• *Is Moonbeam as honest as a boring day is long?*

• *What's my Lavender Lady's story?*

Chapter 18

Jessie opens the door a crack. "I'm busy this morning. Got a list of orders a mile long."

"You could fit a lot of orders on a list that's 5,280 feet long. Could I come in and watch, please and thank you?" I zip my lips.

She opens the door wider, goes to her worktable, and points to the stool beside hers. "Park your keister there."

"Park your keister."

"Sit your bottom down." Then she passes me a bar of soap. White. No smell.

"I had a bath last night." I look around for the bathroom. I think the skinny Flannel Gray building out back with the crescent moon on the door is an outhouse, like the head Nicholas was afraid to use on the *Sally*, only without the ocean underneath.

"This'll be your practice piece," Jessie says. "Soap's a fair bit easier to work with than wood."

"Could you help me learn to coax a creature's soul out of a piece of wood, like Catherine wanted Grandmother to do for her?"

She zips her lips, then gives me a glove like hers—a Kevlar glove she calls it—and a small knife. "You'll be all right without the thumb glove on your knife hand for today. It's tricky to get used to. Now, first thing I do is spray the block of wood with a water and rubbing alcohol mixture. Softens the wood, makes it easier to carve. You can skip this part since you're using soap."

"Wet soap is slippery," I say. "Madame LeBlanc used it to wash out kids' mouths when they said bad words. But not my mouth."

She nods. "Proper thing. Sounds to me like you need to wash that LeBlanc woman out of your memory."

"I have a memory like an elephant," I say. "Especially for mean people."

Jessie laughs. "You and me both. First thing you do is square off the bottom of that bar of soap, keep it flat so it won't topple over."

"Won't topple over." The Kevlar glove makes my hand itch, but I try to concentrate on Jessie's instructions. The handle of the small knife she lets me use isn't an owl, but it's smooth wood that's easy to hold onto.

"Now, the thumb of the wood-holding hand, that's your pivot point. That thumb's going to help push and steer your knife. Just a flick of your wrist, like this. Always away from your body. For obvious reasons. I'll try to go slow so you can follow along."

For somebody who's trying to go slow, she is a very fast carver. Little curls and chunks of wood pile up on the table under her strong hands. "I'm making an owl, but you just concentrate on getting the hang of using the knife. Don't worry about form yet. Focus on not cutting yourself."

I take quick glances up at the owl drawing Jessie has tacked up on the wall, and try to follow her, but it's hard.

When it's time for me to leave, Jessie's wooden owl is finished. And it looks just like the drawing. My soap owl is good only for washing your hands.

"Never you mind," she says. "Rome wasn't built in a day. Carving's a fine art. You'll catch on. As the master sculptor Michelangelo said, 'I saw the angel in the marble and carved until I set him free.'"

"Angels aren't real," I say. "And we're using wood and soap, not marble."

"Never mind about that. The point is, a carver needs to learn to see in her mind's eye, visualize what she's carving in order to bring it to life in the material, set it free. It'll come to you." She puts three little knives, my glove, and some pieces of wood and soap in a cloth bag. "Some practice pieces for you to take with you. Mind you don't cut yourself, now."

Back at The Chickadee, Jo-Ellen tells me Muzzy's gone out for lunch.

"With Jack Jodrey," she says, winking.

I know she means Jack Jodrey, Senior, not Jack Jodrey, Junior. Jack is away at YMCA camp with Ruthie, and JJ was very interested when he heard Allison Pearson was in town. And Muzzy used to be madly in love with him a long time ago.

Does that mean Muzzy used to make out with him?

Thinking about that makes my brain get the balloon-about-to-burst feeling. Mrs. MacKinnon used to make out with Jean-Claude, who was one of my Dislikes because he didn't respect my personal space. And then she had to kick me out of the nest because I was one of Jean-Claude's Dislikes, too.

On TV shows, boyfriends and girlfriends talk about love when they're kissing. Muzzy says love is the same as a very big Like, and that you love the people who make you feel good about yourself. I squeeze my Lavender Lady. Did Moonbeam get rid of me because I didn't make her feel good about herself? Isn't it the law that mothers have to love their kids?

When she gets home after lunch, Muzzy's cheeks are Georgia

Peach Pink, partly because she has a tan, and partly because she's excited and talking too fast. Maybe she had a glass of wine with lunch. Or two. Which she mostly only does at Christmastime when her sister, who is not estranged, comes to visit.

Jo-Ellen puts Muzzy to work chopping vegetables for soup. I take Butterscotch and go down by the harbor. The Captain's blowing on a Coral Dust Pink conch shell as the long Midnight Blue *Eastern Star* pulls away from the dock. Two people are tugging on thick twisty ropes to raise the sails. Muzzy said someday we can take a trip on the *Eastern Star,* only for ninety minutes, not seventeen weeks like Catherine was on the *Sally.* It costs thirty-five dollars for adults and sixteen dollars for children.

I bike along the Phantom Trail. I take a quick look at some people with a dog sitting on the grass. They might be homeless because they have lots of bags piled up around them. Their hair is long and scraggly. I think they're all men, not Moonbeam, who wouldn't have whiskers.

When I get far away from them, I sit on the bank under a big oak tree and look over my shoulder, away from the harbor, up past the Mi'kmaw healing garden, to the fire station. The kids in the daycare next door are screaming and laughing.

I get out my Lavender Lady and look across her crystal bumps at the sparkling water, then I lie on my back and look up at the sky, French Twist Blue, through the leafy branches. I think of some new questions for the Moon.

• *Did Catherine ever carve something from one of this tree's branches?*

• *Did she wear gloves to carve, and can trees live that long?*

• *Is your mind's eye the same color as your face eyes?*

At bedtime, Muzzy sits on the edge of my bed and I show her my soap carving. "It's supposed to be an owl, a saw-whet owl like Chou Chou, but I'm just learning to find the creature inside and set it free. Like Michelangelo—only he found angels inside marble."

Muzzy tilts her head, like Miranda when she is trying to understand people-talk. "I can definitely see some owl characteristics there, especially the big eyes. Was it fun?"

I nod. "Jessie doesn't talk much, and I keep my lips zipped because carving requires concentration so you don't cut yourself."

"Since she never married, I don't suppose Jessie has any children of her own?"

I lift my shoulders. "She used to, but I think it's in the MYOB category."

"MYOB?"

"Mind your own beeswax. I don't think Jessie wants to talk about it. Aggie used to have a niece named Kitty, synonym for

Katrina, and there's somebody named Chouette. Sometimes Jessie calls me Chouette by accident, because she's old and confused."

Muzzy squeezes her eyebrows together.

"It means 'little owl' in French," I tell her. "Jessie would be a good grandmother because she knows how to do lots of cool things."

"My grandmother, my father's mother, taught me how to quilt and make icicle pickles."

"Aggie makes icicle pickles. Only they're made of cucumbers, not ice."

She laughs. "I'm sure Nana Pearson had lots more to teach me, but she died when I was about your age."

"Being left behind is never easy. Did you love her?" I ask.

"Very much. We were two of a kind. I was so sad when she died that I worried I'd never stop crying."

"But you did stop crying."

She nods. "Time goes by. The hurt passes."

"Do you love Jack Jodrey, Senior, too?"

Muzzy leans away from me, shakes her head, tucks her hair behind her ears. "JJ and I are just old friends."

If I could read her face, maybe I would know if she was telling the truth. Or a white lie, a synonym for not telling the exact whole truth. A black lie is the opposite of the exact whole truth. I don't tell lies, black or white.

"I do love *you*, though. And there are always things to be happy about. Right?"

I nod yes. "Listening to Catherine's stories makes me happy. And you, and Jo-Ellen, and Aggie and Jessie, and Ruthie and Jack. I might teach them how to carve when they get back from camp."

"Seems like this adventure is turning out to be a good one for you." She leans in, touches her nose to mine, and gives me a pinky hug. "Me, too. Can you believe it's almost Homecoming Day again? Where does the time go?"

Homecoming Day. July 24th. The anniversary of the foster care people giving me to Muzzy.

After she leaves, I get out my old Science scribbler and write the date, July 21, before I start practice-drawing. I'm trying to figure out what to draw for Muzzy as a Homecoming Day present. Only nine more days until we go back to Montreal. Time goes by too fast in Lunenburg. While I'm thinking, I draw a tiny owl carving knife in space number five on my pie chart.

I turn off my lamp and look up at the sky. Because it looks like a right bracket, I know the Moon is waxing, which has nothing to do with candles or the stuff Sebastian digs out of his ears to eat. Miss Matattall taught us a poem to help us remember the difference between waxing and waning, synonyms for growing and shrinking.

If you see the Moon at the end of the day,

A bright Full Moon is on its way.

If you see the Moon in the early dawn,

Look real quick, it will soon be gone.

• *Do I have a grandmother or did she already die, like Nana Pearson?*

• *Will I get to hear all Catherine's stories before I go back to Montreal?*

• *What are the last six treasures for my chart?*

Chapter 19

I put my carving materials back in their sack. "Do you know about Rous's Brook? My friends Jack and Ruthie took me there once."

Jessie puts the splint box in between us on the loveseat. "I've whiled away many an hour out there, trying to imagine Catherine and her family catching their very first sight of lovely Lunenburg."

"Then, nobody in her family had to get tipped overboard?"

"Hold your horses." She looks over her specs at me. "Synonym for be patient. *Most* of the family arrived in one piece. Now, let me see ..." Her freckly hand disappears inside the box, then reappears holding a giant-sized red and white card, the nine of hearts, between her thumb and two fingers. It's in a plastic jacket, like the hockey cards the boys at school collect.

I lean closer to see it better. "What's that?"

Jessie holds up one finger, synonym for wait a minute. She opens the little notebook. "Catherine's family made it to Nova Scotia in September of 1752, but this bit, Catherine's first thoughts about the New World, is dated April 21, 1753, after a long cold winter living in tents in Halifax. She got to start writing her letters again thanks to a new graphite pencil, a gift from Madame Masson, whose babies she'd helped look after over the winter."

"Do you think Mason's Beach was named after her? Same as the Lunenburg streets were named after the founding fathers?"

"Could be. Now, listen up.

"We believe Elisabeth and her family have also arrived safely on their ship, the Gale, *and are living across the harbor. Halifax is a rough town with fearsome soldiers and unsavory women. Heathens roam the muddy streets at all hours of the night and day. Seamen carrying great wooden cudgels smash the glowing street lanterns for reasons no one can fathom, and people who steal have their hands branded with the Letter* T *for Thief. This is indeed a foreign, rocky land, but we are, nonetheless, grateful to have our feet firmly planted upon the earth once again."*

"Planted upon the earth once again. Catherine Marguerite Langille, formerly uprooted and now transplanted," I say.

Jessie snorts. "Sure enough. After surviving their first snowy winter in Nova Scotia, the French and German settlers were told they'd be moving down shore to Lunenburg. This letter ended with a pile of questions.

"We shall soon set sail for our new home, which the British call Lunenburg. It is said the Indians call it Merligueche, which means milky bay in their language. Will the voyage to Lunenburg be another endless journey? Will I ever again lie in a bed of feathers, rather than prickly straw and pine? Will I ever again taste fresh cheese and milk, or must my taste buds forever be subjected to dried peas and oatmeal, with a trickle of molasses? Has Elisabeth missed me as I have missed her? Please continue to pray for us."

"I'm allergic to feathers," I say. "Not on birds, but the ones inside pillows and duvets. They make me sneeze."

"Thanks to Grandmother's geese, the Langille family had nice feather mattresses back in Montbéliard. But back to this card. In Halifax, the head of each household—" she lifts her eyebrows at me, "—synonym for man—was given a playing card designating the plot of land where they'd build their homes in Lunenburg. This was David Langille's card. Lot 10-A Strasbourg Division. See here? It's written in ink on the back."

She passes me the card and I turn it over. "Why would they write the land lots on cards?"

"Well, paper would've been pretty scarce back then. Who knows? Maybe the British soldiers were great card players, gamblers, so they had a ready supply on hand."

I squeeze my warm Lavender Lady inside my pocket. "Is it the exact same card? From all those years ago?"

Jessie nods. "This card turned up during a house renovation, and the finder turned it over to the Fisheries Museum. Somebody at the Genealogical Society figured out that this lot number was granted to David Langille, our ancestor, and Catherine's papa. And so the card made its way back to us."

I examine both sides of the card, then count my Lavender Lady's nine crystal tips. "Nine is one of my favorite numbers. Was this a lucky card for Catherine's family? Is her house still there? Does it have a nametag?"

She shakes her head. "Ages ago, I tracked down the lot number on Pelham Street. It's just a vacant lot now, up from the Knaut-Rhuland Museum toward Hopson Street." Jessie takes the card from me and returns it to the splint box. "The Jodrey family lived a couple of houses up from there."

"You and Aggie used to persuade Jack's grandfather Alex to play the part of Nicholas in your settler game."

"You don't miss a trick, do you?"

"Was it a long voyage from Halifax to Lunenburg? Because it only takes one hour to drive that distance."

Jessie shakes her head. "There were a few delays, but the *Swan* arrived in the fog and drizzle on June 7th, 1753, more than a year after the Langilles had left Montbéliard. Catherine had gotten too big for all her grimy clothing, and she was wishing for a fresh, clean petticoat. Like me, she had funny extra-long second toes, and she was getting sick of them jamming into the ends of her too-small *sabots*."

Jessie takes off her sock and shows me. The toe beside the big one is her longest toe. "A foot reflexologist told me once that my longer second toe means I'm creative and bossy."

I take off one sock and show her my disordered toes. "But I am not bossy. *Sabots*. Synonym for wooden shoes. Was there a house waiting for them on Lot 10-A Strasbourg Division?"

Jessie snorts. "No such luck. The families had to work their tails off ..."

I sit up straight. "People had tails then?"

Jessie laughs. "Synonym for work real hard. Anyhow, they were building rough log homes for themselves and planting crops for food; the men were kept busy putting up forts and palisades to keep them safe."

"Safe from who? The wild men and wild beasts?" I ask.

Jessie pokes her tongue into her cheek. "I suppose so. Over the winter, Catherine had picked up enough English to understand stories told of settlers being sneak-attacked and scalped by the Natives, Canada's first people. Indians as they were called then. I have my suspicions that the attacking was a two-way street. And, of course, there were moose, bears, wolves, and such about."

"Did Elisabeth's family come to Lunenburg, too?"

Miranda goes to the door and whines. Jessie stands up and opens the door for her. "That's a story for another day. Back to work. I'll see you when I see you, Chouette."

I write Playing Card, Lot 10-A Strasbourg Division in space number seven of my chart. It's an easy one to draw. I'm not sleepy and the Moon's hiding, so I get out my colored pencils and work on Muzzy's present for a while. Then I draw a picture of Catherine and Nicholas on board the *Swan*. I use a painting from the Nova Scotia Archives site to draw the ship. Its sails are squares, not triangles. Catherine ends up looking like me, and Nicholas looks like Jack, since they are both boys with long hair.

When I'm finished, I pull the covers up under my chin and stare out the window.

- *Why did Jessie say most of the Langille family did arrive safely?*
- *Did someone in Catherine's family get sneak-attacked?*
- *Are funny second toes a Langille family trait like the Jodreys' crooked nose?*

Chapter 20

I give Jessie the bag of muffins Muzzy and I made. "These are Morning Glory muffins, but they do not have flowers in them, and they're gluten-free, and we used molasses instead of sugar. I grated the carrots; four carrots for twenty-four muffins."

"Thank you, kindly. That'll be a real treat with our afternoon tea." After we sit down on the loveseat, Jessie puts on her specs, lifts one side of the splint box lid, and takes out something wrapped in white cloth. She unfolds it gently, then holds it out for me to see. "Toddler size, I'd say. Right fancy, isn't it? Made of deerskin."

The shoe is Sand Patterns Brown with a beaded sun in the middle of the toe part. "Can I touch it?"

Jessie nods and passes it to me. "Made by the Mi'kmaw people, I expect. The glass beads must've come from the European settlers, probably the French Acadians who came before Catherine's family, and all the other Foreign Protestants."

"Some of the French Acadians are buried by the Phantom Trail," I say.

"Sure enough. This belonged to some relative of Marie Claire's, I believe. The ivory bits are porcupine quills. Natives used to flatten them using their teeth."

I touch the moccasin with my pointer finger. Like the seed pouch, it feels like the Baby Soft Pink ballet shoes I had when I was nine. I only took ballet for one year because every time I did a spin, my brain spun, too, and dancing on your bum is hard. "Is a real deer this soft?"

Jessie shakes her head. "Not that I've ever come near enough to touch a deer, but the Mi'kmaw people do what's called tanning the hide before making it into moccasins."

"Madame LeBlanc, my foster mother before Muzzy, used to tan kids' hides. A synonym for spanking," I tell her. "But not my hide."

"Sounds to me like you're lucky to have found this Muzzy person. This tanning involves soaking, stretching, and pounding the deerskin with a mallet to soften it up." Jessie wraps the moccasin back up and puts it in the splint box. She takes out the plaid flannel bundle and unwraps the owl knife. She looks at it for a long time, rubbing the little owl's smooth head with her thumb. After she puts it back inside the box, she gets out the yellow notebook, and flips through the pages.

"Anyhow, about two weeks after Catherine's family landed in Lunenburg, the ship carrying her cousin Elisabeth's family finally showed up. Catherine and Nicholas were foolish with excitement, dancing around, waiting for their cousins to get off the boat."

"Were they lip-flapping flutterbugs? And was their boat also called the *Swan*?"

"Beats me. But quit interrupting. Makes me lose my train of thought." She taps one finger against her lips and stares out the back window. "Soon as Peter, Elisabeth's little brother, stepped on shore with his parents, just the three of them, Catherine knew." Jessie takes off her specs, closes her eyes and rubs her forehead. "Let me see if I can recollect her exact words when she broke the news to Grandmother. Agatha used to love acting out this part. She could even make real tears come, drama queen that she was. And no doubt still is."

"Why was it just the three of them?"

After thirteen breaths, she shakes her head and opens the Gothic Gold notebook. "Maybe I can find some of Catherine's words that I scribbled down in here." She flips through some pages.

I pat Miranda while I wait. Rubbing between her eyes makes her fall asleep.

"Ah—here's that sad bit. From the 10th of July, 1753.

"Dear Grandmother, I cannot believe more than fourteen months have passed since I saw you last. Nicholas, Peter, and I sing your Moon lullaby to help pass the time as we work, gathering wood, collecting fresh boughs for our beds (how I long for your ornery geese!), and water from the well. Sometimes I can almost hear you humming along. Neither you nor the Moon will be happy to hear the very sad news I must impart. Until now, I have been unable to force myself to write these painful words ...

"My beautiful cousin-sister has succumbed to the great fever. Elisabeth will never see the Moon again. Never sing with me again. Never share stories and adventures with me again. We were to be neighbors and friends forever, even here in this harsh New World. Yet, here I am alone."

I sit up straight and stare at Jessie. "Elisabeth died? But she wasn't old. Did she die of shame and a broken heart, like Sophia McLachlan?"

"Not exactly. Typhus got her."

I make a connection. "Is typhus like cancer?" I ask. Because a twelve-year-old boy at my school died of cancer last year.

Jessie shakes her head. "More like a real nasty flu with a bad rash. Happens in dirty places, where people can't wash, possibly spread by lice or rats."

"My friend Ruthie has a very old nitpicker comb they could have used on the lice."

"Maybe they did."

"And probably Anne Frank's body was burned after she died of typhus. Because that's what they did in the concentration camps."

"Anyhow, Catherine had real trouble sleeping after that, kept picturing her beautiful cousin-sister Elisabeth being tipped into the icy cold ocean, same as she'd seen other youngsters who'd died from the great fever."

"That's why Catherine got to keep Elisabeth's Moon hairclip, the one inside the snuff jug."

Jessie pokes her tongue into her cheek and nods. "Although I do believe she'd have preferred to have Elisabeth herself, in the flesh. But the world works in mysterious ways. Catherine made her first friend in the New World that very night."

"Was it Marie Claire?"

"How'd you know about her?"

"Aggie told me you used to take turns being Catherine and the other would be Elisabeth or Marie Claire."

Jessie nods. "Catherine had a habit of walking down the beach, toward the end where the healing garden is now."

"By the Phantom Trail."

She nods yes. "Anyhow, Catherine had a favorite rock she liked to perch on when she needed to cogitate. Synonym for think things through."

"Like your flute-playing rock?"

"I suppose so. Anyway, that night, she took Grandmother's leather seed pouch with her so she could soak up the smells of home."

"The smells of home. Lavender, brown-eyed Susans, horse chestnuts, and acorns," I say.

"Sure enough. In the middle of her crying, a girl appeared out of the woods, a Métis girl, Marie Claire, half-Native and half-French. Her father, Cloverwater, was a big help to the settlers in the early years. Him and his uncle, Old Labrador."

"I know they were real people, because I saw their names in the library book I'm reading about the Foreign Protestants."

Jessie nods. "Seeing as Marie Claire had long, shiny black hair, Catherine was scared at first, thinking she was one of the savages she'd heard about."

"Poe's Raven Black," I say. "That's one of my colored pencils."

"Huh. I always wished I had hair like hers when I was young. Catherine did, too."

"What color was your hair, before Silver Sword Gray, I mean?"

Jessie looks at my hair. "'Bout the color of yours, I suppose. Not quite so thick."

"Did Catherine get the hiccups when she saw Marie Claire? That's what happens to me with strangers, remember?"

"Can't say as I recall her mentioning that. Good thing was, the two girls could chit-chat in French. Marie Claire did her best to comfort Catherine, including showing her how to make a wish using a P-shaped rabbit bone—from the hip I think it was."

"Turkeys have wishbones. But they're V-shaped."

"This one you held above your head and tried to poke your finger through the little hole without looking. If you did it, your wish would come true."

"What was Catherine's wish?"

"She didn't tell Marie Claire because everybody knows wishes don't come true once you've blabbed. But Catherine did tell Grandmother in a letter. Let me see if I can remember this part. Guess she figured the Moon wouldn't blab." She closes her eyes and rubs her forehead. I wait. "Said she wished to know happiness again, to get rid of the great lonely cloud of sorrow hanging over her."

She stops talking and pats Miranda's head. "Believe you me, Chouette, I've felt that same lonely cloud of sorrow hanging over me a time or two in my life." She takes off her specs and we listen to Miranda snoring for a while.

"What I wish is that we had those letters. Catherine Marguerite was a darn sight better at telling her story than me."

"Is the P-shaped rabbit bone one of the treasures?"

Jessie nods and polishes her specs on the sleeve of her shirt. "As youngsters, we tried poking our fingers through that hole plenty of times, but I don't know as we ever succeeded. Agatha might have once or twice, but she probably cheated."

"Agatha, the woman formerly known as your sister. A synonym for Aggie," I say.

Jessie takes a tiny P-shaped bone out of the box. "Hard to imagine this came from a critter that lived all those years ago, isn't it?" Miranda sits up to sniff it. "Want to make a wish?"

I shake my head no. "Wishes never come true. Is Elisabeth's Moon hairclip still in the box? I already know it was the other thing you and Aggie found inside Grandmother's jug."

"Can't remember if we left it in the jug or put it in here. It's not here now, anyhow. Darned if I can remember the details. My brain's all full of cobwebs today."

"Did a spider crawl up your nose?"

"Sure do take things real literal, don't you? Just an expression that means my brain's feeling foggy today."

"Maybe the fog eater, synonym for the sun, could help you. And was the hairclip a full Moon or a crescent Moon?"

"Crescent, I do believe." Jessie puts her specs back on. "Now, where was I?" She leans back and closes her eyes. "Those first few months, Marie Claire taught Catherine a whole pile about how to live in the rough New World. That night, she showed Catherine her first lightning bug, flashing because it was mating season. Agatha always liked the part when Marie Claire compared the young men playing their love flutes to flashing fireflies looking for a mate."

"Do your flutes make people fall in love?"

Jessie pokes her tongue into her cheek. "Not so far as I know. Catherine taught Marie Claire a few things, too, over the next while—some English words and a French song. You heard Grandmother's lullaby, yet?"

I shake my head no.

Jessie clears her throat. "Don't speak French myself, and my lullaby-singing days are long-gone, but I'll sing what I can remember. Something about a youngster being cold and lonely in the moonlight.

"Au clair de la lune, mon ami Pierrot.

Preté-moi ta plume, pour écrire un mot."

My heart starts beating faster. I squeeze my Lavender Lady. "I know that song."

Jessie looks over the top of her specs at me, then motions for me to zip my lips. I close my eyes.

"Ma chandelle est morte, je n'ai plus de feu.

Ouvre-moi ta porte pour l'amour de Dieu."

My heart's still doing its *pa-dum pa-dum* when Jessie's finished. I keep squeezing my warm Lavender Lady until my heart goes back to its regular beating. "I do know it. You didn't pronounce all the words right, but I know that Moon song."

"Probably sang it at school," Jessie says. "It's catchy, the kind of tune that won't leave you alone. Odd coincidence that's what I was playing on the flute when you showed up the other day."

I shake my head no, close my eyes, and try to see the picture, but it won't come. "Somebody used to sing it to me when I was going to sleep."

"I suppose it's sort of a lullaby, although somebody's candle going out doesn't seem like a great lullaby topic." Jessie looks at my watch. "I've got work to do. Market day tomorrow."

"Should I come back?"

"Suit yourself. You know where to find me. I shouldn't be too busy on Friday." I follow her gaze out the church-shaped window on the back wall. Far away, through the trees past the small outhouse with a skinny Moon cut out of the door, there's a sliver of gray water, wisps of fog floating on top of it. And a bird's making a long, sad wailing sound. Like ghosts in movies.

Jessie shoves her hands into her overall pockets. "Loons flyin' and cryin' above the pond's a sure sign of rain. You'd best be off home now."

"My friends, Ruthie and Jack, will be back from camp on Friday, but I'll try to come visit you, too."

"I'll see you when I see you."

The almost-half-Moon has a twin in the still harbor tonight. I get out my splint box chart and write *Tiny Moccasin* in space number eight and *Rabbit Wishing Bone* in space number nine.

- *Who was it that used to sing Grandmother's lullaby to me?*
- *Did Catherine ever get rid of the great lonely cloud of sorrow hanging over her?*
- *Why does Jessie call me Chouette?*

Chapter 21

I get off Butterscotch and start pushing because the hill's too steep. "I used to live in a creaky old wooden building like these ones, with Mrs. MacKinnon, my second foster mother. But she got a boyfriend that didn't like bratty kids so I had to leave. Even though I'm not bratty."

"I'm glad Allison's your foster mom now," Ruthie says. "Otherwise, I'd never have met you."

"My family lived in the same house down on Pelham Street for almost a hundred and fifty years," Jack says. "Until Grampy went into the home. It was too big for just Dad and me to look after."

"Muzzy and I have lived in the same apartment for almost three years. One thousand and ninety-six days, because one of the years was a Leap Year. That's a very long time for me."

"The first settlers had church here," Ruthie says, sitting

on a bench in front of a big black and white church, St. John's Anglican. "In the open air before they built a church."

I lay Butterscotch on the grass and sit on the bench beside her. There are twelve stained-glass windows that I can see. "I would like to see inside. Do the windows make rainbows?"

"Sometimes. The big one in the front is 'The Fisherman's Window.'"

"The church before this one got torched in 2001," Jack says.

"Did it get hit by lightning?" I ask. "The tall pointy parts?"

"Nobody was ever charged, but it was supposedly kids playing a Halloween prank," Ruthie says. "They tried to build this one just like the original 1871 church."

"They even left some of the partly-burned pews up in the loft," Jack says. "They still stink like smoke."

"One hundred and forty-four years old. When Madame LeBlanc made me go to church, the itchy dresses were one of my Dislikes, but the rumbly organ music was one of my Likes. Those kids should have gone to jail. That was not a very funny prank."

"Let's go," Jack says, pushing his bike toward the street. "I missed my little fort when I was at camp all week."

Ruthie waits for me. "And Katie's going to give us a carving lesson and tell us all about Jessie, right?"

I nod yes.

"I suck." Jack's carving was going to be a fish, but it's too small to be anything. A minnow, maybe. "But I've got a wicked pile of soap flakes here, unscented, if anybody's interested." The tree house floor is covered with bits of white soap.

"Well, mine sorta looks like a flower," Ruthie says. "Maybe a dying flower."

I hold up my piece of wood. "This is the first gnome I could see before it started coming out of the wood. Like it was hiding inside, waiting for me to find it." They know what I'm talking about because I told them all about Jessie and Catherine's letters and treasures.

"Cool. You should paint it." Jack leans back against the wall. "Think I'll stick to pounding nails and painting houses."

"Carving's fun, though," Ruthie says, putting her soap in her backpack. "You're lucky Jessie's teaching you. What do you want to do now? We have to be home by lunchtime to help Dad build the new chicken coop this afternoon."

"I've never been to the playground by the Bluenose Academy." I put my carving sack in my backpack. "That big spider-web climbing thing looks interesting."

"Hey, maybe we could meet Jessie," Ruthie says. "Doesn't she live out that way?"

I look down at my sneakers. Jessie likes animals better

than people. "I think she's busy working." This is not a lie because she works every day.

"Don't you just love the little owls she makes?" Ruthie says, climbing down the rope ladder we finally got finished. "I wish she'd come to the market herself so I could watch her carve. I saw this video the other day about these kids on a field trip. An owl landed right on their shoulders. It was the cutest thing ever. A little saw-whet."

"Jessie has a saw-whet owl in her family, Chou Chou, who lands on Jessie's shoulder. Catherine carved an owl, also named Chou Chou, for her cousin Elisabeth, who died of the great fever," I say. "Jessie likes animals better than people because they don't give her any guff. A synonym for nonsense."

"An old lady who lives alone in the woods with an owl and doesn't like people?" Jack says, zipping up his backpack. "Not too witchy."

"She's an odd duck," I say. "But she doesn't quack and have webbed feet, and she's not a witch. Witches aren't real."

Jack gets on his bike. "Uh-huh. Whatever you say."

I look at Ruthie's Midnight Mystery Brown eyes. Would she be scared of Jessie? "Do you believe in witches?" I ask.

She laughs and starts pushing her bike back to the trail. "I like kid witches and wizards in stories, like Hermione Granger and Harry Potter."

"Hermione Granger is smart, but she's not a witch because witches aren't real," I say. "But the actor, Emma Watson, is real and smart, too. And the Harry Potter books aren't one of my Likes."

"Are you serious? I LOVE Harry Potter! I've seen every movie and read all the books at least twice."

"I like true stories," I say. "Not fantasy."

"Race ya!" Jack takes off, making his back tire spit up some gravel.

The plastic pyramid roofs and slides beside the tennis courts are Three O'Clock Royal Blue, one of my favorite pencil colors. Maybe whoever built the playground picked that color because kids come here after school at three o'clock. I'm very good at swinging. Better than I am at dory rowing. I pump hard and try to touch the big tree right in front of me. I lean back, make myself flat like a board, and stare up at the sky through the branches. The pale Moon's out early today. There's no breeze, but the fluffy clouds are moving fast.

After we jump off, I try to wrap my arms around the tree's rough Charcoal Gray trunk, but it's too fat. A synonym for too old. With my arms still wrapped, I hold up both my baby fingers. "Pinky hug," I say. On one side, Ruthie hooks her pinky to mine, and Jack does the same on the other side. "A perfect fit!" Ruthie says. "We're a tree necklace."

"Tree necklace." The Royal Magenta sneaker on Ruthie's left foot is touching my right one. Twin feet. I hope the tree doesn't feel like it's suffocating.

"We are serious tree huggers," Jack says.

Ruthie groans. "That is so lame."

Lame. A synonym for limping. "What kind of tree is it?" I ask.

Jack unhooks his pinky. "Dunno. Elm, maybe. Gramps always told me this is one of the oldest trees in town."

"How old?" I ask. "Two hundred and sixty-two years?"

He shrugs. "He didn't say."

"The tallest tree in the world is named Hyperion," I say. "It's in California in the United States of America, and it's three hundred and eighty feet tall, one-third the height of the Eiffel Tower. If you want to see it, you can look it up on Google."

"Cool."

In between the gray stripes, some of the bumpy bark is Amigo Pink. I close my eyes and press my cheek up against the deep grooves. Somebody's humming. I can feel it. But it's not me. I look at Jack and Ruthie, over by our bikes. They're talking, but they're too far away for me to hear. Is the tree singing? Like Grandmother's snuff jug and the little owl carving knife? Only none of those things is alive. Is it the spirit of the person who planted the tree? I close my eyes and try to hum along. There's too much traffic. The tune is full of holes where notes are missing. But I think it's Grandmother's Moon lullaby.

Jessie feels my wooden gnome all over with her thumbs. The dirt under her short fingernails is from what she calls slaving in the garden. She is not really a slave because nobody owns her. "Not half bad. You want to give him a spot of color now he's nice and smooth?"

I nod, and she gets out some small bottles of paint, the dollar store kind. "I use watercolors, mix 'em with water to mute the tone. Keep it as natural looking as possible."

It takes me a long time to choose my colors, then mix them so they're just right. "I wish I could use my one hundred colored pencils," I say.

"Thing about paint is you can mix the colors, get an endless number."

"Endless number. A synonym for infinity."

We work without talking for a long time. My gnome's tall pointy hat is easy, but on the face, it's hard to get the tiny brush to go in all the right places and stay out of the wrong ones.

When I'm almost finished, Jessie looks up from her own painting and whistles. "He's got a lot of soul, that little guy. Don't forget to write your initials under the base. Gonna give him a moniker?"

I look up at her quickly. Her eyes are all squinty. Is she trying to see something, or is she smiling? Mostly she has a serious old-lady face, like me. Only she really is an old lady.

"Synonym for name."

I set my gnome on the windowsill next to my flute, think hard for a minute, and then shake my head. "I'll think about his moniker when I go to bed tonight. Can you tell me some more about Catherine and Marie Claire now? Please and thank you."

We sit down on the loveseat, and Jessie gets the yellow notebook out of the splint box. The page she opens to is almost at the end. "Here's another bit that she wrote after meeting Marie Claire." She picks up her broom from beside the woodstove. "One thing Catherine learned from her was how to make a twig broom, like this.

"What was your saying about the broom, Grandmother? A new broom sweeps clean, but an old one knows the corners best? I have a new friend, but I shall forever miss the old one who knew me best."

"I don't have a broom, but I'm giving my new friends, Ruthie and Jack, carving lessons. I don't have any old friends, except for the Moon." I look at her freckled hands. "And maybe you and Aggie because you're both old."

"Age doesn't much matter when it comes to friends. In my experience, the Moon's not much of a talker, but he's a real good listener." She looks through the notebook. "Not too much left in here. Maybe we should save it for another day. How's about a little music?"

I get our flutes from the windowsill above her worktable. "Do you think the Mi'kmaw flutes looked like ours? Japanese knotweed grows beside the road on Green Street. Maybe it's always grown there."

Jessie nods. "Possible. Spreads like wildfire once it takes hold. Which is nice for me since I sell a pile of flutes at the market, specially around the holidays. Imagine there's lots of folks cursing me once their youngster starts caterwauling first thing Christmas morning. Now, let's see if we can't figure out 'Au clair de la lune,' Grandmother Langille's lullaby. I remember most of it."

I hum the tune while she picks out the notes on her flute. I close my eyes and try to get my brain to give me a picture of somebody else's fingers playing that song for me on a flute. Younger fingers with long Lavender's Blue nails. But I can't see the face. Was it Moonbeam?

I concentrate on learning the notes. When I can play it through without any mistakes, I check my watch. "I need to go home now. It's Homecoming Day and we're going out for supper."

"How's that?"

"The anniversary of the day Muzzy and I first met. July 24th. Three years ago, when I was eight years, four months, and four days old."

"Sounds to me like a pretty good reason to celebrate. I'll see you when I see you."

Miranda woofs.

Biking home, I think about Catherine's story and the three empty spaces in my pie chart. The movie in my brain keeps stopping and starting; it's hard to fill in the pauses. In my mind's eye, Catherine looks like me.

And she's friends with the Moon, like me and Jessie.

Chapter 22

Back at The Chickadee, Jo-Ellen's busy serving the special written on the chalkboard outside. Fresh Adams & Knickle scallops, one of my new Likes. When the scallop boats come in, people line up outside the big red A&K store to buy fresh scallops. I wave to Jo-Ellen, then go upstairs.

On my treasure chart, I write *Missing* beside number two: *Elisabeth's Moon Hairclip*. I change my drawing so the Moon on the barrette is crescent, not full. Four of Catherine's treasures have *Missing* written beside them, and there are only three empty spaces left. If those treasures are missing, too, will Jessie remember what they were?

I lie down on top of my quilt, yawn, and close my eyes to think. A clip-clopping horse wakes me up at 4:22 PM. Ninety-eight minutes before our supper date. I keep my eyes closed and tap out the hoof-beat music on my quilt. It goes from slow to fast, then disappears. That means he's turned the corner leading up to Pelham Street, the same route they always take.

I get Muzzy's Homecoming Day present out of the bottom drawer of my desk. The picture has Muzzy and Jo-Ellen sitting on the front step of The Chickadee, with me in the middle. I'm still trying to get our faces right. Jo-Ellen's wearing her lobster apron, and she's supposed to be laughing, Muzzy's pushing her hair back from her face, and I look the same as always. I try to smile into the seashell-frame mirror beside my desk. I've been working on copying Ruthie's smile. Muzzy used to sit beside me and play "Show and Tell" in the mirror so I could learn to understand faces; I'm still learning.

I want to put Catherine and Marie Claire in the picture, too, on the beach out by Marie Claire's house at the head of the harbor, but my paper isn't big enough. Miss Matattall says you can use artistic license when you draw, which is not the same as a driver's license. She told me that means I should let my imagination run free, like the wild horses on Sable Island. My imagination might be one of the inside bits of me that Moonbeam took with her. Like my tears.

I get out my colored pencils. *Hmmm* ... I need to put Aggie and Jessie somewhere, too. While I'm thinking, I color some of the background—Indian Slipper Blue sky, Dragon Fly Green grass, and Sailor Boy Blue for the harbor.

I think of the humming tree over by the swings. Did Catherine plant it? Trees are easy, so I make it fill one whole side of the paper. Then I draw Aggie holding Grandmother's jug on a big branch on the right side of the tree, since she lives on the right-hand side of the real tree. I draw Jessie on the left side, since she lives out in Mason's Beach, to the left of the tree. Maybe I'll put Miranda on the branch beside her. I draw a ladder leaning up against the tree since dogs can't climb trees.

When the sun starts dropping above the golf course, I stretch, put away my drawing, then look out the window. I can't find the Moon, yet, but I know he's there.

- *Do I have a cousin-sister like Elisabeth somewhere, alive, not dead?*
- *Did the Indians (which Jessie calls the Mi'kmaw people) attack Catherine's family because the British stole their land? Or did Cloverwater keep them safe?*
- *How did the elm tree, the snuff jug, and the owl knife sing to me when they don't have voice boxes?*

Muzzy and I always trade Homecoming Day gifts at bedtime, after we have a special dinner date. Last year, we went to Sushi Fang for spring rolls and green tea ice cream. It's tastier than it sounds, and would be a very good color name for the Felissimo pencil company. Today, I hope we'll go to The Knot Pub, then Sweet Treasures for homemade Toasted Coconut ice cream, one of my new Likes.

But when I get downstairs, Jo-Ellen is alone in the café, dancing with her mop, which is one of her habits.

"Well, that's a sophisticated dress," she says. "Very Audrey Hepburn."

"Audrey Hepburn." Maybe she is a pianist, too, since my black dress has trim that looks like piano keys. "Where's Muzzy?" I ask, checking my watch. It's 5:48 PM. "I didn't hear her come in."

She gives me a wink. "Gone out for a dory-rowing lesson and picnic with you-know-who."

I know you-know-who is not Jack because he's helping Ruthie's father build a chicken coop. So it must be JJ. P*a-dum pa-dum.* "But it's Homecoming Day. July 24th. She has to be here." I sit down because I'm getting the no-gravity floaty feeling. "Can we call her cell?"

"Homecoming Day? I saw that written on the calendar but forgot to ask what it meant."

I explain, then go out on the deck and sit down at one of the little red half-moon tables, looking out over the harbor. Lots of sailboats, big scallop boats, and the *Bluenose II*, but all the dories are parked. I try to play "Au clair de la lune" on the piano keys on my dress. But I keep hitting the wrong notes. And my stomach is making hungry noises. I look back through the screen door at Jo-Ellen. "Did she say what time she'd be home?"

She shakes her head and holds up Muzzy's Pretty Polly Purple cell phone. "And she forgot this. It buzzed a while ago. I tried to answer it, but I was too late. The name of her magazine in Montreal came up on the screen." She takes off her apron and hangs it on the hook beside the cash register. "But, hey—you and I can go on a date. Your choice and my treat. Maybe Aggie would like to join us. Seems we haven't seen her in a good long while."

I nod yes. But Homecoming Day is for Muzzy and me. That's all.

"Oh, my gosh. I'm so sorry I'm late. I didn't have my phone or my watch."

I can feel Muzzy looking at me, but I keep my eyes on the shiny seaweed art on the wall of The Knot Pub. Aggie told me it came from the Lunenburg Foundry, and it's the drippings left over from bronze parts they make for boats. Same as cloud-watching, you can find all sorts of interesting shapes if you look hard enough.

"No worries. We haven't even ordered yet," Jo-Ellen says, squeezing over to make room for Muzzy.

"I thought you forgot," I say.

"Forget Homecoming Day? Our third anniversary? Never! I forgot my phone and I just lost track of time, that's all. I'm so sorry, Katie. I was just having too much fun."

"I'm so hungry I could eat a moose," Jo-Ellen says.

I give her a quick look.

"Kidding. Don't think I'd like the taste of moose. Unless it was chocolate. Let's order."

"I'm on a heart-smart diet," Aggie says. "Caesar salad and chili for me, with a side of garlic bread. Most of that's low-calorie, isn't it?"

I crunch up the last bite of my waffle cone and wipe the sticky corners of my mouth on my napkin. "Thank you, Jo-Ellen ... and Muzzy." I'm sitting between them on the Plum Crazy Red bench outside Sweet Treasures.

"My pleasure, sweetie." Jo-Ellen pats my bare knee. When I thought Muzzy forgot me, I left my Audrey Hepburn dress in my closet. My shorts feel like they're getting too tight. Because I'm growing like a bad weed.

"I'll miss The Knot when we go back to Montreal." Muzzy reaches out to give me a pinky hug. I keep my hands in my pockets and rub my Lavender Lady. I don't look at her because I know her eyes will be shiny.

Aggie stands up and pats her middle. "Best meal I've had in ages. And it was so lovely to get caught up with all of you and to hear that you're enjoying Jessie's company, Katie. And that you're enjoying JJ's company, Allison."

"There's no friend like an old friend." Jo-Ellen winks at Muzzy. "She and Jack are getting reacquainted."

"Better late than never," Aggie says. "Matthew and I had a whirlwind courtship, but we were well into our forties before he got up the nerve for a bended-knee proposal. Before he passed, we had eighteen lovely years of marriage."

Lovely years of marriage. I've seen bended-knee proposals on TV. Is Muzzy starting to love JJ more than me? I had to leave Mrs. MacKinnon's house when she fell in love with Jean Claude, who did not love me because I didn't laugh at his jokes. And once I had to push him out of my personal space when he was babysitting me. Even though I wasn't a baby.

We stop off at the Post Office so Aggie can check her mail. She takes a big envelope out of her box, Pale Purple Periwinkle. She squints at the messy writing on the front. "I rarely get a letter these days, and I don't recognize the handwriting. The return address is in Vancouver. I'll save it as a treat for later. I love surprises!" All the way to her house, I'm sniffing like Miranda. It smells like Jessie's house. Like lavender.

I go straight upstairs to bed when we get home. Muzzy wanted to exchange Homecoming Day gifts, but I told her I was too tired. I can hear her talking on the phone downstairs. Probably to her boss at the magazine, or maybe JJ. The wind is gusty, splatting raindrops up against my window. I start counting the ones trickling down, but there are too many. They're as hard to count as waves. Or tears.

Finally, at ten o'clock, I hear somebody tiptoeing up the creaky stairs. I squeeze my eyes shut, hide both hands under my quilt, and concentrate on not humming. My Lavender Lady is cold. My door creaks open and I can feel Muzzy standing beside my bed. I do yoga breaths and try to keep my eyelids still so she'll think I'm asleep. Am I telling a lie? She brushes my bangs back from my forehead and whispers, "Sweet dreams, Katie love."

Katie love. I watch as she tiptoes out, pulling the door closed behind her. I look out the window and try to find the Moon, but he's hiding in the clouds. The rain has stopped.

- *How could she be late for Homecoming Day?*
- *Is Muzzy madly in love with Jack Jodrey, Senior, again?*
- *Will she send me back to Montreal alone, to the foster care people, so she can stay here with him?*

I watch the clock. A watched pot never boils is what Jo-Ellen says, even though pots and clocks are two different things.

The last time I remember is 12:45 AM.

Chapter 23

In the morning, I wake up too early. In between the foghorn blowing every thirteen seconds, I can hear Jo-Ellen bustling around down in the café, singing along to the radio. Singing is something she's still learning.

I do yoga breaths, fill my lungs with salty air, and try to feel sunny. My brain feels like it's full of black thunderclouds. Or maybe cobwebs. I get up and look at my drawing. I sit down and work a little on the tree bark, Amigo Pink and Charcoal Gray, then fix Jo-Ellen's hair to add her new highlights, August Glow Pink.

Seeing how I drew Muzzy's pinky finger holding mine almost makes me forget to be mad at her. I draw the Moon behind some of the highest tree branches, a crescent Moon for poor Elisabeth. I try to fit Miranda in beside Jessie on her branch. Miranda looks like the Big Bad Wolf, and I have to erase her. Real artists don't use erasers but I'm still learning. I close my eyes and picture Chou Chou, then draw her sitting on Jessie's shoulder. I change Jessie's eyes so she's trying to look sideways at the little owl.

I turn my picture over, then get out my bookmark. I press my Lavender Lady up to my forehead, hum Grandmother's lullaby, and try to see Moonbeam with my mind's eye. My Moon questions for tonight might be:

- *Does Moonbeam look like me? Or is she pretty?*
- *If she lived in Montreal, how come she had this bookmark?*
- *Why doesn't she come back to tell me our Lavender Lady's story?*

When my stomach growls, I go downstairs. Muzzy's wobbly voice makes me stop on the bottom step. It sounds like she's almost crying. Did she sprain her ankle when she was out running? One time that happened to her in Montreal.

"I can't do that to her, Jo. Katie's had too much to deal with already. And she's been doing so great since we came to Lunenburg. I'm still kicking myself for almost forgetting last night."

Kicking yourself would be hard to do. And it would hurt.

"I was thinking to start talking with her about adoption when we get back to Montreal."

Adoption. Synonym for becoming somebody's forever kid.

"But I know she still hopes Moonbeam will come back for her."

"She's a sweetie," Jo-Ellen says. "It's a tough call for you to make."

"And he's only giving me a week to make up my mind about his proposal."

His proposal. I hold onto the acorn-shaped newel post. With both hands.

Proposal. Synonym for asking somebody to marry you. After a whirlwind courtship, Matthew and Aggie were well into their forties before he got up the nerve for a bended-knee proposal.

"It's something you've wanted since you were a kid. But Katie's a creature of habit. Like Bilbo Baggins. And wherever you are, that's her hobbit hole."

Like Bilbo Baggins. I squeeze my Lavender Lady. *Pa-dum pa-dum.* They don't say anything else. I count to thirty, then walk down the hallway and into the kitchen.

Muzzy puts down her coffee cup and rubs her eyes. "Good morning, sunshine."

I hum loudly and walk in behind the counter where Jo-Ellen's making coffee. I stare at the lobster calendar, a red cooked lobster, not a green alive one, rowing a dory. A long time ago, I'd colored the July 24th square with my Lavender's Blue pencil and written in HOMECOMING DAY.

"Oh, Katie. Will you forgive me for being an idiot?"

She is not an idiot because she's very smart. Not with

numbers, or directions, but with words, because she is a journalist who writes non-fiction stories.

Muzzy shoves her chair back and comes to stand next to me. She holds out her pinky finger. I bury both hands in my pockets and squeeze my Lavender Lady. Her points stab into my hand. All nine of them.

"Katie, I'm so sorry."

I want to say it's okay, but that would be a lie. I want to tell her JJ is why she forgot. Because that's the truth. But her not telling me about the proposal isn't the truth. Should I ask? Was I spying? Spying's something nosy people and tattletales do. I wasn't trying to be sneaky.

"We had a real nice dinner in the end, though, didn't we, Katie?" Jo-Ellen rests her elbows on the counter. "And Aggie sure seemed glad for the company."

I nod yes, but keep staring at the black and white floor tiles. It sounds like thunder rumbling inside my brain. I hold onto the counter to keep from floating away.

"I got you something special," Muzzy says.

"I'm not finished your present," I tell the tiles.

"Maybe we can exchange our gifts later on today. Around three-thirty when I'm finished work?"

I look up at her quickly. Underneath her worried W, her eyes are shiny. I nod yes. "Okay. I'm not quite finished yours, and I'm going to Rissers Beach with Ruthie and Jack, remember? I'm meeting them by the library in thirty minutes. I need to return my book about the Foreign Protestants. I didn't finish it because it's not as interesting as Catherine Marguerite's story. But I will be here at 3:30 PM, because I am very good at remembering things. Especially important things."

Her face looks like it does when we see dead animals by the side of the road.

I'm not a mean girl. People crying is one of my Dislikes.

I think she loves me, or at least she used to.

"I can't wait until the library moves up to the Academy," Ruthie says. "Maybe as early as next summer."

Next summer. Where will I be then?

"I am not a very good swimmer," I say, trying to distract myself. "But I can dog paddle, even though I'm a girl, not a dog. Are there shells and beach glass at Rissers?"

"Yup. And it doesn't matter if you can't swim," Ruthie says.

"Mostly we just run in and out since the water's better for polar bears than people," Jack says.

Ruthie holds up a basket full of beach toys. "I brought our old sand-castle-building stuff. Remember the colossal ones we used to build?"

Jack nods and looks at his phone. "Dad should be here soon."

"I have to be home by 3:30 PM," I say, checking my watch. "In five hours and forty-eight minutes. If Muzzy doesn't forget our date again."

"Hey, speaking of dates, your mom and my dad seem to be making out pretty good," Jack says.

Making out pretty good. I look at his face. Is he happy that Muzzy and JJ are making out pretty good? Does he know about the proposal?

JJ drives his car onto a ferryboat that takes us across the LaHave River. "It's a cable ferry," he explains. "There are giant wires pulling the boat across the river."

I look over the gunnel but I can't see any wires. "If Muzzy was here, she would probably get seasick," I say. If JJ likes boats, maybe he doesn't like people who get seasick on them.

He laughs. "Probably not. It's a pretty short trip and the water's calm."

On the other side of the river, he buys us cinnamon buns at the LaHave Bakery.

"Cinnamon is one of my Likes," Ruthie says, giving me a thumbs-up. Borrowing words is something friends do.

"Muzzy makes these at Christmas," I say. "Only hers aren't this good and poufy."

"Baking might not be one of Allison's talents," JJ says.

"But she took to the dory right away. Maybe we can all go out rowing together sometime."

"We're going back to Montreal very soon. I'm not very good at rowing but Jack is teaching me."

"You're getting better every time," Ruthie says.

Jack's too busy chewing to say anything.

At Rissers Beach, I sit down, rest my chin on my knees, and bury my feet and hands in the warm Tippy Toe Beige sand. I sweep my hands back behind me, making half-moons on both sides. "We could make a hundred sandcastles."

"A thousand. A million!" Ruthie shouts. We're using outdoor voices because we are outdoors, and the ocean's roaring every time it pushes a wave to shore.

Jack starts digging with his hands close to the edge of the water, like Miranda. "How about we start with one? If I can remember how."

"I think the tide just turned," Ruthie says, dropping to her knees beside him. "It's on its way out. This should be a good place."

"But the waves are still coming toward us," I say. "Shouldn't they turn around if the tide's going out?"

Ruthie giggles. "I know. Tides are hard to understand. Like gravity."

Right now, gravity is doing a very good job of holding me

tight to the ground. Even though the wind is trying to blow all of us away.

JJ crouches down beside me, but outside my personal space, my sand half-moons. His legs are white and hairy. Did the hair from his head move down to his legs?

"Isn't it amazing how the pushing and pulling of the waves sculpts those beautiful sand ripples? The ocean's a master carver."

"A master carver, like Jessie," I say, showing him the piece of Aqua Whisper beach glass I found. "Like sandpaper on wood, the ocean's waves soften the sharp edges of glass."

He nods. "All that tumbling back and forth on the waves. Who knows how far each piece travels?"

"Like the first settlers who traveled 4,909 kilometers to come to Lunenburg from Rotterdam," I say. "Like Catherine Marguerite, Aggie and Jessie's ancestor."

"That piece is a keeper," Ruthie says. "Usually I only find boring pieces, brown and green bits of beer and wine bottles."

"I'm learning to be a carver," I tell JJ. "I find gnomes in pieces of wood."

"Jack told me you were teaching him. My dad was a wonderful whittler, before he got sneak-attacked by Alzheimer's. Anyway, we have a great collection of birds he carved."

"Jessie is a bird carver," I say. "She finds owls in pieces of wood. And Santa Claus, even though Santa Claus isn't real."

His laugh sounds like Jack's. "Jessie Langille? She and Dad were friends for a long, long time, back before he got sneak-attacked by Alzheimer's and lost his memory."

"Jessie does inversion therapy so her brain doesn't atrophy like the other old fogies over at Harbour View Haven."

"I haven't seen Jessie in a lot of years, but that sounds like something she'd say."

"The Natives did sneak attacks when the settlers came to the New World," I say. "But the settlers lost their scalps, not just their memories. I don't know if that happened to Catherine but I hope it didn't."

"It's so not fair that people from Europe came over here and stole the land the Mi'kmaw people had been living on forever," Ruthie says.

"But we wouldn't be here if they hadn't come," Jack says.

I push myself up, then look back down at my half-moons. They look like angel wings. "There's still lots of empty land in Nova Scotia. Why didn't they all share?"

"It's a controversial issue, for sure." JJ stands up and takes a striped beach towel out of his bag. "Too big a problem for us to solve, especially on my day off. If anybody needs me, I'll be right over there, catching some zs."

"Is that a type of fish?" I ask.

Ruthie closes her eyes and makes snoring sounds.

I'm filling my bucket with wet sand for the eleventh time, when my shovel hits something hard. I dig it out with my hands.

"A moon snail," Ruthie says, as I'm rinsing it off in the sea. "Aren't they beautiful?"

"Beautiful." I nod and dry it off on my T-shirt. It's white with a Sea Rock Blue circle in the centre of the swirls. And it's almost as round as a full Moon.

"Those ones with the dark eye are called shark's eyes. Moon snails are beasts," Jack says. "They have this foot that burrows down into the sand to find clams. Then they drill a hole with their tongues and suck out the clam."

Ruthie holds my shell up to the sun. "There's nobody home in this one."

"I'm glad," I say. "I think I like moon snail shells, but not moon snail beasts." I put it in my backpack, then get back to work.

I'm pressing in broken bits of shell for turret windows, when Ruthie says, "Want to give me a hand? We need lots of flat driftwood for a palisade."

Palisade, like in 1753. To keep out the bad guys. Did it keep Catherine safe? I put one hand above my eyes and look up at Ruthie. "I won't give you my hand but I will help you." I check my watch. Already 1:00 PM. No time to visit Jessie today; maybe tomorrow.

Jack's trying to make some trees out of seaweed and shells he calls razor clams, only they keep collapsing. "They're kind of lame."

I look around for something better. "Lame. Synonym for limping. They don't have any legs."

Jack laughs. "You crack me up. Like Humpty Dumpty."

The nursery rhyme about Jack is Jack and Jill, not Humpty Dumpty. I collect some broken pine branches up by the campground, then stick them in the grounds of our castle, like a miniature forest.

"High five!" Jack holds up his hand. "Awesome idea." I hold my breath and touch my hand up against his quickly. It's warm and sandy. And bigger than mine.

Ruthie stands up, walks backward down to the edge of the ocean, crosses her arms, and squints at our castle. "Perfect!" she says, clapping her hands. "Hey, Uncle Jack—will you take our picture?"

JJ stops catching zs. We kneel down behind the castle. I'm in the middle. Our shoulders are touching. I hold my breath.

JJ holds up his phone. "Say cheese pizza."

Pizza is one of my Likes, so I hope I look happy in the picture.

I know I feel warm, inside and outside. Not floaty at all.

"The sad thing about sand castles is they're so temporary," Ruthie says in the car on the way back. "The ocean's probably already gobbling it up."

"One thing you can count on," JJ says, "is that the sea always comes back, twice a day, 365 days a year."

"Three hundred and sixty-six days during ...

"... a Leap Year," Ruthie says, finishing my sentence.

I hold up my hand and we high-five. Quietly. Our hands are the same size.

Maybe Moonbeam should take coming-back lessons from the sea.

Jack's dad looks at me in the rear-view mirror and gives us a thumbs-up.

I like him. Does he like me? Or is Jack the only kid he wants?

"You're punctual, as usual." Muzzy's sitting on the edge of my bed, a book-shaped present on her lap. My unfinished drawing is still face-down on my desk. "How was the beach?"

"Fun." But I don't tell her the details.

"I'm so sorry, Katie. I didn't realize how much fun dory-rowing could be. I completely lost track of time yesterday, and ..." She pauses. "Well, I've got some other things on my mind."

"It was not fun the first time I went dory-rowing with Jack, Junior," I say. "It was hard work and I fell in."

She smiles. "I remember. But the important thing is, you went back a second time."

"Jack's father bought us cinnamon buns."

"I bet they weren't as good as mine."

I don't answer her because the truth is, they were better.

"I'm going to finish my present for you before we leave. It's a drawing. I gave it a nametag, like the Lunenburg houses. *Lovely Lunenburg, Made by Katie Dupuis Pearson.*"

"Sounds intriguing. I can't wait to see it."

I nod and sit down beside her.

She passes me the present. "I found this tucked away in a back corner of Elizabeth's Books."

"Did Chris say he remembered Moonbeam?"

She shakes her head. "I'm afraid not. But he did help me find this gift."

The tissue paper is Lavender's Blue. I open it carefully.

It is a book. A soft Sand Patterns Brown leather book with three owls on the front. I'm not sure what kind of owls they are, but they might be saw-whets like Chou Chou. They look friendly, not fierce like screech owls that could scare the gizzard out of a person. Inside the cover, Muzzy wrote: *For Katie. Thank you for the most wonderful three years of my life. The best is yet to come ...* The pages are lined but they're all blank.

The best is yet to come. Is that the truth?

"I thought you might like to keep a journal," Muzzy says. "A place for your secret inside thoughts."

"Catherine's letters were like a journal, because she didn't mail them," I say. "Before they went missing, Jessie kept hers in a box that looks like a book, with *Catherine Marguerite Langille's Letters to Grandmother, 1752–1754* carved into the front. Maybe I'll call my journal *Katie Dupuis Pearson's Letters to Moonbeam.* I won't be able to mail mine, either, because I don't know Moonbeam's address."

"Sounds like a plan." Muzzy leans in so our noses are touching. Her hair tickles my nose. "Homecoming Day is still the best day of my entire life," she whispers. "Love you, Katie."

I want to tell her I love her, too, but those words are buried deep inside me. Or maybe they disappeared with Moonbeam, like my tears and my imagination. So I rub my Lavender Lady and hiccup instead.

Because she's my Muzzy, she laughs, then we go downstairs single-file. Together, but separate, at the same time. Like the colors in a rainbow. Like music notes. Like the people in good families in stories.

That night, I hold up my moon snail so it glows like a giant pearl in the Moon's beams.

- *Can Muzzy love me and Jack Jodrey, Senior, at the same time?*
- *If Muzzy marries JJ, will Jack be my foster-brother?*
- *Will Moonbeam ever come back, like the ocean?*

Chapter 24

Jessie's sitting on the mossy boulder, playing her flute when I get to her house the next day. I zip my lips and sit on the damp ground, patting Miranda and watching a rabbit, Autumn Calm Brown, nibble some grass.

"You're up with the birds this morning."

Because all around us birds are twittering and tweeting, I nod yes. But I'm staring at her shoes, moccasins, not clompers. Tippy Toe Brown.

"Deerskin," she says. "With porcupine-quill beading, same as that one Catherine found. I've got a smaller pair inside that might fit you." She puts one finger up to her lips, then points to a naked branch on a pine tree. "Hear that?"

Over top of the bird songs, I hear, *Twhoo-twhoo-twhoo.* Three syllables. Then it stops. I hear a chickadee, too, only it does five syllables. *Chick-a-dee-dee-dee.*

"It's Chou Chou," Jessie whispers. "Mostly she calls at night, being nocturnal and all. Suppose it is a dark morning."

Chou Chou doesn't sound anything like the noisy hooting owls on TV. We move closer and watch her for three minutes, but she stays silent and begins preening, the bird synonym for brushing your hair (or feathers).

"Does Chou Chou have a family? A parliament?" I ask.

Jessie shakes her head and walks toward the cottage. "Never seen any other saw-whets out here lately. Figure she's a loner, like me."

"A loner, like me." Only now I have friends. I follow her inside.

The carved book box is open on the low table, with the Moon-girl carving mostly covered by the flax sack. The colored pencil drawing of the girl, K.L., is beside it. Jessie puts the picture back in the box and puts the box on the shelf. Then she gets a pair of moccasins, just like hers only smaller, out of a wooden chest under her worktable. "Try those on for size. Been fifteen years or better since the last girl wore 'em."

"They're so soft," I say, sliding my feet into them and patting the fur around the edges. Autumn Calm Brown. "Is it rabbit fur? And is the beaded owl a saw-whet?"

She nods twice, then gets out the splint box and sits down on the loveseat.

I keep standing. "And was the last girl your daughter, Aggie's niece Kitty?"

"MYOB, please and thank you." She puts on her specs. "Well, what are you waiting for, Chouette? Came to hear another story, didn't you? Sit your keister down, girl."

I sit my keister down beside her. "It's Katie, and I am going back to Montreal in four and a half days," I say, looking at my watch. "In approximately one hundred and eight hours."

She flips through the Gothic Gold notebook. "Don't need to fret about getting the stories finished. Unless the letters turn up by some miracle, we're just about done."

I look right at her. "Done? Did Catherine die, too?"

Jessie's laugh sounds like Miranda woofing when she's chasing rabbits in her sleep. "By gory, if you don't look like Chou Chou with those big eyes of yours in that tiny little face. Specially with all them freckles. I suppose Catherine did die, eventually. Happens to the best of us. The last letter was written in the spring of 1754. Good thing for us she never found a way to mail the letters, so her stories stayed alive."

"I'm going to start writing in a journal so my stories will stay alive, too."

Jessie nods. "Proper thing. Somethin' I always meant to do but never got around to. Here's what she wrote on the 30th of September, 1753:

"Dear Grandmother, We have been busy preparing for the long ferocious winter the British have promised as a reward for coming to settle this New World for them. Already we must keep the fire burning day and night, and the ground is crunchy with frost some mornings. In Lunenburg, we do not suffer from the same shortage of firewood trees as in France. However the work here is endless ...

"The settlers had no time to be lazy. Kids and all had to work at jamming clay and moss in between the logs of their house to keep the cold outside where it belonged."

"Kids back then weren't flutterbugs." I look at the log walls of her abode. "Did you do that, too?"

"These days, they mill the logs so they fit snug together. Wouldn't be room to stuff anything in between them. Here's another part Agatha wrote down. Her handwriting was just about as perfect as her:

"We tucked your flower seeds in with care so they will remain warm during the winter, Grandmother. Marie Claire helped me gather seaweed to use as a blanket for them. Sprouts unfurling in the spring will be a promise for a better tomorrow. Mama says the brown-eyed Susans' smiling yellow faces next fall will surely be a sign of good fortune. We will plant the trees before the first heavy frost, during the Hunter's Moon. But I have questions, as always. Will your seeds be able to take root in this rocky soil? Will the new trees adapt to this harsh New World? Will I?"

Jessie looks inside the splint box. "Can't remember if there was a treasure for this part. I know she and Marie Claire planted an acorn out by her place. Marked the spot with a fish-shaped stone. Sometimes the Natives had to resort to eating acorns if the winter was extra harsh." She takes out a flat, triangle-shaped piece of birch bark, about the size of her hand. It has a hole in the middle.

"What's that?"

"Part of a toy Marie Claire helped Catherine make as a gift for Nicholas. Used to be a clay ball hooked onto it, but it's gone missing over the years."

"Gone missing over the years. Your estranged sister Aggie read the letters to Kitty, and some of the treasures disappeared over time. Her niece said she didn't know anything about that."

Jessie does a horse snort. "Serves Agatha right, always trying to be everybody's favorite, young and old alike." She holds out the birch bark triangle. "You held this by one corner, flicked your wrist, and tried to get the attached ball to drop down through the little hole. I was always better at it than Agatha."

The hole is about the size of a nickel. Synonym for a five-cent piece.

"Catherine picked up a fair amount about using what the land has to offer from Marie Claire: smoking eels and mackerel, making tea from cedar needles, drying huckleberries, using quills to tap the maple trees, things the Native people have always known. Always wished I had one of their beaver-tooth knives in my collection. Catherine got to be real good at helping people with the healing herbs Marie Claire showed her. Her mama started calling her Dr. Langille. Shaman is what the Natives called it—healer."

"I might be a doctor when I finish school," I say. "But not a surgeon because blood is one of my Dislikes. Remember?"

Jessie laughs, then closes her eyes. "Now, what else can I remember? Her older brother, Jean-Jacques, gave Catherine a fancy comb for her fourteenth birthday. Had yellow flowers painted onto it that she thought might be brown-eyed Susans."

"My friend Ruthie has a really old wooden comb, one of the neat things that came from the old Langille homestead. If it was Catherine's, the painted flowers are gone."

Jessie shrugs. "Possible. Another thing that tickled my fancy, something else Catherine learned from Marie Claire, was the Natives' belief that the shadows given by Grandfather Sun, Nisgam, are the spirits of our ancestors. Seeing my shadow just about always brings Catherine to mind."

"I see my shadow sometimes, but I can't see my ancestors in my mind's eye because I don't know who they are."

Jessie stares at me for six breaths without saying anything.

"If you can track down this Moonbeam person, maybe she'll share that information with you."

I nod yes, then check my watch. "I have to go back to The Chickadee because it's my day to help make muffins. Banana pecan. Mashing bananas is one of my new talents." Before I leave, I take off the moccasins and put them back in the wooden chest.

Jessie picks up her carving knife and nods. "I'll see you when I see you."

I get out my treasure chart and write *Birch Bark Toy* in space number ten and draw a picture. Then I lie in bed, staring up at the Moon. My brain is buzzing like Muzzy's alarm clock, one of my Dislikes.

- *Why didn't Jessie want to talk about the last girl who wore the moccasins?*
- *Did Catherine's seeds survive the winter? Did she?*
- *Did Muzzy make up her mind about the proposal?*

Chapter 25

"That's so nice of Ruthie's family to invite you for a sleepover. Go ahead and call her back."

"Thank you, Muzzy."

I give her a pinky hug, then go upstairs to pack. I check my watch. The sleepover starts at 3:00 PM. I have just enough time to bike out to Jessie's.

I sit on a mossy stone with my lips zipped until she's finished her Inversion Therapy. Her face is red when she drops to the ground. October Leaf Red. She shakes her head and slowly opens her eyes. "Thought I heard somebody. Getting to be a bit of a habit, you showing up out here."

"Is showing up out here a good habit or a bad one, like biting your fingernails or smoking?"

"Depends on the day, I suppose. Gonna be a real scorcher

today." She puts on her clompers and we go inside and sit down. "Don't know how much energy I've got for stories. Got a bit of a frog in my throat." She passes me the notebook. "How 'bout you take a turn?"

I look at her neck, but keep my lips zipped. Does she eat frogs? Like Marie Claire ate smoked eels?

"Don't stick out your *bruddle* at me, missy. My voice is raspy, like a bullfrog's. You can read, can't you?"

"I'm a very good reader. I read seventy-eight books in Grade 5."

"Proper thing." She bends down and scratches Miranda's ears. "Time and tide wait for no man. Or woman. Or girl."

Her face is twitchy, like Muzzy's when she's in a hurry to get going.

"Haven't had a youngster read to me in a dog's age."

"Dog's age. Twelve years is the average lifespan for a dog," I say.

"Sounds about right."

I open the notebook. The Innocent Ivory paper is soft, not crisp like a new scribbler. "Aggie wrote this part, from December 20th, 1753:

"Winter has struck with a fury, and we have been trapped within for the better part of two days as a storm rages without, threatening to scalp the very roof off our sturdy log home. Scalp is what the savages, the enemies, do

to express their anger at the British who have taken over their land. Marie Claire says the British have also taken their fair share of Indian scalps."

I look at Jessie. "Was that true?"

She nods. "More than likely. War is usually about people fighting over land or religion. Most times, both sides share the blame."

I go back to the notebook.

"Papa says there is talk of the British preparing to banish the French Catholics who remain in Nova Scotia, the Acadians, said to number in the thousands. They steadfastly refuse to pledge their loyalty to the British government. We Protestants shall remain unscathed, but I fear for Marie Claire and her family who are half-Acadian ...

"That's all Aggie wrote down. Do you remember anything else? Did Marie Claire's family get banished, a synonym for kicked out?"

"Let me cogitate on that." Jessie gets up and straightens out the stools at her woodcarving bench.

"Cogitate, synonym for think things over."

She nods. "About that same time, Nicholas got real sick, had an infected festering splinter in his foot; Catherine described it so well you could almost feel the boy's pain."

"Did they have tweezers to get it out?"

She shakes her head. "Catherine was able to help her brother because Marie Claire had told her about plantain."

"Is that a plant?"

She nods, then draws something on a piece of paper. "Bright green bumpy leaves, like this. You know it's plantain when you rip a leaf in two and there's little white veins sticking out."

"I think plantain grows in the healing garden by the Phantom Trail."

"More than likely. It's a real useful little plant. Draws out the poison." She picks up a glass jar. "Here's another thing I always keep on hand—red clover tea, something they gave Nicholas to help with his fever."

"Maybe it was named after Marie Claire's father, Cloverwater. If they'd had red clover tea on the ships, kids like Elisabeth might not have died of the great fever."

"Possible. Anyhow, one day Catherine showed up, Marie Claire was busy making what they called *cacamo*."

"Like cocoa, a synonym for hot chocolate?"

Jessie snorts. "Not exactly that sweet. They made it by crushing the dry bones of a moose with stones, then boiling them for a long time. The Natives made a butter with the bone marrow that rose to the top, used it in soups and stews over the winter."

"A moose would have a lot of bones."

She nods. "Didn't I write something in there about the kissing bridge? Always liked that part."

"My friend Ruthie lives on Kissing Bridge Road." I turn the page. "Here's some of your messy writing from April 23rd, 1754. I can read it because my writing is messy, too.

"We have survived our first winter in the New World! Some ice remains yet in the center of the harbor and snow mounds linger in the deep woods outside the palisade. Papa and Jean-Jacques work to clear land for crops and livestock in the North West area where we Montbéliardians will farm. The British have promised we shall soon receive either one cow and one sheep, or one pig, one sheep, and six goats, to be shared by two families. Nicholas hopes to find a new Nellie and sends hugs to his old Nellie goat (and to you, of course).

"We often walk with Papa and Jean-Jacques to the end of the palisade at the edge of town, kissing them goodbye and wishing them Godspeed. A tailor in the Fauxburg area beyond the palisade was recently set upon by Indians. One of the Germans had his trousers returned to him bearing droplets of the tailor's blood! As Mama says, uncertainty is the only constant of life in the New World."

Pa-dum pa-dum.

"Did Catherine and her family get sneak-attacked?"

"Can't say for sure."

"Is there a treasure for that part of the story?"

"Don't believe so." Jessie rubs the frog in her throat, then takes the notebook from me. "Not too much more written in here. Think that's it for today. Might have to take a nap this afternoon. Been a month of Sundays since I last did that."

A month of Sundays is impossible. Every week has seven different days. I sit up straight and look at the notebook in Jessie's scarred fingers.

Why did Catherine stop writing? Did something happen to her? Or did she start mailing her letters? My pie chart puzzle still has two empty spaces.

I find my warm Lavender Lady in my pocket and hum Grandmother's lullaby. Miranda stretches her front paws out long, then pads over beside me, resting her snout on my bare knee. I look at her Truffle Brown eyes, then count the wiry whiskers springing out of her muzzle on both sides of her black nose. *One ... two ... three ...* sixteen altogether.

Jessie coughs, then opens the door. Synonym for time to leave. I check my watch. "I am going for a sleepover at Ruthie's house."

"A sleepover, eh? Could be you might like to have a sleepover out here some night, with me and Miranda and Chou Chou. Could be we'd invite the Moon, too."

I nod yes. "I would like that. I am going back to Montreal very soon but I will ask Muzzy."

"I'll see you when I see you."

Chapter 26

I help Ruthie spread out the plaid blanket on the ground.

"Maybe we'll see a few shooting stars, but the newspaper said next week will be the best for meteor showers," Jack says.

"Meteor showers. A synonym for Perseids," I say. "In the city, there's too much light to see them. This is my first-ever sleepover."

"Really? In your whole entire life?"

I nod yes, then squirm around between Ruthie and Jack, trying to get comfortable on the hard ground, but sharp rocks are poking through the blanket into my back.

Ruthie claps her hands and points up at the sky. "Look! Did you see that? Three shooting stars at once. I'll share them with you guys."

"Shooting star. Synonym for a dying meteorite."

"Quick! Make a wish," Jack says, then pokes me with his

elbow. "Even though Katie doesn't believe in wishes."

Ruthie squeezes her eyes shut and presses her lips together.

I rub my Lavender Lady, squint up into the twinkly blackness, away from the glowing almost-full Moon.

I could wish for Moonbeam to come back for me. Then if Muzzy accepts JJ's proposal, but he only wants one kid, I wouldn't have to go back to the foster care people.

But Moonbeam's been gone now for 2,685 days, and wishes don't come true, anyway.

"I'll share my secret wish if you'll share yours," Ruthie says.

Share yours. Something friends do in stories. Share secrets and have sleepovers.

She pushes herself up onto her elbows so she can look down at Jack and me. Her long blonde hair's almost touching the ground behind her.

"You go first, Ruthie," Jack says, sitting up. "I'm still trying to think of a good one."

"Okay. Give me a minute."

But I'm only at forty-six seconds when she tells us her wish. She closes her eyes and points her face up to the stars, her Coconut Brown skin shimmering in the Moon's light. "I wish ... I wish that ... Katie could always live here." She pats my shoulder, then flops back down beside me.

Katie could always live here. I look at her and swallow

hard. "Maybe your mother could home-school me, too."

She giggles.

"Sweet. Okay, I've got one. I wish ... I could become a math genius." Jack nudges me with his elbow. "Like Katie."

"Like Katie. I'm not a genius," I say, moving closer to Ruthie. "But there are no flies on me. And you told me you don't have much by way of brains."

They both laugh.

"The way you figured out how to make my tree fort ladder was wicked. I've gotta be good with numbers if I'm going into the house renovating business like my dad."

"Jodrey & Son," I say. "Bringing History to Life."

"You got it. I was gonna wish for a new bike, but I've already saved up almost enough money. What's your wish?"

I sit up straight, hug my knees, and try to concentrate on not humming. Nervous humming is different from scared humming. "I don't think this could ever come true, but ... um ... I wish I had roots here, like you."

Ruthie sits up next to me and hugs her knees, too. Our shoulders are touching. "Maybe you do. You never know. I'd *love* for you to be my cousin!"

"Awesome!" Jack jumps up and pulls a flashlight out of his back pocket. "Who's up for some flashlight tag?"

Jessie holds up a basket full of bright green leaves. "What do you figure this is?"

"Spinach?"

She laughs. "Don't think this'd be near as tasty as spinach. It's plantain, like I was tellin' you about last time. Favors this nice sunny spot here in the open. Miranda must've run into some barbed wire somewhere, got a gouge out of one of her back legs. I'll make this into a poultice, draw the poison right out of it."

Inside, I sit on the floor while Jessie crushes the plantain with a stone. Miranda is lying in her throne bed beside me, licking her gouge. Synonym for deep cut. She doesn't move while Jessie covers her cut with the paste, then wraps some cloth around it and fastens it on with string. Miranda licks Jessie's hand, a synonym for saying thank you.

"Another day or two, she'll be right as rain," Jessie says, picking up the splint box and sitting down.

"What's so right about rain?" I take off my shoes and sit down on the edge of the loveseat. "It's wrong when it ruins a sunny day. Are there any treasures left?"

Jessie lifts both shoulders. She clears her throat and passes me the notebook. "Figure it's still your turn to read. *Ribbit!*"

I look at her Blue Green Velvet eyes.

She points to her wrinkly neck. "Still got that bothersome

frog in my throat." Jessie taps the notebook, then closes her eyes. "Let's hear it."

"It's a long part. Some of it is in your messy writing, and some is in Aggie's perfect printing.

"*27th April, 1754*

"*Dear Grandmother, Once again, I must write with heartbreaking news. Yesterday, as usual, I met Marie Claire, my friend and teacher, on our sitting rocks on the beach. Her brown eyes were not their sparkly selves. After telling me that her family may have to flee in advance of the British banishing the Acadian people, she got out her beaver-tooth carving knife and chopped off a piece of her beautiful shiny black hair. Tying a deerskin thong around it, she presented it to me, saying, 'I give you this living bit of me in honor of our time together. We shall always be friends.'*

"*I did the same, using my owl carving knife. As we were saying goodbye, we saw a perfect rainbow—Munkwon, in Marie Claire's native language—above the bush-speckled hill across the harbor. Taking my cold hand in her warm one, she said, 'Each separate color so different, but side-by-side, blending together, they make a wondrous thing. If only people could learn to do the same.' Isn't that beautiful, Grandmother?*

"*The next day her house was cold and empty. Near the fish stone we used to mark the spot, I found a tiny green sprout from the acorn we planted together in the fall. Will Marie Claire ever get to see the tree it will become? Stumbling home along the stony beach, humming your lullaby, I tripped and fell—on a true treasure! A small stone, but not an ordinary* stone, a rough gray egg stone full of crystals. Smoky, lavender-colored crystals, with pointed tips twinkling like stars. Nine pointed tips. It is so beautiful—how I wish you could see it, Grandmother."

I stop reading, fast-look at Jessie, who might be sleeping, then find my Lavender Lady in my pocket. She is warm, very warm.

Jessie opens one eye. "What? You tired of readin' already?"

I shake my head no, wet my lips, then continue.

"And then, something truly magical happened as I held the stone in my hand. All at once, my hand began to warm, the glow spreading through my cold fingers, up my arms, straight to my heart. Like an embrace. Despite losing my friend, this gave me hope that we shall one day meet again. Meanwhile, I cherish Marie Claire's lock of hair and hold our memories close to my heart, as I do my memories of you and Elisabeth.

"I hold fast to my hope that Marie Claire and I shall one day meet again. Perhaps our children will also be friends. I hope this rumored war will never come to pass, and in time her family will return to Merligueche.

"At home, I went to my horsehide trunk and tucked the salty crystal egg stone inside your seed pouch, next to Marie Claire's precious lock of hair. I put my nose to the pouch's opening and breathed deeply. Of home. Both old and new.

"By the light of the Moon, as always, I remain,

"Your loving granddaughter, Catherine Marguerite Langille, formerly uprooted and now transplanted."

After I finish reading, I put the notebook on top of the splint box, close my eyes, and zip my lips for two minutes, one hundred and twenty seconds.

"Bush-speckled hill. I have seen a rainbow over that hill, which is now the golf course, too." I check my watch, then stand up and put on my sneakers. "I need to go."

"Good enough. I'll show you Marie Claire's lock of hair next time. That sparkly stone used to be in the splint box, too, amethyst, but I don't see it here now. Used to be Chouette's favorite." Jessie gets up off the loveseat, sits down at her worktable, then picks up the owl she's working on. "Tomorrow might be a good night for us to have a sleepover, if you're interested."

I nod yes. "I'm very interested, but I have to ask Muzzy first."

At bedtime, I fill in the last two empty spaces on my treasure chart. Number eleven, *Marie Claire's Lock of Hair*, and number twelve, *Catherine's Crystal Egg Stone, Missing.* Missing from the splint box, but warm in my pocket.

- *Did Catherine ever see Marie Claire again?*
- *Did Muzzy make up her mind about the proposal?*
- *Is Catherine's amethyst egg stone a synonym for my Lavender Lady?*

Chapter 27

After I get home from helping Aggie hang her laundry on the line, I get out my colored pencils and work on my Homecoming Day picture. I have to get it finished before we leave Lunenburg. Or maybe it will just be me leaving, if Muzzy accepts JJ's proposal.

I'm not having a sleepover with Jessie and Miranda because Muzzy said two sleepovers in one week is too many. But I am allowed to visit them to say goodbye. In my picture, Miranda looks more like herself than a wolf this time, except her Truffle Brown eyes still aren't right. I try to fix them, then go downstairs.

Muzzy and Jo-Ellen are busy talking and laughing, serving a late lunch to a noisy group of people. I wave, point to my watch, 2:15 PM, and hold up my right hand, all four fingers and my thumb, a synonym for 'I'll be home by 5:00 PM.' I read in the newspaper that the Moon tonight will be a Super Moon, closer to the earth than usual, so it will look bigger and brighter. Maybe tonight will be the night he answers my questions.

Butterscotch has a flat tire, so I jog along the Phantom Trail, around the head of the harbor, then walk slowly up the steep hill past the golf course. It's both sunny and cloudy but windy. I keep my Blue Green Velvet jacket zipped up under my chin. Jo-Ellen fixed the zipper to pay me for being her summer Muffin Maven. Synonym for fast learner.

At the top of the hill, I sit down on a white bench, wait for my heart to slow down. I dig my Lavender Lady out of my pocket and look across her crystals, to the other side of the harbor. There are still some big stones on the beach there, but I don't know if they're Catherine and Marie Claire's. I would like to ask them, but I know they are dead because nobody lives for two hundred and sixty years.

I hold my Lady up against my cold cheek. She's warm. I close my eyes and hum Grandmother's lullaby, the black notes skipping through my mind. What will Jessie say when I show her my Lavender Lady? My puzzle chart is finished but I still need some help. How could the same crystal egg stone go from Catherine's letter in 1754 Lunenburg to Moonbeam in 2008 Montreal?

My stomach feels nervous but excited.

Like before a piano recital, or when Miss Matattall asks me to show the class how to solve a hard math problem on the board.

Hopping across the ditch without getting cut or wet is easy for me, now. Except for the wind rustling in the high tree branches, it's very quiet. Jessie's Inversion Therapy branch is empty. The open door of the outhouse is creaking in the breeze.

Jessie doesn't answer my knock, so I cup my hands around my eyes and press my nose up to the window full of dangling prisms. Some dishes with bits of food on them are on the work table. Jessie never leaves dirty dishes around because she does not want mice in her family. Maybe she and Miranda were in a hurry to go out gathering wood for carving. Or maybe they're at the beach and Miranda is dog-paddling, which she is better at than me because she is a dog.

I walk around the outside of the cottage. It still looks like a fairy tale house, but I know that Jessie isn't a nasty cackling witch like in *Hansel and Gretel*. She does have long gray witchy hair, but she doesn't have a wart on her nose, just freckles like me. And wrinkles because she's old.

Out back of her cottage, I stop in front of a dead gray Y-shaped tree. Jessie rounded out the tops of the two short branches and turned them into twin saw-whet owls. A real family tree. I pat their heads, which are not as soft as Chou

Chou's feathers, then sit on the big flat stone in front of them, and lean back against the bottom trunk part. I close my eyes. Did Catherine and Marie Claire ever wander into these woods, looking for huckleberries or healing herbs? Did Moonbeam?

I sit up straight when I hear something besides the birds chirping, something far away. Is it Jessie playing her flute? I listen harder. No, it's a three-syllable sound. *Twhoo-twhoo-twhoo.* Chou Chou is a loner without a family tree. I check my watch—3:50 PM—get up, and follow her call into the woods. I find her staring down at me from a branch above a skinny tunnel, between the trees and bushes. My eyes try to follow Chou Chou flitting from branch to branch, but it's hard to look at her and the bumpy ground at the same time.

I glance back over my shoulder and think of the birds eating Hansel and Gretel's breadcrumbs. If I get lost, will Chou Chou help me find my way back? The path does a sharp curve. I look behind me once more but I can't see Jessie's house. The Sea Sailor Blue sky is changing to Drizzly Afternoon Gray, and I have to do yoga breathing because the coniferous trees are crowding my personal space, almost touching my shoulders. They look like the Ents in the *Lord of the Rings.* Ents are one of my Likes because they also have strange toes, seven of them. But they're not real. These trees are real. It's 4:05 PM. I have to be home by 5:00 PM. I think I will be late.

I hum but keep my lips zipped in case Jessie is working in the woods, like she does when she needs to let her imagination run wild. I stop a couple of times when I hear a sound like moaning, or like Miranda whining and chasing rabbits in her sleep. But it's only the tall bald trees creaking in the wind, the Mint Tea Green old man's beard, synonym for moss, dangling from their dead branches. Do trees get arthritis like Aggie? Maybe they need a branch replacement.

I stop walking. What's that?

Something crashing through the bushes.

Toward me.

I duck down behind a boulder and peer out around it. Is it a bear? Or a bull moose? A coyote? *Pa-dum pa-dum.* You're supposed to make noise if you think a black bear is near.

"Au clair de la lune, mon ami ..."

I look all around but the trees aren't the climbing kind.

And then I hear barking, excited Miranda barking. She bursts out of the bushes, jumping her front paws up onto my shoulders, knocking me backwards so I sit down hard on a root. *Ouch.* Her tail's wagging frantically, whacking me in the face.

"Where's Jessie?" I ask, even though I know real dogs can't talk. But I wish they could.

Miranda does a head tilt, then takes my right hand in her teeth. Gently. She lets go when I start following her away from the skinny path, keeping my hands out in front of me to push away the sharp branches and sticky cobwebs. There are lots of twisted roots trying to trip me. And I can't see Chou Chou anymore. Miranda looks back every few seconds, like she's making sure I'm still there. Her Burnt Orange fur makes her easy to follow. I've never been in this part of the woods before. It's dark.

After a while, 4:22 PM, I hear water music above the crunching of my sneakers on the needly forest floor. We come to a fast-moving brook and I follow Miranda along its edge, lined with mossy stones. Crocodile Green. I put out my arms to keep my balance. On the other side of the water, there's a hill covered with rusty old car parts, tires, and ripped-open black and green garbage bags. Where the brook gets wider, like a river, Miranda stops and does one loud, sharp bark. She looks back at me, then sniffs at something on the ground. *Bark, look, sniff. Bark, look, sniff.*

Something black and not moving on the ground. Is it just a garbage bag? Or is it a bear?

But wouldn't Miranda be scared of a bear?

Pa-dum pa-dum pa-dum.

Chapter 28

Chou Chou sits silently on a low branch as I tiptoe closer. Miranda lowers her belly to the ground and drops her snout softly onto the sprawling black thing.

Not a thing. A person.

Jessie's eyes are closed but her chest is moving up and down, too fast. She doesn't look like herself, but I've never seen her sound asleep before. This does not seem like a good place to take a nap. I rub my Lavender Lady and try to breathe with Jessie, but I lose my breath. I do some yoga breathing to catch it again.

I crouch down beside her. She's only wearing one moccasin. The other one is on the ground beside her but it doesn't match. It's dark reddish brown. Mojave Brown. Like blood. And there's a long rusty spike sticking out of a board beside it. The ground is dry but Jessie's bare foot is covered with mud.

I get closer and sniff. I think it's blood, but not fresh red blood. It's the same rusty brown as the spike, Golden Pepper Brown. I squeeze my Lavender Lady and rub my thumb across her crystals. Blood where it doesn't belong is one of my biggest Dislikes. I walk away from Jessie, turn the spike board over and step on it, pushing the spike into the ground.

Jessie's other foot, the one still wearing the moccasin, is facing the wrong way, as if somebody really strong, like Ruthie's father, twisted it. Only, the World's Strongest Man is far away on Kissing Bridge Road. And he would never hurt an old lady like Jessie because he is a gentle giant.

Jessie begins mumbling. My eyes jump up to her Drizzly Afternoon Gray face.

"Chouette. Katrina ..." I lean in, put my ear close to her mouth so I can hear. "... born to drive me mad, break my heart ... foolish daughter ... be the death of me ..."

The death of me. Did she say Katrina, or Catherine the French way? Katrina is the real name of Aggie's niece Kitty. I close my eyes to think. When Jessie moans again, I open them and put my hand on her forehead, like Muzzy does when I have the flu. She's hot.

I lean away and cover my ears when Jessie opens her mouth wide and twists up her whole face. Is she going to scream like Joseph at my school? The deep groan that comes out instead sounds like it's coming from the very bottom of her stomach. Her bowels. Her breath smells like Jo-Ellen's too-full compost bucket.

I plug my nose. "Jessie," I whisper. "It's me, Katie. Why are you talking about death? You can't die."

Her lips are zipped. Her eyes stay closed.

I check my watch. 4:45 PM. It took me almost fifty-five minutes to get here from Jessie's cottage. How will I get Jessie back home? If I was like Pippilotta, only real, I could carry Jessie because a lady doesn't weigh as much as a horse.

Miranda woofs and licks Jessie's cheek. I force myself to look at Jessie's bleeding foot with its disordered toes. Like Catherine's. Like mine.

I am not very good at cleaning, but I have to do this. I scoop up some cold river water in my hands and pour it over her foot to rinse away some of the blood. On both the bottom and the top of her foot, the skin around the hole is puffy, red, and oozy. Festering. Synonym for infected.

Like the splinter wound on Nicholas's foot. The gouge on Miranda's leg. Plantain poultice for poison. Dogwood leaves to stop the bleeding. Only I think the bleeding has already stopped. And red clover tea for fever.

I walk around, looking for a sunny spot in the woods, but the trees are too close together. There are lots of other plants but no plantain leaves. They favor sunny spots.

Miranda stares at me with her Truffle Brown eyes. She has Muzzy's worried w between her furry eyebrows.

"I'll be right back."

She tilts her head and woofs. I take off my socks and sneakers and splash across the cold river to an open sunny spot on the other side.

There are lots of dandelions, Sunshine Yellow daisies, Queen Anne's lace, and Ruby Red rosehips. When I spot some shiny leaves, Parrot Green, I tear one in two, check for the thin white threads. I stuff handfuls of leaves into my hoodie pocket, then wade back across the river.

Jessie hasn't moved but she's mumbling again. "Katrina, baby girl ... where'd you get to ... no, no, NO!"

Quickly, I rip up the plantain leaves, crush them against a stone with another stone, then mix in some drops of river water. It looks like the basil pesto Jo-Ellen makes. How will I get the goopy paste to stay on Jessie's foot?

I look around, peel off a thin piece of birch bark, then fill it with the paste. I kneel next to Jessie's feet and wrap it around both the top and bottom of her foot. I try not to look at the hole or at her twisted other foot. How will I tie it on? I don't have a leather thong or string. But I do have a hair elastic. I pull it out and use it to hold the bark in place. Not too tight, because even though it doesn't have lungs, skin needs to breathe when it's healing. And the Band-Aid people are running a scam.

I'm trying to cool Jessie's face with my wet sock, when she says, "Chouette?"

I tuck my hair behind my ears and look at her eyes. They are wide open. She looks more like herself. "No, it's me, Katie."

She snorts and makes her face more wrinkly than usual. "'Course it is. Stupid people dumping their trash out here. That rusty spike best not give me lockjaw." She looks down at the birch bark on her foot. "Plantain?"

I nod. "Because your foot is festering."

She closes her eyes again. "Sure could use some of Clover-water's red clover tea 'bout now. Hot as Hades one minute, cold as ice the next." She shivers, then struggles to push herself up so she's leaning on her elbows. "What time of day is it?"

I check my watch. "5:59 PM."

"What day?"

"Wednesday, July 29th, 2015."

"Been out here more than a day, then. Came to check on that patch of Catherine's brown-eyed Susans across the brook."

Brown-eyed Susans, not Sunshine Yellow daisies with brown middles.

Jessie looks down at her twisted ankle, closes her eyes, and mashes up her face again.

"Should I get the tea from your abode?"

She squints her eyes open. "Wrenched my other ankle pretty bad when I hit that spike. Help me scoot over so I can stick it in the river. Maybe if I freeze it, I can hobble home."

I pick up her legs and we do a backward crabwalk over to the water. Her skinny arms are trembling, like her body's too heavy.

I take off the moccasin and she sticks her foot with the twisted ankle in the water, then shivers all over. "*Oooh.* Gee Willikers, that's cold. Miranda can show you the way back. Chou Chou here will keep me company."

I look up at the little owl and her big not-blinking yellow eyes. "She helped me find you," I say, putting on my sneakers. "I heard her."

Jessie nods, then says, "Git 'er home, Miranda." She looks straight at me. "And don't even think about goin' for help. You and me can handle this."

"But Muzzy said I'm not allowed to have two sleepovers in one week."

"We'll figure it out when you get back. Haven't been to the doctor in umpteen years." She closes her eyes and crumples up her whole face. "Not since the baby had pneumonia."

"Baby had pneumonia." I jog after Miranda along the edge of the brook, then down the path through the woods.

It's hard to figure out a puzzle and run at the same time.

Jessie's had a few loved ones leave her over time.

Was one of them her daughter Katrina, who is missing?

Did Katrina take Catherine's letters with her and some of the treasures?

My brain has the balloon-about-to-burst feeling, and I'm out of breath when we finally get back to the cottage: 6:40 PM. I'm late. I could call Muzzy but Jessie doesn't have a bothersome telephone. Over the loon pond, I see the Super Moon starting to rise. He's Sun Kissed Peach because the sun is setting at the same time.

- *Is Chouette Jessie's pet name for her daughter Katrina, the last girl who wore the moccasins?*
- *Does Jessie call me Chouette because I look like Katrina?*

Inside, I heat some water on the little gas burner Jessie uses when it's a real scorcher outside, too hot for a fire in the woodstove. I walk in circles around the braided rug, rubbing my Lavender Lady, waiting for the water to boil. I don't look at the pot because a watched pot never boils. When it does, I put in some red clover tea and fill the teapot, but I don't wait six minutes for the tea to steep. I tie on the lid, put the tea pot and a tin mug in a basket. I'm looking for a blanket when Miranda woofs.

"Hang on. I'm going as fast as I can."

She woofs again, then takes hold of my hand with her teeth, pulls me over to the low table in front of the loveseat. Jessie's carved letter box is open, and the colored pencil drawing of the ginger-haired girl is inside it, without the frame. I sit down and pick up the picture. K.L. is a better artist than me. On the back, in messy printing, it says:

For Aggie, the best auntie in the world, my other mother. (But don't tell Mama Jessie!) It's signed, *Kitty (Katrina) Langille.*

Miranda pads over and sits beside me, puts one rough paw on my knee. She has something in her mouth. "What's that? You know the rules. No chewing on wood that's inside the house. Give, Miranda, give."

She lets me take the carving from her. I wipe the slobber off on my shorts. It's the MYOB Moon-girl carving that used to be in the letter box. I hold it in both hands and stare at the girl's serious old-lady face. It's even better than Jessie's owl carvings.

Is it me?

But when I saw it before, I barely knew Jessie. I look underneath the flat base that keeps the carving from toppling over. In black ink, it says, "For Chouette, the moonbeam who lights up my world. Love, Mama Jessie." And it's signed, JL, like all her carvings; Jessie Langille.

Pa-dum pa-dum. I close my eyes and squeeze my warm Lavender Lady. The dry, choking feeling is in my throat again. I do yoga breaths to try to make it go away.

Chouette. Moonbeam. Katrina. Mama Jessie's daughter.

All synonyms for my real mother.

When Miranda scratches at the door, I put the carving in the basket, find a blanket, put it on top of the things in the basket, then fast-walk after her, back through the woods. The trees are blocking the sun: 7:01 PM. I think of Little Red Riding Hood with her basket, going to visit Grandma. I hope there aren't any Big Bad Wolves out here. Real ones, carnivores, not made-up story ones.

Jessie opens her eyes a little when Miranda nuzzles her cheek. She lifts her twisted ankle foot out of the brook. "My festering foot's already a little less tender. Expect that plantain's drawing the poison off real good. The other foot's frozen solid."

I try to help her stand up but she's too floppy, so I help her crabwalk back over to a mossy spot, then cover her up with the blanket.

"How will you get back to your cottage?" I ask, while she sips her tea. "I heard the loons flyin' and cryin' so it might rain, and I am already two hours and thirty-seven minutes late for supper."

She does a Bessie snort-laugh. "Sleeping in the rough's not so bad. Done it a time or two in my day. There's a nice early apple tree across the brook. Tumblin' Down Brook I call it. Might find a patch of wild blueberries somewhere, too."

Blueberries are one of my Likes. And I'm hungry. I take off my sneakers again, and Miranda and I wade through the brook. I fill my pockets with the scabby apples, then look for a blueberry patch, but it's getting dark and they're hard to see. We splash back across but Jessie doesn't have much appetite. The juicy apples taste better than they look.

I crunch up my apple and dry my wet feet on the bottom of my T-shirt. Jessie looks like she's sleeping again, with Miranda pressed up against her. Watching them makes me yawn. Chou Chou is still on her branch, watching. Is she tired from helping Jessie today instead of sleeping? Can birds yawn? I finish my second apple, stretch out on the other side of Miranda, and put one arm around her warm, furry belly. She smells like wet dog. Because she is a wet dog.

I hum Grandmother's lullaby and stare up at the giant Moon, glowing behind a giant pine tree.

- *Why doesn't Jessie ever talk about Katrina?*
- *Why doesn't Aggie know if she still has a niece?*
- *Did Katrina die?*

I must've fallen asleep, too. It's almost dark when Miranda woofs me awake. Somebody's shouting, far away. I sit up, rub my eyes, shiver, and look for the Moon. I can see his silvery glow and some of his beams, but he's hiding behind a cloud. I look down at Miranda and Jessie. They both have their eyes closed, and Miranda's back legs are twitching, like she's running in her sleep.

• *Is Jessie really my grandmother?* My *roots?*

The Moon doesn't answer, but this time I don't need him to.

Because I'm very good at solving puzzles.

"Katie?"

It's a man's voice. Maybe it's a stranger. The don't-talk-to-strangers rule doesn't apply in lovely Lunenburg. But how would a stranger know my name? I keep my lips zipped anyway.

Jessie groans and opens her eyes. She shakes her head and closes her eyes. "Bound to be somebody come lookin' for you. 'S'pose I'll end up in hospital after all."

"But your foot isn't festering that much now." I put one hand on her forehead. "And Cloverwater's tea helped your fever go away."

She nods, just as two flashlight beams come bouncing through the trees, followed by Jack Jodrey, Senior, running along the riverbank, with Muzzy right behind him.

"Oh, my gosh! Are you all right, Katie?" She crouches down next to me, pushes my hair back from my face. She's panting and sweating like she just finished one of her half-marathons. Even in the dark, I can see the capital W between her eyebrows.

I nod and give her a pinky hug. "I didn't mean to stay for a sleepover, and I'm sorry I didn't come home at 5:00 PM.

I had to help Jessie who was festering and fevering. She's better now, and she hasn't been to the hospital since the baby had pneumonia."

JJ kneels down beside Jessie, takes off the birch bark, and shines his light on her foot. "That's a nasty-looking puncture, and a dislocated ankle by the looks of it. We've gotta get you to the hospital for a tetanus shot."

Jessie looks at me and shakes her head. "Didn't I tell you that's what would happen?"

JJ tells her who he is, then scoops her up, like she doesn't weigh anything. Because he's powerful.

"You're the spitting image of your father Alex. Katie here did a real good job of healing me up," Jessie says. "No need for any doctor. Too many sick people and germs in hospitals."

Miranda woofs, like she's agreeing with Jessie. Muzzy picks up the basket, then we all follow the flashlight beam shining on Miranda's wagging tail back through the dark woods. I hook two fingers into Muzzy's belt loop so I don't lose her, then glance back at Chou Chou's branch. She's still there, preening in a moonbeam, silently watching us with her big yellow eyes. High above her, the Moon is doing his best to help us find our way home.

Chapter 29

Talking about hard things is easier in the car because you don't have to look at the person. Muzzy doesn't have a diamond ring on her finger, but I need to know if I'm going back to Montreal alone. I do two deep yoga breaths, then ask, "How are you and Jack Jodrey, Senior, making out?" Making out. A synonym for getting along. And kissing.

Muzzy gives me a fast look, then looks back at the road, squeezing the steering wheel with both hands. Her face is Tea Rose Pink. "Well, that's kind of a personal question, Katie."

I keep my hand wrapped tightly around my Lavender Lady inside my pocket. "The week is almost up. Did you decide about his proposal?"

Muzzy looks at me again, squinching up her whole face. "Proposal?" A horn blaring makes her look back at the road.

"I wasn't spying but I heard you talking to Jo-Ellen. Are you going to marry JJ?"

She laughs, then waves her hand in the air like she's trying to push me away without touching me. "Oh, *that*. I was talking about a work proposal. My boss offered me a six-month assignment as a foreign correspondent. In South Sudan. In Africa."

"In Africa." Where it would be hard to take a kid. I close my eyes and do two more yoga breaths. "Did you say yes?"

She shakes her head and pats my knee. "Not this time. I need to be with you right now."

"What about JJ? Do you need to be with him, too?"

She lifts both shoulders. Synonym for I don't know. "We've been having fun together, but you and I are about to go home. He did say he and Jack might come to visit us, though ..."

"Jack is one of my Likes," I say. "And Lunenburg."

She nods and turns into the hospital parking lot. "Mine, too."

Jessie looks too small in the high hospital bed. Her hair is in two long gray braids. "Twenty-four hours in this place is about twenty-three too many for my liking."

Muzzy nods. "Hospitals always make me feel queasy. I think it's the smells."

I put the bouquet of brown-eyed Susans on the little table beside the bed. Ruthie helped me pick them. She still thinks we might be cousins, since we don't know who Moonbeam's father is, and Jessie and Alex Jodrey were real good friends, back in the day. Maybe they loved each other.

I'll ask Jessie someday. But not today. Because maybe that's in the MYOB category.

I put my backpack on the floor and sit down on a plastic chair. Crocodile Green. Muzzy stays standing by the door. "You being away is one of Miranda's Dislikes," I tell Jessie. "Jo-Ellen is giving her lots of treats, but The Chickadee is not her abode. And we are not her family."

Jessie's eyes go shiny. She snorts and tries to poke her feet out from under the white sheet. "Got both feet bound up so tight they can't hardly breathe."

Muzzy helps her pull back the sheet, then sits down beside me and gives me a pinky hug.

I put my other hand in my pocket, take out my Lavender Lady, number twelve, *Catherine Marguerite's Crystal Egg Stone*, and lay it down on the bed.

Beside my grandmother. Not all apple pies and lullabies. But *my* grandmother.

When I get the Moonbeam carving out of my backpack, Jessie's shiny x-ray eyes get as big as Chou Chou's. They jump from the carving up to my eyes. I want to look away but I don't. Her eyes are like magnets holding mine tight. Keeping me from astronaut-floating. Like gravity. Like roots.

"The Moonbeam that lights up your life," I say. "My real mother."

"Guess we got a few things to talk about," she says, slow-nodding and putting on her specs. "Like you, when Katrina had a hankering for somethin', she went after it. Agatha should've known to keep that splint box locked up tight when that girl was around."

"Did someone mention my name?" Aggie pokes her head in around the door. Her Hint of Sun White hair's all fluffy, like she's wearing a cloud.

Jessie closes her eyes, then turns her head away, facing the window.

Aggie sits down on the chair beside Muzzy and leans her loon cane up against the end of Jessie's bed. She looks at my Lavender Lady and the carving, then puts both hands over her cheeks. "Kitty's favorite treasure from our family stories."

"Our family stories." *My* family stories.

"Oh, Jessie. When did you know?" she asks.

Jessie keeps her eyes closed. "I knew they looked alike, even before you sent me that drawing Katrina did, but it seemed too much of a fluke to be possible."

"The Lord works in mysterious ways," Aggie says, tilting her head and looking at me. "I didn't want to raise any false hopes; I thought it was too much to hope for, our long-lost

Katrina coming back to us in this wonderful way. A miracle, really."

I look at her quickly. *Long-lost Katrina coming back to us.*

Is Katrina dead? Pa-dum pa-dum.

I pick up my Lavender Lady and hum Grandmother's lullaby.

Jessie snorts. "It's been, what—almost twelve years since I've heard tell of Katrina?"

Twelve years. Synonym for a dog's age. The age I will be on my next birthday.

"It was twelve years in June." Aggie reaches out for Jessie's hand. But Jessie stuffs it back under the covers. Aggie leaves her giraffe-freckled hand on top of the sheet. "Before she left, Katrina continued to visit me, even after you and I had stopped speaking."

"And you couldn't keep her from leaving?" Jessie asks. "Seemed you were always ready, willing, and able to stick your nose into our business. Trying to finagle me into giving up homeschooling and sending the girl to school with all those flutterbugs just waiting to crush her spirit. She belonged out in the woods with me, happy to be a loner."

"A loner." Like me, before I came to lovely Lunenburg.

"Oh, Jessie." Aggie shakes her head. "Could anybody really have kept that headstrong girl, her mother's daughter, from doing whatever she put her mind to? She was seventeen, ready to see the world, chomping at the bit like a horse wanting to run free."

"Run free," I say. "Like the wild horses on Sable Island."

Jessie looks at me, then back at her estranged sister. "Did you know about Katie all along? Since she was born?"

"March 20th, 2004," I say.

Aggie shakes her head. "I hadn't heard a word from Katrina, not until just last week." She pulls the Pale Purple Periwinkle envelope out of her handbag. It smells like Jessie's cottage, like lavender. "This arrived in the mail. No note, just your copy of Catherine's letters. It's postmarked Vancouver. She did include a return address."

Vancouver. In British Columbia. Not dead, then. I close my eyes and hold tight to the edges of my chair as my heart goes back to its regular *tick-tocking.*

Big Chou Chou eyes. Lavender's Blue fingernails playing Grandmother's lullaby on a bamboo flute.

Catherine Marguerite Langille's great-great granddaughter, several times over.

Moonbeam Dupuis.

Synonyms for my real mother.

Jessie snorts. "Figures she'd contact you and not me."

I look over Aggie's shoulder at the name above the return

address on the envelope: M. Dupuis. Moonbeam's writing is messy, like on my bookmark. If I write to her and tell her I already know our Lavender Lady's story, will she write back to me?

That night, after we have supper at Aggie's and help her finish her Lunenburg jigsaw puzzle, I'm finally ready to finish my Homecoming Day present. Aggie gave me Moonbeam's self-portrait that she drew when she was ten. I draw her, only older, in between Aggie and Jessie. Katrina has the same Apricot Brandy Brown hair, serious face, and big eyes as me. But she's different. We're together but apart, like the colors of the spectrum. Like the good families in stories. I change my arm in the picture, draw it so it's reaching up toward her. She's reaching down for me with her Lavender's Blue fingernails. But our hands aren't quite touching. Not yet.

I put the Pale Purple Periwinkle envelope from Aggie—"Your salary," she told me—inside the front pocket of my suitcase. I know Catherine's lost letters are inside, but I'm saving them for the drive back to Montreal. I finish packing, then sit down at my desk, press my warm Lavender Lady up to my cheek, and find the Moon.

• *Can you have a Muzzy and a real mother at the same time?*

One of the Moon's beams lights up the first page of my

journal. The beginning. And then I start to write, my very first letter to my real mother.

Dear Moonbeam,

Muzzy gave me this owl book for Homecoming Day. Except you don't know about Muzzy or Chou Chou or Homecoming Day, since you haven't seen me for seven years, four months, and eleven days, 2,689 days altogether. Aggie says history cannot be rushed; it must unfold and reveal itself over time, even if you're impatient, like me. This is how my history's been unfolding, starting thirty-one days ago ...

THE END

(or the beginning ...)

Epilogue

Here's what Katie read while she was traveling back to Montreal with Muzzy: Catherine Marguerite Langille's Missing (and now found) Letters.

23rd October, 1751

Dear Grandmother,

As writing helps clear my thoughts and settle my emotions, I have decided I shall write letters to you to as a record of the next chapter in our family history.

When Uncle Leopold and his family made their decision to depart for the New World in the coming spring, I hoped it had been settled that we would remain here. But Mama and Papa have been discussing it yet again. I shall be heartbroken and miss my cousin-sister Elisabeth dreadfully, but Montbéliard is home. We are not rich but, most often, we do not go hungry and enjoy a peaceful life, when people are not squabbling over their preferred house of worship.

Why is it so important to own one's own land, rather than being a tenant, as we are here? It does seem unfair that we must give half of everything we grow to Master Bourgeois, simply because he owns this land we work so hard to farm. And we all live in dread of a repeat plague of sparrows, causing us to spend more time collecting sparrow corpses for delivery as bounty to the Master than weeding. And Papa hopes that somehow Jean-Jacques will be spared having to join the army now that he is sixteen.

Who would do our work if we left? Would you be content to remain here with Uncle Robert? Would another family live in this house Papa built for us?

I must trust that Mama and Papa will make the best decision for all of us, yet I am a creature of habit, uncomfortable with change. And I wonder if it is true, the talk I have heard of wild beasts and wild men in the New World. Nicholas's longed-for pirates and whales may well be the very least of our troubles ...

By the light of the Moon, I remain, as always,

Your loving granddaughter, Catherine Marguerite Langille

6th January, 1752

Dear Grandmother,

Why did Nicholas find those recruitment posters last fall? Their ominous words are printed on the underside of this very paper: "Join your fellow Protestants prospering as land owners in the New World. Mr. John Dick, Merchant, is recruiting settlers for additional sailings in June 1752, out of Rotterdam." Already Nicholas is sad that you and his Nellie goat shall remain here.

While collecting acorns to help Nicholas with his maths this afternoon, a perfect rainbow stretched across the entire sky. Most days I see a rainbow as a sign of all good things to come. But not today.

I am trying to be brave and optimistic, but it is difficult.

By the light of the Moon, I remain, as always,

Your loving granddaughter, Catherine M. Langille (I think it looks better to use just my middle initial, do you not agree?)

13th May, 1752

Dear Grandmother,

I was surprised to awaken to birdsong and sunshine this morning, as I expected I should die from a broken heart after bidding all of you farewell. It is my whimsical hope that perhaps after I read these words to our friend the Moon, he can somehow relate them to you, Grandmother. Mama says Nicholas and I must be brave, but, despite the excitement, our long journey already threatens to be far from pleasant.

The farewell church service last evening felt more like a funeral than a celebration, despite the glowing full Moon. I kept myself busy, rubbing the lambs, stars, and sun on your méreau and counting our softly-thudding footsteps as we walked to the church, marching steadily into our future. Will we need the méreau to prove we are Protestants in the New World? I have memorized the verse on the back, St. Luke, Chapter 12, Verse 32: "Have no fear, little flock, for it is your Father's good pleasure to give you the kingdom."

The Reverend chose a most fitting hymn, the prophetic words of Martin Luther, as we were departing.

Flung to the heedless winds
Or on the waters cast,
The martyrs' ashes, watched,
Shall gathered be at last.
And from that scattered dust,
Around us and abroad,
Shall spring a plenteous seed
Of witnesses for God.

Afterward, we huddled together on the rickety wagon that brought us to this log raft, which is carrying us along the

River Rhine, all the way to a place with the unfortunate name of Rotterdam. We have already had to stop 35 or possibly 36 times to pay a toll. Father is fearful of depleting our savings before we are even aboard the ship for the New World.

Nicholas continues in his constant state of excitement, pointing out castles, wondering if Cendrillon and her wicked stepsisters might live in one of them. I grow weary of him ceaselessly calling out: Minette! Minette! and have taken to meowing in response.

My flax sack containing my quill (a gift from your ornery geese!), my precious bundle of paper, and my tiny bottles of sand and oak-apple ink, is safe in my horsehide trunk. Monsieur Perrault's Mother Goose book is wrapped securely in my extra petticoat, along with your snuff jug, Grandmother.

I shall attempt to find a quiet spot to read these words aloud to the Moon, in hopes you will somehow hear them.

By the light of the Moon, I remain, as always,

Your loving granddaughter, Catherine M. Langille

19th May, 1752

Dear Grandmother,

Rotterdam is the largest, most busy and noisy place I have ever seen. Nicholas and I have been sitting on my horsehide trunk for ages, just watching, as Mama and Papa make the arrangements for our voyage.

The girls dress in beautiful gowns and lace-cuffed jackets with elegant coiffures, like Cendrillon's evil stepsisters. I feel like an urchin with my ordinary apron, pinafore and plaits. You would most certainly require more than a pinch of snuff here to clear your nostrils. The stench of tar and offal fills the air as fishing vessels unload their catch. How could anyone think of eating such horrid, slimy things?

I already miss Elisabeth almost as much as I miss you. She entrusted me with her precious Moon hairpin, in hopes it will keep us connected on our separate voyages. Do you remember how hard I worked, carving that tiny owl for her? She calls it Chou Chou. Remember how she always calls me Chouette? Until we meet again, we agreed we shall both say goodnight to the Moon and rub our noses at bedtime each evening.

A rich-looking man, crowing like a rooster, tried to convince Papa to board his ship, sailing to somewhere called Pennsylvania, rather than Nova Scotia. The stranger described Nova Scotia as an icy wasteland, riddled with rocks and bloodthirsty savages. I hope he is wrong.

Papa declined the rooster's offer. Master John Dick, the agent for His Majesty, King George II of England, is in charge of organizing our voyage. His words sound like German mixed with French and something I assume is English. I do wonder if there will be any French-speakers in the New World.

Already, Grandmother, as you can see, there is much to learn on our journey. New people, new places, new languages.

By the light of the Moon, I remain, as always,

Your loving granddaughter, Catherine M. Langille

30th May, 1752

Dear Grandmother,

We are finally on board! Our two-masted ship is named the Sally. I have already learned the difference between "he" and "she" in English, and, strangely, all boats are referred to as "she."

Nicholas thinks the Sally looks like a pirate ship. One of the rough sailors pretended to be a pirate, showing us a great trunk full of treasure—bead necklaces, brass bells, and ribbons. He began patting his mouth, making strange whooping sounds, like a pigeon, or perhaps an owl. We ran away when he pulled a dagger from his belt, pretending to cut off Nicholas's hair. He used the word "savage" several times. I have already learned that these savages or Indians are something to fear.

My legs trembled as we crossed the ship's deck toward a large hole with a rope ladder leading down to our assigned berth between decks. It is very dark and crowded in the belly of the ship.

Papa and Jean-Jacques signed a redemption agreement whereby they will work for the British Government in Nova Scotia in exchange for our passage across the ocean—seven pounds for each adult, and half as much for children. While on board, we are considered "freights"; Nicholas and I are "half-freights." As if we were trunks or boxes!

Wiggly Nicholas and I share a narrow plank bed and a lumpy straw-filled mattress. Nicholas was happy to discover a cat on board, until a sailor told us its job is to catch rats!

The voyage is expected to take only six weeks. Forty-two days, one thousand and eight hours. Remembering your wise words of farewell gives me comfort, Grandmother, yet makes me weep. "Roots of home for you to carry with you, my child. Memories to plant. No other place on earth shall ever smell so sweet as the place in which you were a child." Remember? Your wise advice to hold the seed pouch close and cherish my memories whenever homesickness flooded my heart, as it does now, is most soothing. Just as you promised, I feel your love and spirit traveling with us, dear Grandmother.

To distract myself from seeing my homeland disappear in the distance as the Sally set sail, I began to count the waves splashing up against the side. I wondered if there were enough numbers in the world to count all the waves between the Old World and the New. And the tears.

By the light of the Moon, I remain, as always,

Your loving (and nauseous) granddaughter, Catherine M. Langille

4th August, 1752

Dear Grandmother,

I have not written for some time as most days we are tossed about on the sea swells like leafy twigs in a gale. Being thrown violently from our berths below deck leaves us with bruises and, for some, broken bones. I believe it has rained for almost forty days and forty nights. I can only pray the Sally proves to be as seaworthy as Noah's Ark.

Pressing your lavender sachet to my nose, Grandmother, provides some solace from the stench of retching, vinegar, and mold. Scurvy, which the sailors call mouth-rot, has begun to spread due to our constant consumption of salted meat and porridge, and the absence of vegetables. Ship's fever, or typhus, has already taken several lives.

Supplies are scant and the rock-hard ship's bread, on which Papa cracked a tooth, is rife with worms and spiders. We collect rainwater when we can as the cask water is black and foul. Some drink Geneva instead, but Father says we must not touch spirits. We add vinegar to the water, but most often we use it to scour our mossy berths.

JAN L. COATES

How I long for the taste of your fresh oat bread and a mouthful of water from the sparkling stream. This supposed six-week voyage has become a never-ending test of both our endurance and our faith.

Nicholas is most fearful of using the "head," a hole in the floor for relieving oneself. I encourage him to count the waves, assuring him the ocean is not interested in consuming such a worrisome boy. He has given up whistling as it is bad luck aboard ship, likely to cause another gale to blow.

Mama and I prepare our meals on deck, using an open fire grate in a box of sand. It is lovely to breathe in fresh air, but I grow weary of boiled barley with a smidgen of watery treacle.

I keep my owl carving knife in a pocket of my increasingly grimy petticoat. How I wish you were here to share your secrets of coaxing the creature's soul from a simple piece of wood, as I struggle to carve a Nellie goat for Nicholas's birthday.

Yet another small child has died of the great fever. During a calm spell last evening, her broken-hearted parents wrapped the girl's tiny body in a tattered blanket and laid her out on a plank, while the Reverend delivered the funeral service. We raised our voices in song as the plank was tipped up, allowing the girl to slip soundlessly into her watery grave, the Reverend pronouncing, "God's Will Be Done. Have Mercy on Her Soul."

Does God not see how we, his people, are suffering? Is this truly His will?

When I am lucky enough to see the Moon, I ask him questions: What is Grandmother doing right now? Shall we ever again enjoy fresh bread, milk, and vegetables? Does God continue to watch over us?

There is much sorrow and little joy on board the Sally. I sincerely hope that when next I write, we will have arrived safely at our destination.

By the light of the Moon, I remain, as always,

Your loving granddaughter, Catherine M. Langille

21st April, 1753

Dear Grandmother,

September last we arrived in the rough town of Halifax. My ink dried up from lack of use, but I am finally able to write again, using this fine new graphite pencil given to me by Madame Masson in gratitude for helping with her four children over the winter.

We believe Elisabeth and her family have also arrived safely on their ship, the Gale, and are living across the harbor. Halifax is full of fearsome soldiers and unsavory women. Heathens roam the muddy streets at all hours of the night and day. Seamen carrying great wooden cudgels smash the glowing street lanterns for reasons no one can fathom, and people who steal have their hands branded with the letter T for Thief. This is indeed a foreign, rocky land, but we are, nonetheless, grateful to have our feet firmly planted upon the earth once again.

Frothing waves smashing violently against a bleak rocky coast lined with trees welcomed us to the New World. Nicholas did get to see one great whale leaping high into the air before plunging back into the dark depths of the ocean. Whale blubber is used for lamp oil!

My heart fell upon our first discouraging sight of Halifax, only a few wooden buildings and a long palisade marching up both sides of the steep hill, with an endless number of trees all around. Papa tried to encourage us, exclaiming about our opportunity to become masters of our own piece of this New World. Jean-Jacques claimed his muscles were tired just thinking about all that work.

"Our gift to the generations who will follow us," Mama said. "Thanks be to God." I hope that we shall survive to allow for those generations to follow us! I give my own thanks to God daily for guiding us safely thus far, begging him to continue watching over us.

We were on board ship for a total of seventeen weeks, one hundred and nineteen days. Upon our arrival, we were not allowed to leave the ship until a doctor had examined each of us. I was grateful to finally scour the layers of grime from my clothing. There were many bothersome biting insects, and Mama said we must plant some of your lavender as soon as possible, as the insects do not care for its perfume. Will the seeds be able to grow in such rocky soil?

We remain sheltered in temporary barracks. Jean-Jacques and Papa labor each day, building more barracks and blockhouses, clearing stumps for roads and extending the palisade to keep us safe. They are paid one shilling a day, and Papa is hopeful they will soon be rewarded for their diligence by having the British forgive them the remaining redemption fee.

Snow fell more days than not over the endless winter, squalling into great solid walls of drifts. Many settlers fell ill, and the carpenters were well occupied building coffins.

We have learned to stretch our rations, dried peas, oatmeal, vinegar, molasses, and bread, to keep the ever-gnawing hunger at bay as we arrived too late in the year to plant crops. The English forbade us from venturing any distance from Halifax, to prevent us from associating with the Natives, as the Acadian settlers before us have done.

Nicholas and I walk the streets on sunny days, admiring the wares displayed on drop-down wooden window shelves outside the shops: cheese, candles, fresh meat, delicate hair combs, sheep skins, and clothing. My own clothing grows snug, but there is no money for anything new, nor do we have the means to make our own. I learned some English from the sailors, and I continue to learn by listening, although the English children are not always friendly toward us. I miss you and Elisabeth terribly, and I long for a friend other than Nicholas.

Will we ever go to school again? Will I learn to read English?

We shall soon set sail for our new home, which the British call Lunenburg. It is said the Indians call it Merligueche, which means milky bay in their language. Will the voyage to Lunenburg be another endless journey? Will I ever again lie in a bed of feathers, rather than prickly straw and pine? Will I ever again taste fresh cheese and milk, or must my taste buds forever be subjected to dried peas and oatmeal, with a trickle of molasses? Has Elisabeth missed me as I have missed her? Please continue to pray for us.

By the light of the Moon, I remain, as always,

Your loving granddaughter, Catherine M. Langille

26th May, 1753

Dear Grandmother,

One recent evening, just before sundown, Papa returned from

a meeting in great high spirits and showed us a playing card, the nine of hearts. We were unable to guess its significance. Finally, he told us it was the card he had drawn, designating the lot we had been given for our new home in Lunenburg. Strasbourg Division, A-10. I do hope nine will be a lucky number for us.

As always, I have questions for the Moon as I read this letter aloud to him. Will the voyage to Lunenburg be another endless journey? Will Elisabeth and her family also move to Lunenburg? Will the summer be kinder to us than the winter has been?

And so, Grandmother, we have survived the first two phases of our journey. Please continue to pray for us.

By the light of the Moon, I remain, as always,

Your loving granddaughter, Catherine M. Langille

20th June, 1753

Dear Grandmother,

Once again, I must apologize for the great span between letters. Our ship, the Swan, carried us safely to Lunenburg, arriving on 7th June, along with six other ships, seven hundred other settlers of both French and German descent. Seven hundred more are scheduled to follow, including Uncle Leopold's family and my dear cousin-sister Elisabeth.

Over the winter, we heard terrible stories of Indians

scalping settlers across the harbor in Halifax, including an eight-year-old boy (thankfully, Nicholas is safe); it is said there are also Indians in Lunenburg ... Once again, we met with great disappointment upon our arrival—no buildings, no farmland, no barns or livestock. Nothing, save low treed hills rising up on both sides of the dull gray harbor. To soothe ourselves to sleep that first rainy night on deck, Nicholas and I sang your lullaby to the Moon, glimmering faintly behind the rushing clouds. Did you hear us?

> *Au clair de la lune, mon ami Pierrot.*
> *Prête-moi ta plume, pour écrire un mot.*
> *Ma chandelle est morte, je n'ai plus de feu.*
> *Ouvre-moi ta porte pour l'amour de Dieu.*

Once again, we are housed in great canvas tents, until the men have completed the building of a palisade and two blockhouses, under the command of Colonel Lawrence. Upon seeing us, some of the German children scratch as though they have fleas, implying we French are dirty and have lice. Papa says the British soldiers speak kindly of us, saying that despite being small of stature, the Montbéliard men are capable of working twice as hard as some others.

When I am not chopping cabbage for yet another kettle of soup, I take my flax sack of writing supplies and walk along the beach, seeking quiet refuge. It is a relief to go barefoot as my sabots are too small, my long second toes chafing against their ends.

Yesterday, I was sketching you and Nellie beneath Great-grandfather Langille's oak tree as a gift for Nicholas. After some time, I felt someone watching me. Nearby, the men were busy constructing the log palisade, paying no mind to me. Over my other shoulder, deep in the forest, I saw the corner of a house, which seemed odd, so distant from where the town is to be.

I went back to my sketch, but soon caught a glimpse of someone running from tree to tree. Was it a savage? Would they be so brazen?

Quickly, I gathered up my things and flew across the stony beach back to the tents. Something pierced my bare foot, causing me to fall to my knees. As I sat rubbing my tender foot, I saw something furry in the long grass. Not a creature, but a tiny shoe like none I had seen before. More beautiful even than the fine leather shoes worn by Master Bourgeois's wife! I dropped the mysterious little shoe into my bag and took it back to the tent.

As you can see, Grandmother, there continue to be many things to wonder about here in this New World. I yet await the Moon's answers. To whom does this little shoe belong? Will I ever have a friend here? Who was watching me in the woods?

We are slowly (and painfully) finding our way in this strange
new land.

By the light of the Moon, I remain, as always,

Your loving granddaughter, Catherine M. Langille

10th July, 1753

Dear Grandmother,

I cannot believe more than fourteen months have passed since
I saw you last. Nicholas, Peter, and I sing your Moon lullaby
to help pass the time as we work, gathering wood, collecting
fresh boughs for our beds (how I long for your ornery geese!),
and water from the well. Sometimes I can almost hear you
humming along. Neither you nor the Moon will be happy
to hear the very sad news I must impart. Until now, I have
been unable to force myself to write these painful words ...
My beautiful cousin-sister has succumbed to the great fever.
Elisabeth will never see the Moon again. Never sing with me
again. Never share stories and adventures with me again. We
were to be neighbors and friends forever, even here in this
harsh New World. Yet, here I am alone.

For two weeks, fourteen days, three hundred and thirty-six
hours, we had been eagerly anticipating Peter and Elisabeth's
arrival from Halifax. We could scarce contain our excitement
as their ship sailed into the harbor.

The Langille family was among the last group to be ferried to land by raft. I waved Elisabeth's Moon hairclip in the air as Aunt Marguerite and Uncle Leopold stepped ashore, followed by Peter and a group of strangers, their excited voices joining a squawking flock of seagulls overhead.

My eyes darted about from face to face in the great crowd milling about on the rocky beach. Arm-in-arm, Nicholas and Peter danced in circles beside me. Aunt Marguerite laid a gentle hand on my shoulder, the other caressing the round bump of a new baby growing inside her. She smelled of the sea and her blue eyes, Elisabeth's deep blue eyes, were shiny. "Oh, my dear. I am so sorry. We thought you had received word ..."

Refusing to believe, I jerked my shoulder away, closed my eyes, and began humming. But I could not block out the noise, the rushing of the blood draining from my breaking heart. Oh, Grandmother, I have never felt such sorrow.

Uncle Leopold stood in front of me, head bowed. "Our beloved Elisabeth did not survive the crossing. The ship's fever took her, only three weeks into the voyage."

I slipped away, stumbling along the beach, escaping the joyful swarm. At the harbor's head, I dropped to the ground, squeezing Elisabeth's hairpin, trying to push away the memories. Stark images and sounds of the children being buried at sea. Not Elisabeth. Not my beautiful cousin-sister. I covered my ears, rested my forehead on my knees, and hummed your lullaby. Elisabeth will never see the Moon again. Never sing with me again. Never see the New World.

And now, Grandmother, I must say goodnight. I am too weary of body and soul to write any more.

By the light of the Moon, I remain, as always,

Your loving (and lonely) granddaughter, Catherine M. Langille

12th July, 1753

Dear Grandmother,

I am sorry to have ended my previous letter so abruptly, but I know you will understand.

Back at our tent that night, I worked in silence, helping to prepare the bland evening meal of colcannon—boiled turnip, potatoes, and cabbage. On that day, it tasted of mud and swamp water.

After the meal, I escaped again to the head of the harbor where I had first glimpsed the girl with the long black hair. We had not yet spoken but sometimes spent time together on the pebble beach. Separate but together. I had come to presume the girl was part of the safe Indian family of which Papa had spoken.

I climbed up onto one of two side-by-side boulders, the spot I had hoped to be sharing with Elisabeth that very night. Hugging my knees, I stared at the gray water lapping at the shore, clutching your seed pouch in one hand, willing the tears to come, releasing my sorrow.

I was startled when the girl approached me, speaking French, offering to help.

Marie Claire is beautiful, with long black hair hanging in a single plait down her back. She wears shoes similar to the tiny one I found, moccasins made from deer skin and rabbit fur. Her people call this place Merligueche, milky bay, because of all the white clam shells here.

After some time, Marie Claire pulled a thin white P-shaped object from her pocket. I thought perhaps it was for needlework. She told me it was a wishing bone from the hindquarters of a rabbit. Holding it above your head, with your eyes closed, you attempt to poke a finger through the tiny hole. Success means your wish will come true.

I was successful, but I did not share my wish with Marie Claire, as told wishes seldom come true. I wished simply to know happiness once again, for the great cloud of sorrow hanging over me to disappear.

Marie Claire's mother is French and her father, Cloverwater, is Indian. Her father and his uncle, Old Labrador, assist the

British soldiers in their dealings with the Natives, who are angry the British have claimed this land as their own. Her people believe that the Creator, Kisúlkw, made the earth for all people to share, that the land is owned by no one.

I told her our Creator is named God and that Elisabeth has gone to live with him in the Kingdom of Heaven, which I pray is a more gentle place than this harsh New World.

Pointing to the early stars twinkling, Marie Claire told me her people believe the spirit world is a place of peace and that those who go before us travel to the spirit world along the Milky Way.

I hope she is right, especially because Elisabeth so loved the Moon and the stars.

The Native people's stories of the Creator are written down by the Elders on birch bark scrolls, ensuring they will be passed down over time, like our stories in the Bible.

Grateful for a French-speaking friend, I shared stories with Marie Claire of our life in France, and of how I read my letters aloud to the Moon. Her grandmothers also live far away, and she explained that her people have a special name for each Moon. This is how they divide the days. Right now it is between the Feather-Shedding Moon and the Fruit- and Berry-Gathering Moon.

Promising to show me the best huckleberry patches when we meet again, Marie Claire gave me the tiny bone as a gift.

It is inside my trunk, along with the tiny moccasin. Elisabeth's Moon hairclip, I put safely inside your snuff jug.

Oh, Grandmother, how I wish you were here to comfort me on this darkest of nights.

By the (dim) light of the Moon, I remain,

Your sorrowful granddaughter, Catherine M. Langille

15th July, 1753

Dear Grandmother,

Papa and Jean-Jacques are becoming impatient with the British, who will not allow us to begin building our own log houses until the building work for them has been finished. Uncle Leopold is anxious to begin building his own sawmill so he can return to his cabinet- and tool-making trade. In the spring, it is expected we shall move out to the big lot we have been given to the north and west of here, where the soil is less rocky and better for crops.

Marie Claire is teaching me many things about life in this New World. Last night, I met the firefly, a homely insect that flashes brightly when seeking a mate, similar to the young Native men who make flutes, believing their music will attract a mate. Marie Claire says she intends to remain a girl forever. Sadly, Elisabeth will also remain a girl forever …

Our area in the tent is cleaner than most, as Marie Claire

helped me make a new broom from twigs. I have delayed telling Mama and Papa about our friendship, as I am fearful they may forbid it because of Marie Claire's Indian roots.

What was your saying about the broom, Grandmother? A new broom sweeps clean but an old one knows the corners best? I have a new friend, but I shall forever miss the old one who knew me best.

By the light of the Moon, I remain, as always,

Your loving granddaughter, Catherine M. Langille

30th September, 1753

Dear Grandmother,

We have been busy preparing for the long ferocious winter the British have promised as a reward for coming to settle this New World for them. Already, we must keep the fire burning day and night, and the ground is crunchy with frost some mornings. In Lunenburg, we do not suffer from the same shortage of firewood trees as in France. However, the work here is endless ...

We tucked your flower seeds in with care so they will remain warm during the winter, Grandmother. Marie Claire helped me gather seaweed to use as a blanket for them. Sprouts unfurling in the spring will be a promise for a better tomorrow. Mama says the brown-eyed Susans' smiling yellow faces next fall will surely be a sign of good fortune. We will plant the trees before the first heavy frost, during the Hunter's Moon. But I have questions, as always. Will your seeds be able to take root in this rocky soil? Will the new trees adapt to this harsh New World? Will I?

I have finally told Papa and Mama about Marie Claire. They were speaking of Old Labrador and Cloverwater aiding the British in their dealings with the Native people. Papa said the British did not respectfully negotiate the treaty and land agreement in accordance with the Indian traditions, including a ceremony that involves burying a hatchet and washing away their face paint as symbols of peace.

Without thinking, I said that the Native people believe all people should share the earth, that no one owns the land. Of course, Mama wanted to know from where I had received this information. After I explained, Mama gave our friendship her blessing.

Marie Claire continues to teach me about using Mother Earth's gifts. Jackstraws, a clever game she showed me, is one of Nicholas's new favorite pastimes. I hope he is learning patience, attempting to withdraw one wheat straw without disturbing the others in the pile!

By the light of the Moon, I remain, as always,

Your loving granddaughter, Catherine M. Langille

15th October, 1753

Dear Grandmother,

The first shop in Lunenburg, owned by Mrs. Born, is simply a wooden trunk full of ribbons, lace, hair combs, and stitching supplies. Sadly, we have no money with which to purchase any of her beautiful things, but it is free to look and admire. Mrs. Born told Mama and me that the British have ordered hundreds of pairs of leather shoes for the settlers. My sabots have been too small for a very long time, but each pair of shoes will cost three shillings, money we do not have.

I ensure your seeds are yet covered with their seaweed blanket, imagining fields of lavender rimmed with yellow borders of brown-eyed Susans—someday. We planted the acorns, elm seeds, and chestnuts further from the house. I saved one acorn for Marie Claire, as she told me they once resorted to eating acorns in the dead of winter.

A great arrow of geese flies overhead as I am writing. "Toqa'q" is the Native name for autumn. It means "birds migrating season." Perhaps they are flying to Montbéliard to winter with your ornery geese, Grandmother. If only they were carrier pigeons, they could deliver my letters to you ...

By the light of the Moon, I remain, as always,

Your loving granddaughter, Catherine M. Langille

5th November, 1753

Dear Grandmother,

Today, I have met my first porcupine, a fearsome, prickly beast! Marie Claire says his sharp quills are welcome gifts, used as needles and to decorate their moccasins. She flattens the quills with her teeth, then stitches them onto the moccasins with deer sinew.

Marie Claire asked me today why I never laugh or smile. I tried to explain that I am happy inside, but my face does not know how to show it. Remember how you always told me I was born with an old soul, Grandmother? Perhaps that was why we were always such great friends.

I have made a new toy for Nicholas, using a triangular piece of birch bark and a clay ball attached with the fibers of the basswood tree. Holding the triangle by the corner, you flick your wrist and try to get the ball to drop down through the hole cut in the birch bark. Marie Claire also has her own knife, made from the split tooth of a beaver, another strange, yet not so fearsome, creature that can fell large trees by gnawing through the trunk.

Mama has begun calling me Dr. Langille, as I am learning much about using Mother Earth's healing gifts. Last week, I made a sweet fern poultice to help ease Jean-Jacques's itching after an encounter with poison ivy. The Native word for doctor is "shaman," which means healer.

Mother Goose and I are helping Marie Claire learn to read. We both hope to be able to attend school one day, and she is a very good student.

The Native name for Grandfather Sun is "Nisgam." Marie Claire told me that the shadows he gives us are the spirits of our ancestors, who are always with us. I will always think of you, Grandmother, when I see my own shadow.

Marie Claire's home has many healing plants as well as long eels hanging from the rafters now, drying for use in stews, along with mackerel, a type of fish Cloverwater catches and smokes for winter use. We collect seaweed and marsh grass for use in making soap, as well as mattress filling. I think I prefer the turnips, potatoes, and cabbage provided by the British, to the eels and mackerel ...

We planted the acorn, my gift for Marie Claire from Great-Grandfather's oak tree, and marked it with a fish-shaped stone. I hope the winter will pass quickly, and allow the new trees to begin to grow.

By the light of the Moon, I remain, as always,

Your loving granddaughter, Catherine M. Langille

20th December, 1753

Dear Grandmother,

I trust this letter finds you keeping warm and well. Winter has struck with a fury, and we have been trapped within for the better part of two days as a storm rages without, threatening to scalp the very roof off our sturdy log home. Scalp is what the savages, the enemies, do to express their anger at the British who have taken over their land. Marie Claire says the British have also taken their fair share of Indian scalps.

Papa says there is talk of the British preparing to banish the French Catholics who remain in Nova Scotia, the Acadians, said to number in the thousands. They steadfastly refuse to pledge their loyalty to the British government. We Protestants shall remain unscathed, but I fear for Marie Claire and her family who are half-Acadian …

All is well now, but Nicholas managed to get a splinter buried deep inside his foot and was feverish for several days. He complained of the bitter taste, but thanks to shaman Marie Claire, we made him red clover tea, which helped with the fever. Mama was worried about sepsis, poisoning of the blood, because it was festering and oozing.

The Natives use a healing plant called plantain, which they make into a paste to draw poison from wounds. Although the snow was deep in the woods, I donned Mama's heavy cloak with its warm rabbit-fur-trimmed hood, my woolen petticoat and Marie Claire's too-small moccasins, newly waterproofed with bear fat, and went in search of some plantain. I knew I'd found it when I ripped a frozen leaf in two, and saw the white thread-like veins, as shown to me by my friend.

I gathered several handfuls and stuffed them into my cloak pockets, then hurried home to make the paste. Before the next sunrise, Nicholas's fever was gone, and his foot was already less swollen and red. Perhaps I shall think of becoming a doctor one day!

A troublemaker named Patriquin caused great unrest by spreading rumors that the promised supplies are here in Nova Scotia, but that Colonel Lawrence is hoarding them, ensuring we must continue in hunger, struggling to stretch our meager supplies until the next victualing day. Soldiers, summoned by Colonel Lawrence, arrived and have now returned with the troublemaker to Halifax where he will be imprisoned.

Marie Claire was making cedar tea and a delicacy called cacamo when I called on her yesterday. The dried bones of the moose, a great horned creature similar to deer, are pounded into powder, then boiled for an entire day, until the bone marrow rises to the top. The butter, cacamo, adds rich flavor to soups and stews. The skin of Monsieur Moose will be used to make new moccasins and perhaps a rucksack for Marie Claire.

I cannot imagine how I could have survived without my new friend during these past months. As the British threaten to banish the Catholic Acadians, I fear for Marie Claire and her family.

314

By the light of the Moon, I remain, as always,

Your loving granddaughter, Catherine M. Langille

23rd April, 1754

Dear Grandmother,

We have survived our first winter in the New World! Some ice remains yet in the center of the harbor, and snow mounds linger in the deep woods outside the palisade. Papa and Jean-Jacques work to clear land for crops and livestock in the North West area where we Montbéliardians will farm. The British have promised we shall soon receive either one cow and one sheep, or one pig, one sheep, and six goats, to be shared by two families. Nicholas hopes to find a new Nellie and sends hugs to his old Nellie goat (and to you, of course).

We often walk with Papa and Jean-Jacques to the end of the palisade at the edge of town, kissing them goodbye and wishing them Godspeed. A tailor in the Fauxburg area beyond the palisade was recently set upon by Indians. One of the Germans had his trousers returned to him bearing droplets of the tailor's blood! As Mama says, uncertainty is the only constant of life in the New World.

We work hard and play little, although it seems Nicholas and Peter frolic constantly. Most days I feel as if I left my own childhood behind with you in Montbéliard …

Jean-Jacques is courting a girl named Henriette, like the Countess Henriette of Montbéliard. He has also started a small business, carving tree-nails to sell to the British and the wealthier settlers. He gave me my very own wooden comb for my fourteenth birthday. It is beautifully painted with yellow flowers, perhaps brown-eyed Susans.

I grow impatient as we have seen no signs of life yet from the seeds. Mama tells me that life can unfold no more quickly than one day at a time, no matter how deeply I may long for it to be otherwise. One day, twenty-four hours, one thousand, four hundred and forty minutes. I wonder yet how many days will pass before I shall start to feel at home once again.

Nicholas discovered a delicate flower the other day, hiding beneath the bits of crusty snow remaining in the woods. The blossoms resemble tiny pink and white trumpets, perhaps heralding the arrival of spring! Marie Claire told me they are called Mayflowers, a sign that the time of the Maple Sugaring Moon, Siwkewikús, is near. Marie Claire's people use quills to tap the sap flowing in the veins of the maple trees. They boil it until it becomes a thick, sweet syrup. Nicholas and I cannot wait to taste that!

What we call the month of May, Marie Claire's people call Birds Lay Eggs Moon, Penamuikús, the Moon under which true growth begins. She showed me some tiny green plants unfurling, shaped like the end of Uncle Leopold's fiddle. The Native people eat them, after cleaning them well in the sea. Rubbing them on the skin also keeps away biting insects, as does lavender. Our people are the same, yet different, in many ways.

Yesterday, as we sat in unusual silence on our boulders, Marie Claire said quietly, "These stones are most fortunate to be so firmly rooted here, in the same place, year after year. This has been my home for most of my life. And you have been my first and only real friend here."

After I assured her we would be friends forever, she pushed herself off the boulder abruptly and walked to the water's edge. "That is what I had hoped, but I fear change is in the air."

She was not referring to my family moving out to the big lots to plant our crops, as I'd hoped. She told me her family may well be included among the French Catholic people the British will soon expel. When I protested, pointing out that they were here long before the British, she said, "We are few and the British are many. Although we are not Catholic like the Acadians, Papa says we may be painted with the same brush because we speak French."

I do not understand religion, Grandmother. Why does it matter if a person is Catholic or Protestant? It seems religion causes a great deal of trouble.

Marie Claire said her Papa's greatest wish is that all people could learn to live together peacefully in this vast land, continuing to share our knowledge.

I agreed. Surely there is room for everyone.

And now, although there is more to tell, I must say goodnight, Grandmother, as my eyelids droop.

By the light of the Moon, I remain, as always,

Your loving granddaughter, Catherine M. Langille

27th April, 1754

Dear Grandmother,

Once again, I write with heartbreaking news. Yesterday, as usual, I met Marie Claire, my friend and teacher, on our sitting rocks on the beach. Her brown eyes were not their sparkly selves. After telling me that her family may have to flee in advance of the British banishing the Acadian people, she got out her beaver-tooth carving knife and chopped off a piece of her beautiful shiny black hair. Tying a deerskin thong around it, she presented it to me, saying, "I give you this living bit of me in honor of our time together. We shall always be friends." I did the same, using my owl carving knife. As we were saying goodbye, we saw a perfect rainbow—Munkwon, in Marie Claire's native language—above the bush-speckled hill across the harbor. Taking my cold hand in her warm one, she said,

"Each separate color so different but, side-by-side, blending together, they make a wondrous thing. If only people could learn to do the same." Isn't that beautiful, Grandmother?

The next day her house was cold and empty. Near the fish stone we used to mark the spot, I found a tiny green sprout from the acorn we planted together in the fall. Will Marie Claire ever get to see the tree it will become? Stumbling home along the stony beach, humming your lullaby, I tripped and fell—on a true treasure! A small stone, but not an ordinary stone, a rough gray egg stone full of crystals. Smoky, lavender-colored crystals, with pointed tips twinkling like stars. Nine pointed tips. It is so beautiful—how I wish you could see it, Grandmother.

And then, something truly magical happened as I held the stone in my hand. All at once, my hand began to warm, the glow spreading through my cold fingers, up my arms, straight to my heart. Like an embrace. Despite losing my friend, this gave me hope that we shall one day meet again. Meanwhile, I cherish Marie Claire's lock of hair and hold our memories close to my heart, as I do my memories of you and Elisabeth.

I hold fast to my hope that Marie Claire and I shall one day meet again. Perhaps our children will also be friends. I hope this rumored war will never come to pass, and in time her family will return to Merligueche.

Acknowledgments

Although inspired by history, this is a work of fiction. All incidents, characters, and dialogue are products of the author's imagination and are not to be construed as real. Where real-life historical figures appear, the situations concerning those persons are entirely fictional and are not intended to depict actual events. In all other respects, any resemblance to actual persons, living or dead, is coincidental. Any errors are the author's alone.

The following people, all great Likes of mine, were integral to the telling of Katie's story. Thanks to all of you for shining your bright lights on my little corner over the past five years.

First and foremost, thank you to the ever-wise, all-seeing, and patient Peter Carver for graciously encouraging me to step aside and allow Katie to tell her own story. You always ask the difficult questions that lead to me doing the hard, but necessary, work. I continue to learn *so* much each time I have the great privilege of working with you; thank you for believing in me and my stories and for never accepting anything less than my best.

Thanks also to the other dedicated people at Red Deer Press and Fitzhenry & Whiteside who work so diligently to get my books into the hands of readers, especially Red Deer publisher, Richard Dionne, who keeps me in the loop. Special thanks to Penny Hosey for doing such an excellent job of copy-editing.

The proud people of lovely Lunenburg were incredibly helpful and welcoming to me, especially during the two months I got to live among them, researching and writing. Thank you to Gill Osmond (I hope Marie Claire doesn't mind that I used her name in the book) for providing me with a perfect place to write and for introducing me to Charlie Guy, my distant relative, and Foreign Protestant enthusiast. Big thanks to Greg Ernst for showing me what he believes to be the disassembled 1757 home of Leopold Langille. I hope you'll one day get to reconstruct it on your property! Ruth Ernst was kind enough to allow me to use her name in this novel; thank you for showing me your ancestral treasures one sunny summer day.

Thank you to the South Shore Genealogical Society and Ralph Getson, Catherine Norman Donovan and her summer students at the Knaut Rhuland Museum, the Fisheries Museum of the Atlantic and the cast of their production, "Glimpses," the staff at the Lunenburg Public Library, and a random woman who walked the harbor trail with me one day, telling me of its reputation as the Phantom Trail. Thanks also to the Savvy Sailor, the restaurant on which I modelled The Chickadee. They have delicious food, especially their breakfast muesli!

Cheers to Chris Huntington and Charlotte McGill who were most generous in sharing their 1805 Cape home, filled with their collection of 18th- and 19th-century Lunenburg County antiques, several of which found their way into this story.

To my writing ladies, Jill MacLean, Jackie Halsey, and Marcia Barss—thank you for your good company and friendship during our Port Joli writing retreats, where I finished the first draft of this novel (and worked on the second, third, etc. ...). A shout out to my good friend, Laura Best, who really gets me, both as a writer and a person; our Vittles Café meetings are essential!

To my Pen Sisters, Andrea Schwenke-Wylie and Carolyn Mallory, thank you for being willing to talk books and writing endlessly, and for reading and giving feedback on an early draft of Katie's story.

Thank you to Tom Chapin and John Forster for giving me permission to use a perfect line from their song "Family Tree." If you don't know Tom's music, you should check it out!

Thank you to the ever-young Jean McKiel of Lunenburg, who helped me conquer (almost) my lifelong fear of water, a feat almost as satisfying as finishing my first draft.

Thanks to Erzsi Deak and Rubin Pfeffer for reading and giving invaluable and succinct advice that caused me to rethink the manuscript.

In researching this novel, I read too many books and articles to list here, but thank you to everyone who has written about the Lunenburg Foreign Protestants, and the many people whose work I delved into on the subject of Autism Spectrum Disorder, especially Temple Grandin. Thanks to Arts Nova Scotia and the Access Copyright Foundation who supported this project in its research stage, and to Ontario Heritage Trust, who granted me a residency to spend an entire month working on this novel at Fool's Paradise, former sanctuary of iconic Canadian landscape artist, Doris McCarthy. Thank you, Doris!

Huge thanks, as always, to booksellers, librarians, teachers, parents, and readers, especially young readers I'm lucky to meet during school visits. Writers get to do what we love because of all of you.

And, of course, my family tree: Liam and Rachel, Shannon and Peter, and Nance—knowing you're always there for me, loving and supporting, during good times and bad, keeps me going. You are my world. And thanks, as always, to my invisible roots: Bob and Ada Mingo, my Pearson and Mingo grandparents, and my Montbéliard Langille and Mingo ancestors. You are who I think of when I see my shadow.

And, last, but never least, love and thanks to my partner in all things, Don, who keeps me fed, prevents the dust bunnies from carrying me away, keeps Charlie happy, and, for better or worse, shares in every aspect of my life, writing and otherwise. None of this happens without you.

Interview with Jan Coates

What first drew you to this story?

In the 1990s, my grandfather and father went to a farm auction, expressly to buy a clay jug they knew had been brought to Nova Scotia in the 1700s by our Mingo/Menegaux ancestors, one of the original Foreign Protestant families to settle in Nova Scotia. I now own that jug, and I've always been curious about its story. My whole life, I've felt lucky to know the names of my ancestors dating back to that time, but I didn't know any details of their leaving Montbéliard (near the French/Swiss border) and crossing the ocean to settle here. I began researching and soon discovered I also had Langille Lunenburg roots. I was hooked and knew I had to give the jug its story. I set out to write a work of historical fiction, but then Katie wandered into Catherine's story. Her voice was so powerful that I knew it was her story I needed to tell, entwining it with Catherine's.

To what extent do you have a personal connection with Lunenburg—and with the essentials of this story?

My long-lost relative, Charlie Guy (our Langille ancestors were brothers back in the 1700s) introduced me to the term "Sudden Lunenburg Love Syndrome." I've always liked Lunenburg, having lived in Nova Scotia most of my life, but when I had a chance to live in the town for two months, researching and writing, I succumbed to the Syndrome. It's so beautiful, and I love its history, charm, and energy. My grandfather and father were so proud of our long Nova Scotia roots, and I grew up believing that my Mingo ancestors had been among the original settlers of Lunenburg.

While researching, I found that our Mingo ancestors, in fact, had gone to Pennsylvania before returning to Nova Scotia in the late 1700s, settling in the River John area. But I am directly descended from David Langille, one of the 1,453 original Lunenburg Foreign Protestant settlers. I've had a chance to visit Montbéliard, France a couple of times, and it was truly moving to visit the homeland of my ancestors. It's also a lovely, quaint town—a few hundred years older than Lunenburg.

Writing a story set in this town, you have chosen to include a lot of details that come from the history of Lunenburg— names of people who live there, buildings and their markers, stores and eating places, actual historical events. Why was it important to you to include so many of the real details of this setting?

Because this became Katie's story, I wanted to include the description of this new-to-her town as she would have experienced it for the first time, giving color names to the painted houses, noticing the plaques indicating the original owners of the buildings, all things she does to help herself become comfortable in yet another strange place. She likes true stories and history, and Lunenburg is so full of both. A perfect place for anyone seeking their roots to find home, transplant themselves.

How do you, as a writer, know how to balance your pleasure in inventing characters and situations against the temptation to write about real people and their adventures?

In this case, at the outset, I was hopeful I might discover an actual diary or letters from the 1750s, but other than a church diary kept by a minister, I didn't come up with any personal written accounts, but I did find many artifacts from that time, which I used to enhance Katie and Catherine's stories.

Ultimately, I'm a fiction writer because I've always liked to play make believe; my imagination hasn't failed me yet, but I hope including factual details adds authenticity to my writing.

Why did you want to include Catherine's letters as an afterword to the story of Katie?

Katie is dogged in her pursuit of things, and I think that would extend to Catherine's letters, as read to their mutual friend the Moon. Katie has kept track of Catherine's twelve treasures, heard snippets of her story, and when the letters reappear by the novel's end, Katie would be eager to read them on the drive back to Montreal. As a young reader, I know I'd want to read those letters along with her, to see what else Katie finds out about her ancestor, fellow friend of the Moon. Because the (fictional) letters have been a significant part of Katie's Lunenburg experience, it seems logical to have them available for reading now that they've reappeared.

Why did you choose to make someone who is on the autism spectrum the major character in your story?

It's hard to believe, but I didn't actually make that choice, not consciously at least. The story was originally to be Catherine Marguerite Langille's, and it was to be told through a series of historic letters.

When I later decided I wanted to set the story in the present day, while still including the history, Katie just appeared in my mind one day. I'd been doing some substitute teaching at that time, and had the opportunity to work with some extremely bright students living with Autism Spectrum Disorder. As soon as Katie began talking, I realized she, too, was on the autism spectrum. I did a fair amount of research, and I hope readers will like Katie, and appreciate her view of the world. I love the idea that we all have family traits, quirks, and habits that may have been passed down from generation to generation, as is the case with Catherine and Katie.

In several of your books, you have delved into stories that have strong roots in the past. Why do you find historical settings and events so intriguing? And why do you think it's important for young readers to gain interest in such stories?
There's an African saying I like: *When an elder dies, it's as if an entire library has burned to the ground.* When my parents and grandparents died, I knew I'd miss being able to ask them questions about the past. I continue to miss that and wish I had recorded interviews with them about their lives, as a permanent record of both their memories and their voices.

Those who came before us worked hard to create the Canada we know and love. This Foreign Protestant history, which hasn't yet been told for young readers, is important; their descendants, numbering in the hundreds of thousands, are scattered throughout North America. This is, in part, a refugee story; kids whose families have lived in Canada for many decades, even centuries, probably don't often think about their uprooted ancestors who made the perilous journey across the ocean, similar to those new Canadians arriving today. I suppose most of us are immigrants, our roots transplanted in that way, but few of us know our ancestors' stories, the importance of which is summed up nicely here by author Madeleine L'Engle :

If you don't recount your family history, it will be lost.
Honor your own stories and tell them, too.
The tales may not seem very important,
but they are what binds families
and makes each of us who we are.

Thank you, Jan.